Praise for
Gods of the Highlands

"This is the perfect blend of medieval romance and hot passion."

"You find yourself in a world where there are immortal and mortals who are at war with each other and seek revenge."

"From the start, this story had me on the edge of my seat."

"I love this series and can't wait for the next book."

"The Gods of the Highlands *series by Ms. Bambi Lynn just gets better and better."*

Books by Bambi Lynn

Mask of the Highlander
Camulus
Sirona
Tanis
Lucan
Marek
Broken Armor
The Valiant Viking
Wrath of the Fire God

Solid as a Rock

Bambi Lynn

Published by Bourdeilles Books

ISBN – 978-0-9974337-2-2
eBook ISBN – 978-0-9974337-2-2

Cover Design by Patricia Schmitt (PickyMe)
www.pickymeartist.com

www.bambilynn.net

for My Family

PROLOGUE

Eleven months ago…

THE SLAM OF PRISON DOORS CLANGED IN HIS EARS.

The memory of that sound washed over Michael Munro as he stared down at the body. He rubbed one hand over his throbbing forehead. He would never go back. He had made a vow, and it was one he intended to keep. The searing pain that had originated behind his eyes radiated to the back of his head and spread to his neck and shoulders. Images flashed across his vision. He closed his eyes against them, but they only became more distorted, more confusing. The tiny nerves and muscles of his eyes ached at trying to see them all at once, yet he could no more stop himself from trying than he could prevent his heart from beating.

Forsyth Park, the pinnacle of Historic Savannah, was usually quiet this time of night. Even the tourists had called it a day. Opening his eyes, he looked around, peering into the darkness for further signs of trouble. But he didn't have to. Amidst the blurry, random images causing havoc in his brain, he saw them emerge from the shadows an instant before they actually did.

They had come for him, and there were too many to fight off this time. Any advantage his gift might have afforded him was swallowed up by the chaos in his head.

He had barely defeated the man who lay dead at his feet, a decoy or a test, apparently. Either way, he was far outnumbered now, and the power inside him was out of control. If only he could slow the images down, organize them, make sense of them. Then he could use his gift to kill these bastards and be on his merry way.

Among the scattered scenes in his mind, he noticed one man in particular closing in behind him, a vicious-looking knife poised to slice him open down the length of his spine. Michael waited, his gaze on the men before him, his hearing tuned behind. He detected the subtle difference when the men in front of him tried to distract him rather than engage. He strained to hear his attacker's footsteps closing in. Just as the man lashed out to bring the knife down, Michael whirled and landed a powerful upper thrust to the man's nose, his strength sufficient to shove bone and cartilage into his brain. The man dropped like a stone.

Michael retrieved the discarded knife. The throbbing in his head intensified as the swirling images came faster and faster. There were so many, he no longer made the effort to see them clearly. Instead, he tried to block them out, knowing before he did so that he could not. The images came and went, seemingly random visions that could appear at any given moment, usually the wrong moment, yet were impossible for him to recall or make sense of.

The dead man's companions closed in. Michael resisted the urge to squeeze his eyes shut against the blinding pain in his head. He swayed on his feet, his knees threatening to buckle beneath him. A wave of nausea swept over him. He swallowed the bile that burned the back of his throat. He needed all his wits about him if he had any hope of getting out of this alive.

Jaw clenched, he took up a stance with the dead man's knife held menacingly before him. He took several steps back as they moved closer, anything to keep them from surrounding him completely. He wondered briefly if he could outrun them, but that was not his style. Michael had faced death before. He was not afraid.

He *was* going to die. It was inevitable considering the odds. But he would take some of these bastards with him.

Would she be saddened by the news? Would word of his death even reach her?

He had not thought of her in days. Quite a feat as he had thought of little else since she left without so much as a "fuck off" nearly six years ago. The devastation of her rejection had nearly driven him mad. The prospect of death was almost a relief.

Suddenly, darkness blocked the images from his mind. He could no longer anticipate his attackers' next moves, but blessedly the pain vanished, too. He stood taller, gripped his weapon tighter. Every muscle in his body was poised and prepared to fight to the death. No distractions.

Michael felt a presence at his back. Had one of them gotten around behind him? Were there others hiding in the shadows he did not know about? For once, his *gift*, if it could be called that, failed him. He saw nothing, no clue as to what approached nor the danger it posed.

The air thickened with power. Michael could sense the change even before his attachers' hard glares changed to wide-eyed fear. The men, who only moments before had been about to kill him, scattered like cats in a sudden rainstorm. None of them took more than a few steps before falling down dead.

It was over in seconds.

A man strode past him, surveying the carnage for signs of life. He was taller than Michael, easily over six and a half feet, with thick black hair. He nudged a few of the bodies with the toe of one black boot before turning his attention to Michael.

Even in the darkness, the man's gaze commanded attention. The intensity of those eyes raised his hackles, setting off warning alarms in his head. Michael stood his ground, wondering what new threat this man posed.

"Doona linger, lad. There could be more."

The thick Scottish brogue caught him off guard, but Michael ignored it. "Who are you?"

One corner of his mouth tilted up, but it could hardly be called a smile. "I am the one man who can teach ye to control yer powers, channel them, and seek retribution against those who would cause ye harm."

CHAPTER ONE

Ellie King stormed out of the hangar. How dare he ignore her like that? She could see the flight instructor through the window of the tiny office on the back wall. He knew she was there. Ellie gritted her teeth, considered going back in there, then changed her mind. She had less than an hour to get to work, and she still had to return Gran's SUV. She pulled her cell phone from her back pocket and checked the time.

Her heart dropped. Way less than an hour. She was going to be late. It would take her ten minutes just to get back to the highway.

Tucked away in the back corner of the Savanah Hilton Head International airport, the hangar housed the business office that primarily dealt with smaller aircraft, prop planes, and private jets. One of those jets was currently descending towards runway 10/28, flying in from the west. Her heart did a somersault as the high-pitched wail of jet engines reached her. The one time she'd been up in a plane it had been an old Beechcraft Bonanza, not a jet. But the experience had been no less sensational. Maybe flying was in her blood. Maybe she had been an airplane pilot in a previous life. Or maybe a bird.

Or a bug, the way her life was going these days. Whatever the reason, that single flight had lit a fire inside Ellie. She held up one hand to block the late afternoon sun and watched the Falcon 7X make its descent. She parted her lips, her breath shallow and sporadic as the engines squealed. Wheels materialized from the belly of the jet moments before they touched down.

She turned from the runway as the plane coasted toward the hangar. *One day*, she vowed. *I will be in the cockpit of one of those, suspended in midair, soaring through the sky.* Ellie was focused on little else.

She hurried over to the Durango, hitting the unlock button on the key as soon as she was within range. She was never going to make it. If she was late again…

She considered taking backroads and side streets to avoid traffic, but decided the interstates would be faster. She wasn't in Atlanta anymore. Overcrowding and nightmarish traffic hadn't reached this far south. She zipped onto the highway and merged into the far left lane.

Atlanta had been such a fantasy. Bright lights. Big city.

Bullshit.

From the time her mother dumped her on Gran's doorstep, Ellie had dreamed of nothing but her return. She had been five at the time. Ellie barely knew the old woman, and her house smelled funny. She had clung to her mom's leg, crying and begging her not to go.

Gran had wrapped her arms around her and held her prisoner while Mama escaped to the waiting car. Gran was strong for such an old woman. Eleven years later, Ellie's prayers were answered. Her mom had sent for her, asked her to come live in Atlanta with her. Ellie hadn't been able to pack a bag fast enough. That was six years ago. Now she was back, and more glad than she wanted to admit.

She pulled off the highway, grateful not to have encountered any cops, and turned right to skirt Forsyth Park. Going through the Historic District would be shorter by half, but maneuvering one perfectly groomed square after another and avoiding the numerous horse-drawn carriages would take three times as long. She loved Savannah's charm now that she was old enough to appreciate it. If only the city wasn't so overrun with tourists.

Moments later, she parked along the curb in front of Gran's hunter green Victorian and dashed inside to drop off the keys. The familiar smell greeted her as she pushed open the door, a combination of cleaning ammonia and gardenias. As a child, Ellie had hated that smell. It served as a reminder that her mother didn't want her, that she had left her there like a basket of dirty laundry. She stopped inside the doorway and inhaled. Now the smell reminded her of home. She had been such a fool.

"Ellie-lamb? Is that you?"

"It's me, Gran. I'm rushing off to work now."

The older woman came out from the kitchen. She wasn't so old as Ellie had first thought all those years ago. Gran was only in her late forties when Ellie had come to live with her and even now, pushing seventy, she hardly seemed *old*.

Ellie planted a kiss on her cheek. Gran gave her arm a squeeze as she hurried on past and headed for the back door. "I have to run. I'm already late."

"Be careful, sweet-"

The sound of her voice was cut short as the door slammed shut. Ellie would bring her a pastry from Betty's to make up for her abrupt behavior. She slipped on her backpack, pulled her bike from inside the shed and took off, spinning her wheels as fast as her legs would pump.

Ellie zipped down the alley behind the Bier Haus and turned right onto Price Street. No squares broke the pace of Price, so she was able to make it to Jones Street in record time. A car alarm went off as she sped by, startling her and nearly causing her to crash. She righted the front wheel and took a right on Jones. The overhanging trees and cobblestone street made it one of the most picturesque in Savannah. Ellie would go out of her way for a ride down Jones Street, but today she had no time to enjoy the view.

By the time she reached the diner, it was ten minutes after four. Not *so* late but late enough that Joe would give her a hard time. Hopefully, he wouldn't fire her.

Walking in without being noticed was impossible. The tinkling bell sounded like a death knoll. An alarm also sounded in the kitchen just in case no one heard the bell. Morgan stood anxiously at the hostess stand waiting for her. Before Ellie was hardly in the door before Morgan handed her an apron and a hair band.

"Welcome to Betty Bombers. You're late. Again." She handed Ellie a tray of dirty dishes and pulled several wisps of hair from the ponytail Ellie had just tied it into. "Take these back and pretend like you've been here the whole time. Maybe Joe won't notice."

Fat chance. "Thanks, girl." Ellie took the tray and lifted it overhead as she maneuvered through the tables. If she was lucky, she could dump the dishes and start taking orders before her boss even realized she was there.

She rounded the corner and her gaze crashed into that of Michael Munro. Gold eyes stared back at her, intense and unsettling. He sat alone at a two-top casually eating his eggs and grits. He seemed just as shocked to see her as she was him.

Before she could mask her surprise, Ellie slipped and went down hard in a crash of broken dishes and pinging silverware. While several smartasses nearby applauded, Michael jumped to his feet and rushed to her aid.

Ellie stared up at him. He was still as gorgeous as she remembered. And bigger. From her position on the floor, he looked to be about seven feet tall with shoulders as wide as a barn. She took a deep breath and swallowed hard.

Things were going from bad to worse.

She ignored his offer to help her to her feet and got up on her own. "What are *you* doing here?" She began collecting the scattered utensils and shards of broken dishes and tried not to look at him. He still made her jumpy and tingly, but far more than when she was fifteen. He had been a gangly teen back then, awkward and lanky. Now that she was on her feet, he still seemed to be about seven feet tall, but more like six and half, she guessed.

Michael stood back and smirked down at her. "I wondered the same thing about you."

His voice, rich and silky, washed over her. It couldn't be good, the way he made her feel. All warm and wet. Achy. *Needy.* "Working," she snapped. Why was she angry at him? She had been the one to leave. Mama had called, and Ellie had been on the first Greyhound out of Savannah the next morning, 5:20 am. She'd not had time to say goodbye. What if Mama changed her mind?

What if seeing him one last time made Ellie change *her* mind?

She couldn't take that chance. Michael Munro was bad news, an outcast, a loser who was going nowhere fast and threatening to drag her along. So in the end, she had said nothing. Just disappeared like fog on a sunny day.

"I mean why are you in Savannah? How long have you been back?"

Ellie could guess what he really wanted to know. *Why didn't you call me?* It wasn't like she hadn't thought to. She had, hundreds of times in the three weeks since she'd come home and even before, while she'd still been living with her mother.

She shrugged. "I've been busy." She brushed her hair away from her face and tried to look anywhere but into those golden eyes that so easily sucked her in. "Like now. I have to get back to work." She glanced at his table. His food was surely cold. "I'll send your server over with your check."

She couldn't resist. Glancing up, she found him staring at her with such intensity, she felt both scared and excited at the same time. It was an intoxicating combination. Those eyes fairly glowed against the contrast of his dark hair and golden tan and made her insides melt, her mouth go dry, her body crave things it shouldn't. Nothing had changed in the years since she'd last seen him. Old yearnings rushed over her like she'd never been gone. She tried not to look at him as she pushed backwards through the kitchen door, but Ellie couldn't tear her gaze away from his. The familiar veil was still there in those golden depths, hiding the pain and loneliness he always tried to bury.

She was relieved to escape into the bustle of the kitchen, but she couldn't resist a peek back into the dining room. Michael had returned to his seat and now sat staring out the window, his expression a mask of indifference. What was he thinking?

It was a question that had always plagued her. Michael Munro had been a loner, keeping himself apart from the other kids. His mother had died while they were still in elementary school, and he'd been passed from one foster home to another. Not because he was bad. Michael had been a well-behaved kid. Quiet in class. He didn't always complete his work, but he followed directions, never giving the teachers any trouble. He got in fights from time to time, but only when he was forced to defend himself. The fights didn't usually last long as Michael always had his opponent on his back in just a few seconds.

There was something strange about him, something different that made people uncomfortable to be around him. By middle school, the fights had stopped. Occasionally some new kid would try to pick on him but would soon discover there were other, safer ways to torment the boy everyone shunned.

"What are you looking at?"

Ellie jumped at Morgan's voice behind her. Her friend peered through the thick window.

"Oh, that guy."

Ellie balanced her tray of broken dishes and tried to look nonchalant. "Who's table is that? He needs his check."

"He just got his food. He can be done yet."

"Believe me, he's done and needs to go."

Morgan shrugged. "It's your table. I asked Erica to wait on him since you were late, but she pitched a fit about it. Said he was a weirdo, and she wasn't getting near him. So, I had to do it."

Ellie glanced back out the window at where he sat, alone. Her heart melted a little like it always did. A few times she had joined in the name-calling when they were younger, ignoring the guilt that assailed her. She sensed a connection to him, even as a child. They had both lost their mothers, though under different circumstances. Ellie had clung to the hope that her mother was coming back for her. Michael Munro had no hope.

"So who has his check?" she asked.

Morgan pulled a pale green slip from her apron pocket and handed it to her, taking the tray of broken dishes in exchange. "You take it. I don't care how hot he is, Erica was right. There's something strange about that guy." She leaned in and lowered her voice. "Plus I heard he's been in prison."

Ellie huffed. "He was in the county jail for thirty days. I'd hardly call that prison."

Morgan gave a little shudder. "Close enough. He still gives me the creeps. You'll have to take care of him." She walked away to dispose of the dishes, leaving Ellie with little choice but to go back out there.

She stuffed his check into her apron, grabbed a pencil from the empty tomato sauce can at the server's station, and stuck it behind her ear before pushing back through to the dining room. Michael now sat glaring at her, like he'd known she was about to come through the door. It unnerved her, the way he seemed to know what she was about to do before she did it. She tried her best to ignore him as she took drink orders for her other tables. But it was like trying to ignore the cry of cicadas on a hot night.

That guy. The way Morgan said it irritated her. So he was a loner, an introvert. That didn't make him weird, just…different. Gran had told her about Michael's arrest. Apparently he had beat the pulp out of some tourists. No doubt they had started it. Some things never changed.

She growled and headed over to where he sat. Why did she defend him? First to Morgan, now in her own mind, making excuses for him and trying to justify his bad behavior. He was a loser, and Ellie refused to fall under his spell.

Again.

Pulling the green ticket from her apron pocket, she tossed it on his table. "Pay at the register," she said.

Michael grabbed her hand before she could walk away. Heat shot up her arm and zeroed straight to her core. Ellie had had more than one lover since she'd left Savannah, but no man had ever excited her with nothing but a touch of his fingers. She inhaled a sharp breath at the sensation and found her feet frozen in place.

He didn't say anything. Just rubbed the pad of his thumb over the top of her hand, those unsettling eyes boring into hers. The diner seemed to fall away, the noise disappeared, the silence rang in her ears. When she tried to pull her hand from his grasp, he squeezed tighter.

"Why did you leave me?"

The hurt in his voice was nearly her undoing. Part of her wanted to apologize. To tell him how much she'd thought of him over the years. How much she'd missed him. Instead, she snatched her hand from his.

"Don't be so full of yourself. It had nothing to do with you." She ignored the hurt that flashed across his face. He masked it so quickly anyway, she wondered if she'd imagined it. "The opportunity to go live with my mom came up, and I took it." She picked up his plate of uneaten eggs and cold grits. "You would have done the same thing."

She turned on her heel and carried the dirty plate to the kitchen. After dropping it off with the dishwasher, she called out the orders she had just taken. By the time she returned to the dining room, his seat was empty. A hundred-dollar bill lay on the table.

***

Michael parked his Heritage Softail in the alley behind the Dresser-Palmer house, stashing his helmet beneath an azalea bush covered in bright pink blossoms. His Uncle Lucan had bought the run-down duplex for his bride, even though she didn't know about it yet—neither Lucan's purchase of the house nor his intention to make her his bride.

The light scent of wisteria assailed him before he even breached the gate. Lavender flowers hung from overhead, a jumble of thick, woody vines and sea-green leaves left untended to overtake the courtyard's canopy. A Koi pond to his left sported dark, murky water, the fish long gone. He strode carefully to the steps, avoiding the once smooth cobblestones that had been pushed above the surface by time and neglect or left gaping holes where they'd disappeared completely. He had tripped on them more times than he could count.

He lifted one corner of the mat with the toe of his black Timberland boot, but before he could stoop to retrieve the key, an image of his uncle opening the door flashed behind his eyes. The visions no longer caused him so much pain. Just a nagging ache at his left temple, nothing like the debilitating migraines he had gotten before. Michael had learned much this past year, not the least of which was how to channel the images into a coherent vision and reduce the pain that threatened to split his skull in two.

Seconds later, Lucan Munro opened the door. He filled the frame with his massive size. Thick black hair hung to his shoulders, unkempt and framing a firm jaw covered in at least two days' worth of stubble. "That dinna take ye long," he said. He turned without waiting for a response and headed back through to the living room.

Shutting the door behind him and sliding home the three deadbolts, Michael followed. The back door opened into a foyer of sorts. Like so many of these old Victorian houses, he could see straight through the dining room to the front of the house, where Lucan ignited a fire in the hearth with nothing more than a wave of his hand. Being the grandson of an ancient Celtic god afforded Lucan many powers, the extent of which Michael was sure he would never know.

His stomach rumbled as he passed the kitchen. His encounter with Ellie had cost him his appetite, but it came back in full force. He stuck his head through the door, but the room was as stark and barren as the rest of the house. Not a lingering morsel in sight.

"The least you could do is keep some food in the house," Michael said, joining Lucan in the living room. Or would they have called this the parlor? He sat on a faded loveseat near the fireplace. It may be spring, but with no heat in this monstrosity of a house, the chill was ever-present.

"I eat when I get hungry. Whiskey?" Lucan poured two fingers of amber liquid into a heavy-bottomed glass and lifted it to his lips. He closed his eyes as he sipped it, no doubt recalling his days in the Highlands.

When his uncle looked back at him, raising the glass in his direction, Michael shook his head. Lucan joined him near the fireplace but did not sit. "I need ye to go to Atlanta," he said. "This eve. A situation is forming, and I ken we are too late as it is."

Michael's stomach knotted. He just wanted to go home and nurse his wounds, to crash in his own bed and sulk over his Ellie. No one had the power to hurt him the way she did. He had been bullied and shunned for most of his life. He'd grown accustomed to it. But the sharp sting of *her* rejection left him raw and hurting.

It always had. Since he first met her more than fifteen years ago.

First grade. He had been fascinated by her ability to control the classroom. She had a way of getting everyone organized and assigned to the task for which they were best suited. If the teacher needed to leave the room, she always left Ellie in charge. And Ellie King ruled with an iron fist.

While the other kids ignored him or made fun of him, Ellie never shied away. She wasn't afraid of the weird boy who kept himself apart from the others. They sensed that he was different. Michael knew it, too. He *was* different. Other kids didn't have the visions he did, images of events moments before they happened. The images started coming soon after his mother died. By the time he hit puberty, they came on so quickly he couldn't track them all. That's when the headaches started. Compelled to make sense of the visions flashing through his mind, he sometimes focused so hard the pain caused him to pass out. More than once he'd awakened to find himself sprawled on the ground, passersby apparently taking him for a drunk or a homeless man and trying hard to ignore him.

The visions frightened him, although sometimes he managed to use them for good. He'd once pulled a toddler from the path of an on-coming car. Her mother had snatched the little girl from his arms and hurried away. No 'thank you'. Nothing. Just that familiar glare of discomfort and fear.

But not Ellie King. She had glared at him for other reasons. Usually she was pissed off at him about something. No one wanted to hold his hand during Red Rover. The other kids refused him when Ellie was dividing them into teams. If he made the mistake of hiding during a game of hide-and-seek, no one would look for him, and she'd be forced to find him herself and bring him back. Why she got angry at *him*, he'd never understood. He was just glad to get her attention.

When he'd spotted her at the diner, his first thought had not been one of anger or resentment, nor even the animalistic need he had for her. No. His first thought was *home*.

Ellie had come home, but it was more than that. When they were young, he'd seen her as the embodiment of everything he longed for in life: acceptance, commitment, loyalty.

Belonging.

She was his home, and now she was back. He felt a sense of calm he had not felt in a long time. He wanted to scoop her up and whisk her away, bury himself inside her until they were spent and boneless, showing her all the things he'd learned in six years.

He wanted to claim her, to never let her go again.

Ellie had shattered that fantasy with a single sneer. Old insecurities shot to the surface. What had he done to make her leave? What was wrong with him that warranted her disdain? He gripped the arm of the loveseat. He would not let her make him feel inferior or guilty. He had done nothing wrong. She had been the one to leave. She had been the one who...

He took a deep breath, letting it out slowly and releasing his death grip on the furniture. Maybe a trip to

Atlanta *would* be better than sitting home feeling sorry for himself. A midnight ride along the backroads of Georgia. Distancing himself from long buried memories. The potential for violence and danger. Self-pity had never gotten him anywhere, never curbed his anger nor thirst for vengeance.

Ridding the planet of the unworthy–different story. Michael was always anxious to test the power and strength Lucan had been teaching him to summon. After he had a chance to calm down, then he could decide what to do about Ellie, for no way in hell was he letting her off that easy.

"What's the job?"

CHAPTER TWO

Ellie forced herself not to look at the door when the bell rang. She kept her gaze locked on the customer at Table Five. The woman's lips were moving, explaining in great detail what she wanted from the menu, but Ellie heard nothing. Every instinct in her body urged her to see if it was *him*. It had been more than twenty-four hours since their surprise reunion. Ellie had thought of him every minute of those hours.

Damn him!

Unable to resist any longer, she glanced away, drawn to the new arrival like a bee to honey. A mad combination of relief and disappointment engulfed her. It was only that rich guy who'd bought the Dresser-Palmer house a few years back. Ellie had never waited on him, but the other girls who fought over having him seated in their sections, claimed he was beyond generous with his tips. It didn't hurt that he looked like the covers of *Muscle & Fitness*, *GQ*, and *NFL Today* all rolled into one. Ellie hoped Morgan sat him in her section. Her tips so far tonight had been little more than pocket change.

Her heart tripped when bell tinkled again. This time the flight instructor walked through the door. *Forget the rich guy with the big tip.* She finished taking the woman's order and hurried over to the hostess station, indicating that Morgan seat the instructor and his guest at her only available two-top. The man said nothing when Ellie caught his attention, but rolled his eyes at her big smile as he followed the hostess to his seat.

She barely approached his table before the man had one hand in the air, as if that would stop her assault. He shook his head as she drew closer. "I know what you're going to ask, and you can forget it."

She hated when people made assumptions about her. She forced a smile. "Good evening, Mr. Osborn. Nelson. Can I call you Nelson? I feel like we know each other." Ellie whipped out her pad and pulled the pencil from behind her ear. "My name is Ellie. I'll be your server." She looked pointedly at him. "Ellie King. I was *going* to ask what you'd like to drink." She smiled at the man's companion. "Ma'am?"

"I know perfectly well who you are," Nelson Osborn said. "You've left so many messages on my voicemail, I can't delete them fast enough. And if you don't quit stalking the hangar, I'm going to file a restraining order."

She released a slow breath, forcing herself to be calm. "I'm not a threat, Mr. Osborn."

"Oh, yes you are. A threat to my sanity."

"Well, if you'd talk to me– "

"Can we have a few minutes to look at the menu?" he interrupted.

Hiding her frustration, Ellie turned her attention back to his companion. "Your drink, ma'am?"

The woman frowned and glanced back and forth between them. "Coffee, please."

"The same," he barked, dismissing her and staring down at his menu. "And water," he called as she walked away.

Ellie pulled a tray from beneath the counter and slammed it down next to the ice machine. Nelson Osborn was a stubborn man. He'd laughed her out of his office the first time she'd asked about flying lessons, humored her the second time when she'd cornered him at the terminal, and avoided her ever since.

She glanced up when a shadow fell across the tray. Her mouth dropped open, but she snapped it shut again. The rich guy had taken a seat at the counter. It was unnerving, seeing him up-close. He was so gorgeous, it had to be a sin just to look at him. It was no wonder most of the girls who worked here had offered him much more than pie for dessert.

"Hey…um," she looked down the line, searching for Erica, who was supposed to be working behind the counter tonight. But there was only the new kid Joe had hired to bus tables. She turned back to the man with a tired smile. "What can I get you to drink?"

"Tea, please."

Did she detect an accent? English, maybe? Or Scottish? Ooo, a Highlander. Drop-dead gorgeous in his Canali suit. Rich enough to pay cash for one of the oldest houses in town, or so the rumor went. Could he be more perfect?

Now here was the kind of man a girl should lose her mind over. Not some outcast with no ambition, no future.

Erica came out from the back and took the glass of tea from her hand mid-air. "I've got it," she practically sang as she set it on the counter in front of her customer.

Ellie rolled her eyes and picked up the tray she'd filled for the flight instructor. Crossing the busy dining room with the tray held overhead was no easy feat, but she carefully made her way through the traffic and set their drinks on the table. "Might I suggest the *Unconditional*

Surrender?" she asked sweetly. It was Betty's most popular burger.

He held up the menus. "Two Chicken Cheesesteaks."

Gritting her teeth, Ellie took the menus and left them alone. Her other tables kept her busy, but she still glanced at the clock every few minutes and tried to ignore the continuous ringing of the bell. Betty's closing time of *'til late* was an irritant to say the least. They sometimes closed as early as eleven or as late as two in the morning. Still, she enjoyed her job most days. Betty Bomber's was one of coolest restaurants in town, a fun place to work. The food was great. There was always a variety of people in and out, both locals and tourists. She had gotten to know some of the other girls well enough that she could almost say she had friends. While she'd been popular enough in school, she hadn't been close to anyone except Michael. Most people considered her too bossy. She hadn't kept in touch with anyone after she left.

Morgan and Erica were the closest things she'd had to friends in a long time. Both of them had moved here to go to school. Morgan attended the Savannah College of Art and Design while Erica was apparently studying the effects of alcohol consumption at whichever bars were having the biggest parties on her nights off.

She watched Erica now, leaning over the counter, her uniform top unzipped further than usual. The rich guy seemed captivated by their conversation but never once looked down at her exposed cleavage. When she excused herself to help another customer, he looked over at Ellie. Had he sensed her staring? He rolled his eyes at Erica's back and shook his head.

They shared a conspiratorial smile.

Nelson Osborn's companion caught her attention with a quick wave, and Ellie hurried over. "Can I get our check, please?"

"Where's Nelson?" she asked, pulling it from her apron pocket. She was reluctant to hand it over.

"In the restroom." The woman pulled a twenty from her purse and handed it to her. "You can just keep the change."

A whopping buck, twenty-five? Was it any wonder she couldn't *pay* for flying lessons? Ellie smiled. "Thank you." She walked over and stood by the men's room door, tapping her foot while she waited.

He jumped when he walked out and found her there. "Jeez, Miss King. This is harassment."

Ellie followed him as he wove his way through the diner. "Mr. Osborn, if you'll just give me five minutes–"

He stopped so abruptly, she almost collided with him. "What you're asking is ridiculous. No one is going to give you free flying lessons. Why would anyone do that? Because you're passionate? Enthusiastic? Welcome to the club." He turned and stormed toward his companion who waited patiently by the door.

Ellie watched him leave, taking her dreams with him.

***

She pushed away the sense of defeat that taunted her. She would not give up. There had to be a way. She turned away, more determined than ever to get what she wanted.

This time, she found *him* staring. "What are you looking at?" she asked. He was Erica's customer, not hers. She didn't have to be nice to him.

"Why do ye need flying lessons?" he asked.

Definitely Scottish. "Why else would I need lessons?" she huffed. "I want to fly airplanes." She lifted her chin towards his plate. "You finished with that?" At his nod, she set it in a plastic tub to be taken back to the dishwasher later.

"But ye dinna want to pay." He sipped his coffee.

"It's not that I don't want to," she said. She wasn't about to unload her financial woes on a stranger, especially one who probably had no idea what it was like to hurt for cash, but Gran's limited income was not enough to cover their living expenses. No, all of her money was spoken for before she earned it, which left none for her to pursue her dream or a way to a better future. "Money's tight, that's all.'

He nodded, as if in understanding. "Why not join the military?"

She shrugged. "I think I'm too old. Plus, I barely finished high school." She missed too many days taking care of her mother to have any real success. She'd had to take an English class her senior year just to have enough credits to graduate. She twisted the water from a clean towel and began wiping the counter.

Erica rushed over to see if he needed anything else. He handed her a couple of bills. *Probably twenties*, Ellie thought with disappointment. He reached into the inside pocket of his jacket and pulled out a business card.

"Perhaps I can help," he said, handing the card to Ellie. "It just so happens I have an airplane. And I ken a pilot or two. Give me a call tomorrow." He winked at Erica, then turned and left.

Her heart racing, Ellie looked down at the card in her hand. Lucan Munro. Yep, the address was the Dresser-Palmer house. Plus, his private cell phone number. It said so: *private.*

"Oh. My. God." Erica tried to take the card but, Ellie pulled it out of reach. "I just want to see," she said.

"Maybe he's going to let me fly his plane. Or...or teach me." She could hardly keep the excitement from her voice.

Erica's laugh held a touch of resentment. "I bet he is."

"What's that supposed to mean?"

"You have to ask? It has been a long time for you, hasn't it?"

Ellie shook her head. "It wasn't like that." At least she hadn't thought so. Lucan Munro was beautiful to look at, but her mouth hadn't gone dry at the mere sight of him. Her heart hadn't flip-flopped when he smiled at her. He hadn't made all the blood rush to her core when he brushed her fingers while handing off his business card.

Only one man had done those things to her. She wondered suddenly if he and Michael were related, but Erica broke into her thoughts.

"You know he'll be expecting *something*," she said. "No one's going to teach you to fly for free."

Ellie sighed and stuck the card in her pocket. "You're not the first person to tell me that."

"Why do you want to fly planes, anyway? Seems like a lot of responsibility."

Ellie finished wiping the counter. "I was in the cockpit of a plane once. There's nothing else like it. The drop in your stomach when the plane leaves the ground. The adrenalin rush at being suspended in midair. The view. The freedom." She pulled a wad of singles from her pocket. "And did I mention the pay is much better than waiting tables?"

"I hate to fly," Erica said. "Fear of heights will do that to you. You could do worse than Lucan Munro, though. You definitely need to get laid, and who better than him?"

I can think of one. Ellie had thought her feelings for Michael had faded, right along with acne and the drama of high school. But seeing him yesterday had dredged up old memories, memories she'd tried to lock away. "He's probably married," Ellie said.

Erica shook her head. "I don't think so. He always comes in here alone."

"That doesn't mean anything."

"He doesn't act married," she said. "A little strange, I think. Always alone, quiet. I mean, he'll chat and all, but very subdued. Constantly looking over his shoulder and checking everyone out while acting like he's not."

"Adam and Eve on a raft," the cook shouted across the counter that separated the kitchen from the dining room.

"That's me," Erica said sashaying down the line.

What was it about a quiet man that made people think there was something wrong with him? She had watched Michael suffer the judgment of people for years. To her, his solitude was one of the things that made him so intriguing. His efforts to be invisible were exactly what made him stand out. While others took his dark demeanor as a threat of sorts, Ellie had found him fascinating and mysterious, more exciting than any other boy at school.

She felt a connection to him she had not felt before or since. Neither of them had friends to speak of. She'd had a number of 'fake' friends, people seemed to gravitate towards whoever took charge, but none of them were close. Michael displayed the same cold, harsh demeanor she had been afflicted with as long as she could remember. She didn't mean to drive people away. Her brusqueness and pushy manner were simply the upshot of her take-charge personality, her ability to see the big picture and know how to get things done.

Michael had seemed to appreciate that about her. Her strength and assurance gave him confidence he said. She had wondered at the time how such a cute guy could lack confidence. He had that thick dark hair that she loved and those golden eyes made her insides melt every time he looked at her. She was curious about what made him tick. What did he think about? What did he want out of life?

After she left for Atlanta, she realized the answer was nothing. Michael had no drive, no dreams. He seldom spoke of the future, expecting no more than the here and now. She suspected he was afraid. Afraid to dream or hope for a better life, security, acceptance.

Love.

Yes, he was her first love. Her teenaged self, rebellious and self-assured, was impatient to learn the joys of sex. And who better to have as her first than the boy who set her nerves on fire? She'd known Michael would be discreet. Who would he tell? So she'd bucked up her courage, did some research on the topic, and organized an evening of discovery that had left her thrilled and eager for more.

She hadn't expected to fall so hard for him.

She'd known of course that Michael had a crush on her. He always had. But that didn't bother her nearly as much as the feelings that welled up inside her. She knew she was in trouble when she caught herself doodling his name on her notebook during Science class.

She tried to distance herself from him, afraid of the hold he had over her. He never pushed her, never made demands on her time. As long as they were together he seemed satisfied. His lack of concern over her refusal to be called his *girlfriend* should have settled her fears. Instead, it was her first indication that Michael Munro was a *wait and see what happens* kind of guy.

She, however, was determined to settle for nothing less than what she wanted. It was a philosophy Ellie had taken to heart. If you wanted something in life, you had to take it. No one was going to give it to you. She had wanted more out of life than living in this slow, Southern town with her grandmother. She envisioned herself as the primary caregiver for an aging invalid and vowed that that was not going to be her life. The only threat to her future plans had been Michael Munro.

***

It was after midnight. By now the diner had cleared out, and Joe locked the door. Finally. While Joe reconciled the money, Ellie organized everyone who was closing the diner into teams based on their skills. Morgan was in charge of the dishwashers. She could get speed out of them when all they wanted to do was lolly-gag about, taking their time and turning closing into a party. Erica was happy enough to supervise the wait staff. She had them hopping within moments, filling salt and pepper shakers, marrying the condiment bottles, rolling the requisite twenty sets of silverware.

Ellie ran around, being extra careful not to slip where the floor had already been mopped, ensuring that there were no slackers and helping out where needed. Closing the diner was a team effort. The sooner the place was ready for opening the next day, the sooner they could all leave for the night. Everyone had to do his or her part.

She was exhausted by the time they headed out to the parking lot. Ellie shouldered her backpack and unlocked her bicycle, ignoring the flash of lightning that lit up the distant sky. With any luck, she would make it home before it started raining. But even if she got wet, she wasn't going to let it ruin her good mood. Things had finally started to look up, and a little rain wasn't going to spoil that.

She waved goodnight to Morgan and Erica before turning onto Bull Street. Ellie was so excited about tomorrow, she doubted she'd be able to sleep at all tonight. She considered cruising up and down some of the more picturesque streets in Savannah's historic district. The majestic, moss-draped trees lining the roads, the centuries-old Victorian houses, the perfectly groomed squares all made for a magical place.

She cut through Forsyth Park. Gran would lecture until the cows came home if she knew she was riding through the park at this late hour. Ellie had blown off her concerns time and again. This wasn't the most dangerous part of town. There were certainly worse. With so many tourists about at all hours of the day and night, citizens of Savannah could usually find a police officer within shouting distance. Besides, she had her handy-dandy canister of pepper spray tucked into the pocket of her Betty Bombers uniform and another dangling from her handlebars.

She had started carrying it almost as soon as she had gotten to Atlanta. During the bus ride that morning after her mother called for her, Ellie had let herself imagine the wonderful adventures the two of them would have in the big city. Gran had tried to warn her, tried to convince her to stay. Ellie had ignored the tears in her eyes, convincing herself she was better off with her mom than wasting her life in this boring town with an old woman. What a great time she and Mama would have together.

The reality had hit her the moment she stepped out of the cab she'd taken from the Greyhound station to the address her mom had provided. She wondered briefly if she had the right address. Surely her mom didn't live in the dilapidated four-story building in front of her. Iron bars covered every window. A homeless man lay curled on the broken sidewalk. Trash tumbled up and down the street before being lodged against a wall or fence, doomed to spend the next few years decomposing, for surely no one had cleaned this street in decades. It was a far cry from the manicured lawns and squares of Savannah. Her mom hadn't picked her up at the bus station. That should have been her first clue that life in Atlanta wasn't going to be all she dreamed. She had barely closed the cab door before the driver spun away.

The crack of gunfire nearby had made her jump. She hoped it was just a car backfiring and not a gun shot. Without waiting to find out, she made a mental note to get pepper spray as soon as possible and hurried into her mother's apartment building. She found what she hoped was the right door and knocked, then knocked again, and finally banged loud enough to wake the dead. After long, uncertain moments, Mama had opened the door. Disheveled and irritated, her only comment, by way of a greeting, was that she hadn't expected Ellie to show up so soon. She had turned away, gone back to her bedroom, and left Ellie to get herself settled.

Even in those early days, Ellie had known she'd made a mistake. She had been blinded by her fantasies. It had taken until a few weeks ago for her to admit it.

Emerging from Savannah's most famous park, Ellie went straight a couple of blocks until she reached Monterey Square, then followed Bull Street around until she was back on Jones. The sky, void of moon and stars, was inky black. Shadows seemed to jump out at her from the hanging moss and dim street lights.

A bright flash of lightning blinded her followed immediately by a deafening clap of thunder. The air crackled for a few seconds before all went dark and silent again. Ellie took a deep breath, trying to calm her nerves. *Get it together, Ellie-lamb. Just a storm brewing.*

Fat drops of rain smacked against her cheeks, further discouraging a midnight ride around the Historic District. The trip from Betty's to Gran's house only took about twenty minutes by bike, but by the time she arrived, the rain was coming down harder. Frequent streaks of lightning illuminated the sky, the resulting thunder crashed and rumbled non-stop.

Ellie coasted around to the back of the house and put her bike in the shed. She was soaked now and shivering. No doubt Gran waited up for her with a hot drink. She felt a familiar twinge of guilt at her own lack of appreciation for all the things Gran had done for her. It couldn't have been easy—raising a child in her twilight years, supporting them both on a small income, putting up with a rebellious teenager. Gran really and truly loved her, unconditionally.

Ellie had been a jerk to her her whole life. A mistake she vowed to remedy every day that Gran remained on this earth.

She pushed open the back door and stepped inside the eerily quiet house. It was unlike Gran not to wait up for her, but the house was dark as well as silent. No sound came from the television she normally had turned up too loud. No lights to chase away the gloom of the old house. Only the soft glow from a single lamp in the front room.

Ellie pulled the bag from her shoulders and fished out the pastry she'd brought home. She set it on the counter in the kitchen, let the bag drop to the floor, and continued toward the front of the house. The tiny hairs on her neck stood up, making her light-headed and jumpy. She tiptoed across the wood floor, careful to avoid the planks that squeaked.

She found her grandmother on the sofa, instead of in her comfy chair, the handset from the old-fashioned telephone in her lap, discarded and putting off a beeping sound.

"Gran?" Ellie turned on another lamp. "Are you alright?"

"They killed her," she said, her voice barely above a whisper. A single tear slid down her cheek. "My baby girl is dead."

Gran only had one baby girl.

Ellie's mother.

CHAPTER THREE

Ellie stood on the landing at the top of the stairs. She could see her mother's apartment door just down the hall. It was easy to pick out. It was the only one with remnants of crime scene tape stuck to the frame.

Forcing her feet forward, she moved toward it, compelled by sounds of shouting, glass breaking, feet stomping up and down the stairwell. She didn't like being here alone, never had. She ripped the remaining yellow and black tape off of the door and shoved her key into the lock. It didn't turn right away, and Ellie stood there fiddling with it for what seemed like long moments. Panic swept over her. Had Mama changed the locks? That seemed unlikely. Besides, she could feel it give a little.

Adjusting her bag over her shoulder, Ellie grabbed the handle with her other hand and tried pulling and pushing as she worked the key around to the unlocked position. She grew more frantic at the sound of footsteps on the stairs. In a near panic, she began yanking on the door, twisting the key so hard she feared it might break off in the lock. She didn't want to be caught out here alone. No one would come if she screamed.

When the bolt finally released, she practically fell into the apartment. She closed the door quickly as the footsteps drew closer and closer, and slammed each of the six deadbolts home. She pressed her ear to the door, but heard no further sounds of threat.

Heaving a sigh of relief, Ellie leaned against the door and closed her eyes. She had hoped never to come here again. Nothing had changed, except maybe the building was even more run-down. Bars still covered the windows. A homeless guy still slept on the sidewalk.

She had left Savannah early that morning after a quick call to the diner to let them know she wouldn't be back for a few days. She took Gran's SUV for the three-and-a-half-hour drive. Gran had wanted to come, too, but she was in no condition to be of any help. Ellie had convinced her to stay home and let her take care of everything.

It was a long and tedious trip under the best of circumstances, but today had been especially difficult. She couldn't believe her mother was gone, murdered. It was too horrible to be real. She told herself it wasn't true. They had identified the wrong woman. She could hardly wait to get here and prove it.

She had gone first to the morgue where a police detective had been waiting. She followed him and the coroner into a cold, sterile room where an aide in a white lab coat pulled out a long, shiny stainless steel drawer.

Strangely, Ellie had had no reaction as she stared down at her mother's face. Gone was the garish make-up. Her lips, usually bright red and slightly smeared, were as pale as the rest of her skin. She reached out and brushed a lock of bleached blonde hair off of her forehead, then turned and nodded to the detective. She swallowed hard, not looking back when the aide slid the drawer closed.

Numb and afraid to speak for fear of breaking down, she gritted her teeth and let the men usher her from the room. She would not be allowed to collect her mother's body until after the autopsy, a few days at the most. Plenty of time for her to pack up her things and get them loaded in the car. After making arrangements for her mother's cremation, Ellie left the morgue and came straight home.

Home.

She shoved away from the door. This was not home. It never had been. Nothing had turned out the way Ellie had hoped. Her mom had made her get a job right away. Everything she earned went to rent and food. At least Ellie hoped that was all she was spending it on. She had never witnessed her taking drugs, but that wasn't proof that her mother was clean.

Every few months, she would bring home a new man. Inevitably, he would make a move on Ellie. Her mother always blamed her. *Ellie had flirted with him, come on to him, walked around in skimpy clothes in an effort to lure him away.* Soon enough he would be gone, subsequently replaced by another.

Ellie turned and faced the darkness. The apartment had few enough windows, and those were always closed with blinds or curtains. The glow of the daylight that managed to seep in lent an eerie glow to the scene, punctuated by the chalk outline on the living room floor.

Choking back a sob, Ellie stumbled into the room. She stood over the spot, imagining her mother lying there. What had she seen in her last moments? What had she felt? Ellie glanced around. The apartment was in disarray, but when had it not been? Her mother had never been the homemaker type. She didn't clean. She certainly didn't cook.

It was difficult to tell if a struggle had taken place. There was no DNA, no evidence of a break-in. So, it was probably someone she knew.

Ellie swallowed, blinking quickly at the tears that burned behind her eyes. Had death come suddenly, or had her mom been afraid in those last moments? How had she died? Strangulation? Poisoning? The police didn't like to make assumptions. Better to wait for the autopsy.

What if Ellie had not left? Would her mother still be alive? Would she too be dead now?

Guilt assaulted her. She pinned her arms against her stomach, wrapping herself in a protective hug that was little defense against ill feelings. She should have stayed. She should never have left her mother alone and unprotected. Mama was vulnerable, had always been too trusting. She allowed men into their lives with little more than the promise of paying the rent that month. It was a wonder something bad hadn't happened before now. Maybe if she had been there, it wouldn't have this time either.

Who was she kidding? Her mother had gone from dating a hot-shot pilot to shacking up with a truck driver from Cordele. Could one of them be her killer? The police said the truck driver was in route to Minnesota on business. But what about the pilot? Of all her mother's boyfriends, he had been Ellie's favorite. He'd been the one to give her her first and only taste of flying. Not long after that, he'd wanted to give her a taste of something else. He'd turned out to be not so different than the others, just worse.

When her mom had taken up with the truck driver so soon after the pilot's departure, Ellie accepted that her childhood fantasy, the one filled with family and adventure, was never going to happen. For years, she overlooked her mother's shortcomings, making excuses for her and accepting her weaknesses as a cry for help.

But Mama didn't want her help, not the emotional kind that might get her out of the rut she'd been living for too long. As soon as one man was gone, another would take his place, and Ellie would always take a back seat.

The pilot's betrayal was especially disappointing. Ellie had had such high hopes. He'd promised Mama, promised both of them, the moon. Stability, security, family.

At the age of twenty-two, Ellie was forced to reflect on her past and make some decisions about her future. Her mother relied on her, it was the real reason Ellie had not left before now, but not for the things that were important. Bills, bills, bills...Mama could always find a man to cover those things.

She had known her decision would not be good for her mom, but she had to do what was best for *her*. Didn't she? Wasn't she entitled to that? Otherwise, Ellie feared she would find herself following in the same path of destruction that was leading her mother to an early grave.

Ellie took a deep, pained breath and closed her eyes. The tightness in her chest merely squeezed a little more. Was it so wrong to want more? To want to make something of her life? Would her presence here have made any difference? Ellie would never know. If she could go back, she wouldn't have done differently. She would have to live with that.

She knelt down, placing one hand on the floor in the center of the outline but keeping her other arm wrapped protectively around her. Unable to hold them back, tears flowed freely down Ellie's cheeks now. She let them fall, crying for her mother with a despair she'd never known before.

***

After a long, hard cry that left her breath hitching and her eyes swollen and burning, Ellie pulled herself together and got down to business. Her mom had few belongings, so it didn't take long to organize her things and pack them into boxes. She stacked them by the door, anxious about the several trips she'd have to make to load them into the SUV.

She filled several trash bags and piled them in the kitchen where she intended to leave them. She doubted her mom had ever paid the rent with actual money and was certainly not entitled to refund of a deposit, so the landlord could take out the trash. She scrubbed away the outline the police had drawn around her mother's body, relieved that at least there hadn't been any blood.

She had to trek up and down the stairs several times to get everything loaded. Each time, she shoved the box in the SUV, slammed the rear door, and bolted back up the two flights of stairs. She was exhausted.

Sunlight outside the now open windows was fading fast. She wanted to be out of here before it got dark. She had one more box to take down. She made a final sweep of the apartment to be sure she hadn't missed anything. Satisfied she had gotten everything that belonged to her mother, she opened the door to her own room. She hadn't been in there yet—certain she'd taken everything the first time.

She stared down at the bed.

It was there he assaulted her, the pilot. There her mother found them, tangled up in her bedspread, Ellie's skirt wrapped around her waist. The remains of the speaker her mom had grabbed and thrown across the room when she opened the door still lay on the floor where it had landed. Her mother had barely spoken to

Ellie after the pilot stormed from the house, ranting at them like he was the victim, even after she'd moved on to the truck driver.

Ellie shoved the broken speaker beneath the bed with her foot and tried to block out the unpleasant memory. She rattled the drawers of her empty dresser. Yep, still empty. She had taken everything when she'd moved back to Savannah. She didn't expect to find anything in there.

Until she tried to close one of the drawers and it caught against something behind it.

Pulling out the empty drawer, she set it on the floor and reached blindly inside the cabinet. Her finger tips came up against a crumple of paper that must have fallen behind the drawer. Ellie pulled it out and caught her breath as she started down at a bulky gold envelope.

She had forgotten all about it.

She plopped right down on the floor and dumped out the contents of the envelope. Her heart flip flopped and tears blurred her vision as she stared down at the mementos scattered around her.

Ellie King didn't keep mementos, so why had she kept all this junk? Why would a person want to be reminded of things they no longer had? And by 'things', she meant people. She had avoided personal relationships most of her life. She realized now it was to avoid the pain when those relationships ended.

When she was younger, she had figured most people didn't appreciate her abrupt manner or her reluctance to get too close or care too deeply. She now realized those weren't personality quirks, but deliberate measures to keep people at a distance. She was sad to admit she had been lonely as long as she could remember. Apparently, her defense mechanism worked.

Except on Michael Munro.

Spread out on the floor were dried flowers, a gum wrapper, a straw, the torn halves of two movie tickets, worn notes on scraps of lined paper. Her heart clenched at Michael's familiar scrawl. He hadn't had a cell phone in high school, so they'd been forced to pass notes the old-fashioned way. She had known him since they were children, but they'd only done anything that could be called dating for about a month before their one night of discovery.

Three days later she left.

Her mother had called a few times over the years, but she had never given any indication of her whereabouts, much less offered for Ellie to come and live with her. Ellie had gone without hesitation.

Better she left before he did.

Wasn't that always the way it was? Sooner or later, everyone left. Ellie had found it easy enough to keep a tight rein on her feelings for others. Don't have any—that was the bottom line. If you didn't care about people, it wouldn't hurt when they left.

The more she let herself fall in love with Michael, the more it was going to hurt in the end. A change in tactic had been in order, and her mother's phone call couldn't have come at a better time.

She gathered up the memorabilia and shoved it back into the envelope. It wasn't like her to get all sappy. Ellie blamed in on her still tender emotions over the loss of her mom. It was enough to make a hardened criminal sappy.

She tossed the envelope onto the pile of trash in the kitchen as she walked by, then hefted the box she'd left by the door. She stuck her head into the hallway before stepping out, but couldn't make her feet move. With a sigh, she set the box down and went back to retrieve the envelope.

She hurried down the stairwell as fast as possible while balancing the envelope on top of the box. She fiddled with the SUV's rear door handle, wishing it was one of those you could open with your foot. She forgot to pull her head back in time and almost got hit as the door lifted with a whoosh.

An eerie sense of being watched flowed over her. Ellie glanced around, but saw no one except the man asleep on the sidewalk. She shoved the box into the SUV and slammed the door.

It didn't close. Frustrated, Ellie hefted it open again and shoved harder at the box, but it didn't budge. She dropped her purse on the bumper and worked at the box with both arms. Still no luck. She would have to go around to the passenger door and try to make some room near the front.

Just as Ellie stepped back, she sensed she was not alone. A scream welled up inside her at the sensation of someone behind her. Before that scream could be let loose, a hand clamped over her mouth.

***

Michael was forced to drag her across the sidewalk. How could a woman dig her heels into concrete? In his mind, he saw her fumble for the canister at her waist and clamped a tighter hold on her arms. He anticipated her stomping his foot and pulled it out of the way just in time. All of this would have been much easier if she wasn't struggling like a wet cat.

Just as they faded into the shadow of the building, voices could be heard coming from the vicinity of Ellie's SUV. Michael pressed her against the building. Damn! He needed her to be still. He kept his hand over her mouth and turn her around to face him. Recognition flared in her eyes, quickly replaced by the anger he knew so well. She stilled instantly.

"She was just here."

"See if she went back inside."

Ellie pressed her eyebrows together. Did she know that voice? Was the man who spoke someone she knew? The first man's hurried footsteps drifted away, leaving the growing darkness in relative silence. *Only two men, then,* Michael guessed. Two men were no threat at all, but his first concern was for Ellie's safety.

He removed his hand from her mouth and held a finger to his lips. He grimaced at the imprint of his fingers on her cheek, but then his attention was drawn to her parted lips. An image of those sweet lips wrapped around his cock jolted his entire body to attention. Was is a vision? A premonition? Or was it just wishful thinking?

Thankfully, she remained quiet. When her tongue darted out, slid all the way around her lips before withdrawing again, he thought it would be his undoing. He was excruciatingly aware of her firm body pressed against him. It molded to his in all the right places. Soft mounds and curves contrasted with her toned muscle, the combination causing an uproar of sensations throughout his own body.

She seemed little relieved to realize it was he who had assaulted her and now held her captive. Was she afraid of him?

He relaxed his hold but not enough to let her go. He could feel her trembling which only made him more driven to protect her. He had been surprised to find her here. He never would have guessed, when Lucan gave him this assignment, that the woman who had lived upstairs had any connection to Ellie. Now, he realized she must have been Ellie's mother.

He had always known of Ellie's longing to be with her. She had spoken often of the day her mother would send for her. He shouldn't have been surprised when she left. But he had indulged in stupid, adolescent fantasies. He believed he could give her the security she craved, make her forget her deadbeat mother and choose him. He was aware of her abandonment issues and refusal to get close to people, but he would change all that.

Then she was gone. Just like that. She had left him and never looked back. He had meant nothing to her in the end.

So why was he so acutely aware of every inch of her body? Of the way her freed hands rested on his hips? Of the smell of her shampoo and the scent of that soap with the baby oil in it? The intense beat of her heart vibrated against him. Michael was distracted by a vision of the two men driving off in the SUV, premonitions of what would happen in the next several minutes, frustrating when he wanted to focus on Ellie.

After their one night together, he'd had three days to dream up new and exciting ways of making love to her. He wanted to please her in ways she'd never imagined. He wanted to make her come again and again, writhing beneath him and crying his name. Three days until she shattered his dreams.

He had imagined her in his arms so many times. Not quite under these circumstances, but Michael had learned to appreciate the gifts offered him. And Ellie King was indeed a gift. She oozed sex appeal, even more prominent now than when she was sixteen. He hadn't thought of her in that way until they'd both hit puberty, but when he did, he could think of little else.

He had loved her since the first time he'd seen her, and no matter that she'd bossed him around like she was a queen, tormented him emotionally for most of his life, and dumped him in a snap for a better offer, he loved her still.

And oh yeah, he was thinking of her *in that way* real hard right now.

He stifled a groan against the painful heightening of his senses, the raw need of his cock. He could see desire in her eyes, as well, even though it was full dark now. They were so close, he could see her pupils, black as jet and obliterating the rich brown he had lost himself in so many times before. What he wouldn't give to lose himself now. He wanted to bury himself inside her.

Michael ground his teeth against the twitch in his balls. How did she still have the power to affect him like this? Did the blood of the gods flow in her veins, as well? Was she descended from Demona, or some such goddess with the power of seduction? Why did he allow himself to care about her when she so obviously didn't feel the same way about him? Resentment flared inside him at the betrayal of his own body. After all the hurt and anger…and time.

It had been more than six years. Years of deeper solitude and bitterness than he'd ever known before. He should be over her by now.

He wasn't.

To lessen the pressure on his painfully hard cock, he shifted, dropping his head a fraction. Encouraged when she didn't shy away, he lowered his head a little more. The warmth of her breath brushed his skin. Michael swallowed against the ferocious dryness of his throat. If he kissed her, he would be lost forever.

She didn't close her eyes as his mouth approached hers. He could read her emotions so well. She was frightened and excited at the same time. The rapid hiss of her breathing, the pounding of her heart, the occasional slide of her tongue across her lips…

Arduinna have mercy.

"She's not there."

They both started. Michael was surprised he had not anticipated the man's return. He marveled at how much his ability to focus had improved under Lucan's coaching.

"It doesn't matter. Look what I found." The jangle of keys rang in the darkness.

Ellie's eyes widened, and she stiffened in his arms. Michael tightened his hold, shaking his head and pressing a finger to his lips. She glared daggers at him, but remained quiet. And still—thank the gods.

One door slammed, then another. Moments later, the SUV sped away.

CHAPTER FOUR

Ellie pushed Michael away and darted out onto the sidewalk. "Hey!"

Michael rushed to her side. "Stop yelling. Do you want them to come back?"

She turned her fury on him. Her fear had quickly turned to anger when the men had stolen the SUV. "Yes, dammit. That's my grandmother's car. My purse in there." She choked on a sob. "And all my mom's stuff."

He reached out, but she twisted away from him. "Don't worry. They'll dump it as soon as they realize that what they're looking for isn't there."

"What *are* they looking for?"

Michael stared after the SUV. "I don't know," he finally said.

He was lying. "Then how do you know it's not there?"

He seemed reluctant to answer. What was he hiding? Did he have something to do with Mama's murder? Was her dismissal at the diner the final straw? Was he so incensed that he would...she almost laughed at the thought. Michael Munro wasn't capable of killing another person.

Was he?

"I already searched your mother's apartment."

She took another step away from him and fiddled with the can of pepper spray at her waist. "You rifled through my mom's things for something—you don't even know what." She narrowed her eyes at him. "How do you know you didn't find it? And why were you looking for it in the first place?"

"My uncle sent me here to protect her. But when I arrived, she was already dead. Naturally, I searched the place."

"Naturally." Each revelation only brought up more questions. "What uncle? I thought you didn't have any other family."

"He's a distant relative of my father's. He tracked me down a few months ago and...brought me into the fold, if you will."

"How did he know my mother?"

"I'm not sure. I didn't realize who she was until now."

Realization suddenly dawned on her. "One of those men could have been the one who murdered her. They were looking for me."

Michael shook his head. "They've only been watching the building for about half an hour. You were just coming down when they first arrived, so they hung back." He pointed to the side of the building where they'd just come from. "I waited there in case they threatened you, but I honestly don't think it was you they were after."

"I'm calling the police." Her phone was in her purse. "Please tell me you have a cell phone."

He smirked at her, but reached into his back pocket and pulled out his phone. Her fingers brushed his skin when he handed it to her, sending a jolt of heat all the way up the back of her neck.

"Best not to mention that I was up there," he said, nodding towards the upper floors of the building.

"Or that you were spying on me?" He didn't respond, and Ellie didn't expect him to. She used the Emergency Call feature on the phone without having to ask for his security code. How many times had she ignored that button on her own phone, never thinking she'd have to use it?

"9-1-1. What's your emergency?"

After giving the operator all the information, she handed the phone back to Michael. "They'll be here any minute."

They were silent for a while before Michael said, "I didn't know she was your mother, Ellie. I'm sorry."

She had many questions but one in particular was nagging her. "Why would your uncle send you to protect my mother?"

Again he had that guarded look. He hesitated, like he was trying to decide how much to tell her. "It's just something he does. He likes to—look after people. Mostly kids who are being mistreated, but sometimes adults, too. He sent *me* because I'm the best...if I get there in time."

She wondered how many other times he'd been too late. "So you're his...what...hired thug?"

He grinned, a forced smile that was far from sincere. "Something like that."

They turned at the sound of a car pulling along the curb. She was surprised to find an unmarked car instead of the familiar blue and red sedan of the Atlanta police. Mr. Blackburn, the detective from the morgue, stepped out of the passenger side.

"Miss King." He indicated the driver of the vehicle who joined them. "This is Officer Calvert." The officer took out a note pad and pencil and prepared to take notes. "Are you all right, Miss King? Were you hurt at all?"

"No, I'm fine. Please call me Ellie."

He nodded. "Would you like to go inside?" He continued when she shook her head. "Or prefer to sit in the car."

"I'm fine, really."

He looked at Michael. "And who are you, son?"

Michael drew up, but relaxed when Ellie placed her hand on his arm. "This is a friend of mine. He came to help me get my mom's things."

"What's your name?"

"Michael Munro."

Officer Calvert wrote it in his notebook.

"Okay, Ellie," Blackburn said. "Tell me what happened."

She glanced at Michael. "We were hiding over there when they came up." She pointed to the side of the building where Michael had used his rock hard body to press her into the shadows and shield her from harm.

"Why were you hiding?"

"We came down and found them rummaging through the boxes in the truck," Michael answered when she couldn't think of a response quickly enough. "Unfortunately, Ellie had left it unlocked with her purse and keys inside."

Officer Calvert wrote furiously in his notebook.

Ellie narrowed her eyes at Michael, but didn't contradict his story.

"Understandable," said Mr. Blackburn, "considering the trauma you've been through. Luckily, neither of you was hurt."

"Do you think they're connected to my mom's murder?" Ellie asked when she found her voice.

"Anything's possible." He asked them several more questions, details about the SUV and descriptions of the men, while the other policeman continued to scribble in his notebook. They took Michael's cell phone number, since she no longer had one.

Ellie promised to call if she had any more information. Mr. Blackburn promised the same if he had news. Moments later, she was alone with Michael.

It was awfully quiet for a big city neighborhood. Her stomach rumbled, reminding her she hadn't eaten anything since Gran had shoved a left-over pastry into her hand before Ellie'd left Savannah that morning.

"How about we find a place to stay and get something to eat?"

She still wasn't sure she could trust him, but she was intent on finding out more about his involvement. "I'm not staying in hotel with you."

"I could let you use my phone to call a cab, but then what? How are you going to pay for it or a hotel for that matter? Would you rather sleep up there tonight?"

She hated to admit he had a point. For the next little while, at least, she was completely dependent on him. She glanced around. "Do you have a car?"

***

Ellie clung to Michael with such a death grip, she wondered how he could breath. Every time he hit a bump in the road or swerved, her motorcycle helmet crashed against his. He was probably ready to toss her off the back of his bike by now.

Fear of such a ridiculous notion kept her arms locked around his waist. She'd tried to swallow her anxiety when he informed her they'd be riding his Harley. He was hard as a rock, broad-shouldered with a waist that tapered to the best looking ass she'd ever seen in a pair of jeans. She couldn't help but notice it when he stretched one leg over the iron monster and straddled the beast. Her fear was momentarily forgotten by the distraction but had quickly returned when he handed her a spare helmet.

Now she couldn't decide which was more unnerving: the excitement of gliding through open space, the warm night air against her skin, or the sensation of her thighs spread around him, squeezing so hard she knew she would be sore tomorrow. While the machine between her legs vibrated with relentless abandon, her nipples hardened against his broad back, her palms tingled where she had them splayed across his rock hard torso.

By the time they stopped, she was ready to drag him into whatever flea-bitten motel room he was taking them to and ride him until dawn. But the building he pulled up to rose what looked like one hundred stories into the air. Its round shape made it stand out among the other high-rises in the sky overhead as did the fact that it seemed to be made entirely of glass. The city lights twinkled in the windows.

A crystal palace in the sky.

Ellie had seen the Peachtree Plaza many times as she rode by. It was a familiar landmark on Atlanta's skyline. But she'd never been this close nor dreamed she'd be staying here.

Michael removed his helmet and held out his hand to help her off the motorcycle. She stood next to it on unsteady legs as he pushed down the stand and dismounted. "You okay?"

Ellie regained her bearings and nodded. The weight of the helmet was awkward. She reached beneath her chin to unbuckle it. She only fiddled with it a few seconds before he pushed her hands away and took over. His fingers caressed the tender skin where her pulse throbbed. The buckle was undone too quickly, and he pulled his hands away. When he pushed up the visor, she pulled in a deep breath. Ellie hadn't realized how hard it was to breathe in there.

Michael gripped the bottom of the helmet. "Are you wearing earrings?"

Ellie snapped out of her trance. "What? No."

He pulled the helmet gently over her head. "Let's go check in before we park the bike."

Ellie could only gape as they passed through the lobby to the front desk. The jeans and t-shirts they wore, Michael in a black leather biker jacket, seemed inappropriate for the luxury of the hotel.

The girl behind the desk glanced up and away, but immediately looked up again. Her too-bright eyes raked Michael from head to toe. When she looked back at his stunning gold eyes, she greeted them with a look that made Ellie want to rip the girl's hair out. What happened to the boy girls shied away from because he was *too* dark and mysterious?

Ellie watched him lean against the counter. She paid no attention to his words as he spoke to the girl. She heard him ask for a single room, but was too mesmerized by the movement of his lips to protest.

Michael Munro had turned in to a man women were hungry for. Maybe not the superstitious women of small-town Savannah, but here in the big city…

The girl cleared her throat. "Would you like a room as well, ma'am?"

Before she could answer, Michael said, "That won't be necessary." He gave Ellie a wink. She had to stifle the smirk she wanted to give the girl. Without taking his eyes off Ellie, he continued. "But do gives us two beds. You know, in case something happens to one of them."

Ellie's smug demeanor quick changed to something else. Need rose up in her, red hot and suppressed for too long. Heat spread from between her shoulders, all the way up the back of her neck until she had to resist the urge to fan herself with one hand.

The clerk continued to glare at Ellie with envy throughout the transaction, but finally they were on their way up the long ascent to their room. The silence in the elevator was deafening and so tense, Ellie jumped at the *ding* that indicated they had reached their floor. The hush continued down the hall to their room.

Michael opened the door, and when she stepped inside it was like stepping into another world. Floor to ceiling windows made up the wall on the other side of the room. From the ground, she had thought there were other equally tall buildings surrounding this one, but as she strode across the carpet, her view was unobstructed.

She spread her hands against the glass, pressing right up to it. The sheer drop sixty-nine floors to the ground took her breath away. She let her gaze travel back up and scan the Atlanta skyline from a vantage point she'd had only once before.

"It's just like flying," she said over her shoulder. She grinned at his reflection when it appeared next to hers in the window. "The one time I went up in an airplane, it was just like this. Exhilarating. Terrifying and thrilling at the same time." Ellie realized it was what had always drawn her to Michael.

And still did.

"You like it?" His rich voice washed over her in the darkness.

Their gazes locked in the window's reflection. Ellie nodded and swallowed hard. She turned to face him then. "Thank you for saving me. I could be dead right now." She shuddered.

A look of anguish flickered in his eyes but was gone just as quickly. Concern for her?

"Did you recognize either of them? Their voices?" he asked.

Ellie shrugged and stared back out the window. "I thought one of them sounded familiar, but it was hard to tell."

He moved away, grabbing his keys off the dresser where he'd tossed them. "I'll go park the bike and scrounge up something to eat. Don't let anyone in. Don't even respond if anyone knocks. Got it?"

She suddenly didn't want to be left alone. "What if you need me?"

He turned at the door and gave her a look so hot, so scorching, Ellie feared she'd burst into flame. He winked, then stepped into the hall and closed the door behind him.

***

Michael didn't want to leave her alone, but he had to get out of there fast. It was on the tip of his tongue to tell her just how much he needed her. That was a mistake he *would not make*. He closed the door behind him, pressing his forehead against it and heaving in deep breaths. What was she doing to him? He checked to be sure the door was secured before heading downstairs.

Rushing as he did, it wasn't long before he was back, waving the key card over the sensor and juggling the cold sandwiches he picked up from the coffee shop in the lobby. His heart pounded with the unwarranted fear she would not be there.

He need not have worried. She still stood next to the window where he'd left her. She turned at his entrance.

"That was fast." She pulled two bottles of water from the mini fridge and exchanged one for a sandwich. "I didn't realize how hungry I was until you left. Glad you made it back so quick. I'm starved."

Did he sense relief in her demeanor? Was it hunger that made her glad he was back...and quickly?

Whatever the reason, he felt a sick pleasure. It had always been that way. It didn't matter why she paid attention to him—anger, sympathy, frustration—he was happy to get it. The thought irritated him, boosting his resolve to remain indifferent to her *charms*.

She sat on the corner of the bed, one bare foot propped beneath her, and opened the package. She picked at the contents but didn't take a bite. Michael wolfed his down in just a few bites, chasing the food with the entire bottle of water.

Tossing his trash into the tiny wastebasket, he secured every lock on the door, peered through the peephole, then checked the one adjoined to the room next door. Confident that they were as safe as could be expected, he grabbed the television remote and fell back onto the empty bed. Hopefully, stretched out as he was, he could hide the hard-on that had plagued him since they first entered the room.

"I thought you were hungry," he said, noticing she still hadn't taken a bite of her sandwich.

"I'm...um...sorry," she said.

He flipped to his favorite channel and was lucky enough to find a show that might distract him from the enticing woman in the bed next to his. "Sorry about what?" He tried to focus on the t.v. couple's search for a cheap beach front home, but their words were drowned out by the roaring in his ears. Could she be sorry for deserting him, for using him and leaving him a broken excuse for a man? He tried to sound as flippant as possible. "It's just a sandwich."

Ellie set the container on the end table that separated the two beds and put both feet on the floor. "I'm sorry for being mean to you all the time."

Not what he'd hoped for, but it was something. "You weren't *always* mean to me." He pressed her with his most smoldering look. "There was that one time…"

He was rewarded when she blushed. Her mouth dropped open before snapping shut again. She glanced away and quickly regained her composure. That was his Ellie. Strong. Resilient.

"Yes, well, before that, I wasn't what you'd call nice."

He shrugged. "I didn't think it was personal. You weren't nice to anyone."

Her face fell. "Really?" Her voice was barely a whisper. "No wonder people don't like me."

His heart hitched at the sadness he heard. He shouldn't blame her for jumping at the chance to be with her mom. He would give up anything to see his own mother. He'd been so young when she died, he didn't even remember what she looked like.

But that didn't excuse her for leaving without a word.

"Why, Ellie? Why are you so mean to people?" What he really wanted to ask was why she hadn't said goodbye, why she hadn't kept in touch. Why wasn't he as important to her as she was to him? Thank the gods she answered his question, saving him from making a fool of himself.

"I just feel angry all the time. It seems like I always have. I don't know why. Something inside me makes me feel like I'm mad at the world, and I just take it out on whoever's around.

"I always thought I was just angry about my mom leaving me, but it's never gone away, that anger. My mom is dead. I'm heart-broken and sad. I'm not angry at her anymore, so what is it?" She looked at him with questioning eyes. Questions for which he had no answers.

Michael turned his gaze to the television screen, if only to keep from getting lost in those deep, rich eyes of hers. "Maybe it's just like you said. When someone leaves you like that, you feel like garbage, worthless, like you don't matter. That's enough to piss anybody off." He clicked off the television and tossed the remote onto the end table. He sat up, swinging his legs over the side of the bed, and met her gaze. "That kind of anger just gnaws and gnaws at you, eating away at your gut. That kind of anger—you may never get over it."

For once, she had nothing to say. He noticed the muscles of her throat moving as she worked to swallow. Good. He hoped he had a least made her uncomfortable. The silence stretched on, until finally she found her voice.

"Guess we'd better get some sleep."

Michael stood and pulled his t-shirt over his head. He forced himself not to smile at her sudden gasp. Having the blood of an ancient Celtic god coursing through his veins gave him strength and power most men couldn't claim, a benefit that sometimes came in handy with the ladies. Until they decided they had him figured out. Then they made a hasty exit. He was glad none of them wanted to hang around afterwards. At least that's what he told himself. Michael Munro vowed to never let another woman get under his skin the way Ellie King had done.

She tried to hide her reaction to his naked torso. Michael made no effort whatsoever to relieve her discomfort. He tossed the shirt across to where he laid his leather jacket on the chair. He kept his gazed locked on her lovely face as he stripped down to his boxers, forgoing his sense of modesty, and taking great pleasure in her distress. She never looked away, watching him unbuckle his belt with a fire in her eyes that made Michael burn from the inside.

Her breath hitched with each button he undid down the length of his fly. Her tongue darted out often, moistening her lips and making him want so badly to kiss her, he wondered at his own restraint. Her gaze followed his waistband to his ankles, slowing starting the trek back up his body when he kicked his jeans away. Her lips curved into an erotic O as she took him in, naked except for his boxers, flimsy black cotton material decorated with tiny skulls that did nothing to hide his raging hard-on.

Before he lost all control, Michael pulled back the sheet and bed spread. Raking all but one of the seven pillows to the floor, he climbed into bed and turned out the light. "Good night, Ellie."

He turned his back to her, aware of every move as she got settled and grew quiet. It seemed like hours before her breathing slowed enough to indicate that she'd fallen asleep. Only then did he turn back, watching her sleeping face in the light from the window.

He wouldn't sleep. He couldn't. He had too many thoughts racing around in his head combined with the overwhelming need to protect Ellie. He couldn't afford to let his guard down, not even to sleep.

It was his last coherent thought before he woke to the sound of Ellie screaming.

CHAPTER FIVE

Ellie calmed down the instant Michael got into her bed. It had only been a nightmare, but she had never felt so safe as she did the moment he took her in his arms and used his strong hand to smooth back her sleep-tousled hair.

"Shhh. I'm here. I'm right here."

Outside the window, the sun was just beginning to enlighten the morning sky. She took a deep breath, letting it out slowly and allowing herself a moment to wallow in his embrace. God, he felt good. His body was hard as solid rock, bulky with muscles he didn't have before. He must have pumped a lot of iron over the years. But more than the way he felt physically was how he made her feel inside. Like for once she didn't have to be in control. She could let someone else take care of everything.

No—not just someone else. Michael. She didn't realize how much she'd missed him, how much she'd needed him.

Still she wasn't immune to the effects he was having on her long-neglected libido. Ellie hadn't been with another man in three years. She was just so picky, and no one ever seemed to measure up. Then after the pilot assaulted her, she hadn't thought she'd want another man to touch her for a long time, if ever.

She snuggled against him. His skin was hot, and she could feel his hard-on pressing against her stomach. It was probably because he just woke up and had nothing to do with her. Either way, Michael was definitely aroused. Having dropped her jeans and bra on the floor after Michael had bid her goodnight, she now wore nothing but her t-shirt and panties. He groaned when she wedged her knee between his and molded herself to his side.

Maybe it was her, after all.

Michael threaded his fingers in her hair, cupping her cheek in his palm and tilting her face up. The look in his eyes was almost scary. It *was* scary. And thrilling and seductive and held the promise of unimaginable pleasure. It was a look that threatened to possess her, and for the moment, she couldn't remember why that was a bad thing.

Ellie parted her lips when he brought his mouth down on hers. The moment their tongues met, tiny jolts of pleasure struck all the most intimate spots of her body. Her nipples hardened, the taut peaks of heavy breasts that ached and tingled. Heat swept over her skin like a tidal wave. Moisture slickened her pussy as the tiny nub at her core throbbed with a need so great she found herself grinding against Michael's muscled thigh.

She let him roll her over onto her back, whimpering when he dragged his mouth away from hers. Chills shot down her body when his lips found the sensitive skin of her throat, contrasting with the inferno radiating from inside her. Ellie threw her head back, giving him better access and abandoning all thoughts of resistance.

She splayed both hands across his broad shoulders, holding on for dear life. She felt like she was drowning, swirling down a whirlpool of pleasure that rocked her to her core. She held on as he trailed further down, dragging his teeth across her collar bone before capturing one hard nipple in his mouth.

Ellie sucked in air, then let it out in a loud moan as Michael began to suckle her, working her nipple against the roof of his mouth with his tongue. Where had he learned to do that? Jealousy flared in her at the thought of him with another woman, but when he worked his hand beneath the elastic of her lace panties and slid one finger inside her, she forgot about everything else.

Suddenly, he stopped, lifting his head and staring off at nothing.

"What is it?" she asked. He pressed his eyebrows together, listening. "What?" she asked again. Still he ignored her.

She jerked away from him, suddenly remembering a crucial part of her dream. "I know that voice." She scrambled off the bed, dragging the sheet to hide her near nudity. Clarity came back in a rush, and she felt an overwhelming sense of relief that she had stopped before things got out of control.

Michael came out of his trance. "Where are you going?"

"The men who stole my SUV? I thought I recognized one of them by his voice. It was one of my mom's boyfriends. The pilot who took me flying." An idea took hold. "He must have killed her. Why?" Michael didn't answer, but she hadn't expected him to. Her eyes widened as realization dawned her. "And he would have killed me...if not for you."

They stared at each other in silence for a moment. Finally, she shook her head. "We have to call the police."

Michael got up and started to get dressed. "No need." He pulled on his jeans. He looked no less enticing than he had in only his boxer shorts. "They are about to call you." He pulled his phone from the pocket of his jeans and tossed it to her.

No sooner had she caught it than it vibrated in her hands. She swiped the green button and frowned at him as she held the phone to her ear. "Hello?"

"Miss King. This is Detective Blackburn. I'm calling to let you know we found your vehicle."

She stared at Michael. How had he known that the police were going to call? Unsated desire throbbed painfully between her legs, but she tried to ignore it. "That's good news, detective."

"Nothing appears to have been ransacked, but we'll need to impound the vehicle for a few days, it being a crime scene and all."

"A crime scene?"

"Yes, ma'am. Two men were found with the vehicle. Murdered. The victims were a Jonathon James and a Wilson Chambers. Either of those names mean anything to you?"

Ellie's heart dropped. One she had never heard of, but the other... "Yes. Jonathon was one of my mom's ex-boyfriends. He worked for Southeast Airlines." Jonathon was dead. She didn't feel saddened by the news, but could that mean someone else had killed Mama? Who?

"We'll check that out. You can pick up the vehicle when you collect your mother's remains. I'll be in touch to let you know when that will be. Good day, Miss King."

She pulled the phone away from her ear and stared at the black screen. "He hung up."

"Well, what did he say?"

She handed the phone to Michael and shrugged. "They found Gran's SUV. Nothing seems to be stolen." She looked up at him, making no attempt to hide the worry that had begun to gnaw at her. "I don't think it was the pilot who killed my mom."

***

Ellie clasped her hands together as the waitress set an oval-shaped plate on the table. The left side of the plate was covered in a lake of grits. On the right, two perfectly cooked, over medium eggs. Four triangles of toast, no butter, were piled on top. She waited for the woman to set down her large side of bacon before digging in.

After setting the toast on the plate with the bacon, she hacked the eggs into bite-sized pieces and mixed it with the grits. When everything was ready, she took a bite of everything—eggs, grits, bacon, toast—and closed her eyes. God she was starving. How long had it been since she'd eaten? And here she sat at the Waffle House, eating her favorite breakfast. She chewed slowly, relishing the savory flavors going on in her mouth.

Ellie peeled her eyes open to find Michael staring at her and swallowed. "What?"

He raised his brows and shook his head. A smile touched his lips, one of the first she'd seen. "Is it good?"

"Oh, yeah." She took another bite then waved her fork at his plate. "Why aren't you eating?"

"I was distracted by the show."

Ellie let him tease her, refusing to take the bait. She was happy to have some caffeine in her system, some food in her stomach, and a cushy seat beneath her ass. They had been on the road for hours, tedious enough in Gran's plush SUV. But on the back of Michael's Harley…she had been relieved when he stopped for breakfast half way into their trip.

"Have you thought of anything your mother might have been involved in, anything she had that someone would want bad enough to kill three people?"

She'd thought of little else since they'd left Atlanta. Ellie had never known her mother to do anything illegal. She drank far too much, but the only other addiction her mom had had was men. The wrong men. A string of losers and scumbags had tramped through their lives. None of them had brought along anything of value, not even themselves.

Only the pilot had given Ellie any sense of hope for her mother, that maybe she had finally found a reliable man who would love her. He'd turned out to be even more worthless than the rest.

She shook her head. "I can't think of anything. Why would someone kill the two men who stole Gran's truck? Wouldn't they be working together?"

"Whoever killed them may have known that whatever they are looking for was not with your mom's things."

She finished off the last of her breakfast and motioned the waitress for more coffee. "You mean like you did?"

Michael took the opportunity of the waitress interrupting them to ignore her question. Ellie wasn't about to let him get away with that. As soon as they were alone, she asked again. "Well, what did you mean by that?"

"Nothing. I can just...sense...things sometimes and if whoever killed the pilot and his friend is...like me...maybe he could sense it as well."

"You think you can *sense* this mysterious object? Because you have some kind of powers?"

He shrugged. "Well, my powers aren't sensory, but sometimes—"

"Wait. You have some kind of powers?" Was she hearing him correctly? Had he had an emotional breakdown in the years since she left?

Michael let out a huff. "This isn't how I wanted this conversation to go."

Ellie sat back in her cushy seat. He was deranged. When had that happened? And why hadn't she seen it before now? "Why don't you start over. From the beginning."

He glanced around then stared out the window. "I can see things that are about to happen." He looked back at her, waiting for her reaction, no doubt.

She raised one eyebrow and cocked her head. "So you can tell the future?"

"No, not really. I know what's about to happen moments before it does, sometimes too late for me to do anything about it. Like, I know an old guy in overalls is going to come in with his granddaughter. They could be pulling into the parking lot right now, or it could be another ten minutes."

She looked through the large glass window. There was no one in the parking lot who fit that description. Except for Michael's bike and two pick-up trucks that had been there the whole time, the lot was empty.

Ellie forced herself not to smirk at him. "How long have you had this power?"

"It started after my mother died. Just random visions at first that didn't make any sense. After...you left, they became so frequent and so jumbled, I started having headaches, debilitating migraines that left me dysfunctional. I would lock myself in a dark room for days at a time."

Ellie's heart broke to think of him in so much despair. She envisioned him curled up in pain, left to suffer alone in the dark. Guilt washed over her like an avalanche. "What did you do?"

"My uncle found me, saved me. He taught me how to control the images, to channel them and use them."

"Use them for what?"

He smiled, a wry, sardonic smile that made her heart trip. "Turns out I have some pretty powerful ancestors. I inherited some of their strength, their *talent* for dealing with others."

"Is that what you do for him in return? Deal with people?" She looked up when the door opened and caught her breath at the sight of a heavy set man in overalls. He looked to be in his sixties. With him was a young girl, no more than ten or eleven, in a tank top, cut off shorts, and flip flops. They sat in a booth near the door.

She turned her attention back to Michael who had turned to look at them. Was he telling the truth? He wasn't lying. He definitely believed the story he'd told her, but was it real?

He turned back with a troubled frown. Had he seen something else? Some tragedy about to befall the little girl or her grandfather?

"So now you work for your uncle who likes to protect people. How's the pay for kind of work?"

"I get by."

They were silent for a moment. Ellie was in no hurry to get back on the motorcycle, so she sat quietly sipping her coffee.

"What if it was the pilot?" he asked. At her frown, he continued. "Maybe the pilot had something valuable, something someone else wanted. He could have found it, stolen it..." he shook his head. "Maybe he hid it somewhere in the apartment."

"But you said it wasn't there."

"It could have been there earlier." He pressed his brows together, thinking. "You said you found him in your room."

"He could have hidden it there, but I was sure I took everything when I left." *Except for a faded envelope full of things that would remind me of you.* She would never tell him about that. "I didn't pay much attention when I was packing. All I wanted to do was get out of there. I just threw everything in some shopping bags and walked out, so I could have missed it."

"Where's all your stuff now?"

Ellie felt the blood drain from her face. She choked on her coffee.

"Gran!"

***

Michael opened the throttle and peeled away from the Waffle House. Going the speed limit, they were still about an hour outside Savannah.

He had no intention of going the speed limit.

The sun beat down on them from nearly straight overhead. It was hot for April. The temperature was more like he would expect at the end of May. Combined with the heat rising up from the pavement, Michael couldn't remember ever being so hot. He tried to ignore it as he tore down Interstate 16, overwhelming concern for Ellie's grandmother spurring him to faster and faster speeds. If his suspicions were correct and whoever, or whatever, had killed her mother was on Ellie's trail, her grandmother was in serious danger.

It was going to be a long ride. Made worse with Ellie's legs spread around him.

The tight clamp of her thighs against his hips held him like a vice. Her torso melded to his back, making his already tense body rock hard. It was incredible to feel her body against his again. Astonishing to think that just that morning, he'd been in bed with her, nearly naked, her tits in his mouth and his fingers in her pussy. Her moans of pleasure had driven him to a state of arousal that threatened to destroy any sense of will power he had left. Her puckered nipples had tightened even more against the roof of his mouth. She was wet and excited, and he'd been ready to drive into her until she was screaming his name.

He had to adjust himself on the seat. He'd been so…lost…in her, for once there were no visions clouding his thoughts. None except the one of him making love to her, something he'd dreamed about for years.

Michael had wanted to rip the detective's throat out when an image of him calling interrupted the one of Ellie's head thrown back on the pillow, her ankles locked behind his back, her hands braced against the headboard. The vision had barely started before it was over. He'd barely tasted her.

He could tell she was relieved. No doubt he was a mistake she didn't want to make again. Ellie had made it clear he didn't fit into the plan she had for her life, whatever that plan was. She was done with him and had moved on. The realization ate at him, but sadly didn't make him want her any less.

She clung to him, more tense now than she had been before they stopped to eat. She had actually begun to relax and seemed to be enjoying the ride, even if it was a little uncomfortable. But now, her every muscle was stiff, and every so often she would lean forward as if urging him to go faster. His ass cheeks had grown numb from the grip of her thighs. She had her hands locked in front of him. From time to time, they would brush his cock through his jeans. Michael would have to tighten his hold on the handle bars to keep from losing control of the bike. How could she be so blind to her effect on him?

He was surprised she'd held up as well as she had. She must have known more violence in the last forty-eight hours than she had her whole life. Yet she handled it all with that same self-assured focus that allowed her to see what needed to be done and make a plan to do it. She operated with clarity and precision, just as she always had. He should have expected no less. Still, he had seen grown men break down when faced with overwhelming fear and heartache.

Michael was used to it. He saw death nearly every day and had been forced to defend himself against violence for a long time. Only recently had he learned to channel his power, turning him into a fighting machine that could deliver justice as swiftly as an eagle seizing a rattlesnake, even if swift wasn't always his method. Sometimes justice was best delivered slowly, allowing death to come near, but shutting the door and allowing more time to ensure sufficient retribution.

He'd taken a few seconds to deliver such a threat to the old man in the diner, a quick warning that Michael would be watching, and if he made further 'advances' towards his granddaughter, or anyone else, justice would be slow...and frightening.

Ellie sat up straighter when he slowed and pulled off the highway. They were in the historic district within moments. The roar of his Harley echoed through the close streets, bouncing off the centuries-old houses like a freight train through a mountain tunnel. She was chomping at the bit to get to her grandmother's rescue. Regard for her own safety seemed to be non-existent.

There was a strength inside Ellie King, a strength he'd been drawn to from an early age. A strength that kept most people at arm's length. And here she had her arms wrapped around him, holding on like she'd never let go, and damned if he couldn't help wanting it to be so.

He screeched to a halt in front of the green Victorian, grabbing Ellie's arm to keep her from rushing inside before he could assess the danger. To her credit, she stayed behind him as they silently climbed the steps to the massive double front door. He peered into the bay window that pushed out next to the front porch, but all he saw was the empty sitting room. He tried to scan his thoughts forward, but the only vision that came to him was one of Ellie wasting her time lifting flower pots in search of something, probably a key.

Before she even started looking, Michael turned the ancient knob and pushed the door open.

Her eyes widened. She looked at him with newfound interest. "How did you do that?" she whispered.

He could have attributed it to his power, anything that might impress her, but he decided against it. Ellie was not easily impressed. "It was unlocked."

She rolled her eyes. When he crossed the threshold, Ellie grabbed the back of his jacket. She clung to him, following along as he stepped into the entry and crept through to the sitting room. He held one finger over his lips when she started to call out. Suddenly, he stopped, sucking in a sharp breath. Heat raced down his spine. Pain shot through is skull, a sure sign of mortal danger in the immediate area.

"She's in the kitchen," he said, no longer trying to trying to maintain the element of surprise. They raced through the house, skidding to a halt at the sight that greeted them.

Ellie's frail grandmother was sprawled on the hardwood floor. Over her loomed a man so beautiful, even Michael had to admire him. The ethereal connection between the man and the old woman was evident as the demon sucked her soul from her dying body.

"Gran!"

At Ellie's shout, the stunningly handsome demon turned, breaking the fragile connection between him and his victim. His lips curled into a lecherous smile. Hollow, depthless black eyes bore into her.

CHAPTER SIX

Ellie screamed as Michael grabbed her arm and yanked her behind him. She needed to get to Gran. Her heart wrenched at the sight of her lying there on the kitchen floor, unmoving. She squeezed her eyes shut against the reminder of the chalk line on the floor of her mother's living room. *This can't be happening. Please be all right.* They snapped open again at the sound of Michael's voice.

"Stay away from her," he snarled.

The man stood, never taking those haunting, black eyes off of her. Ellie began to shiver, fear racking her whole body. *What is this...thing?* She cringed, clinging to Michael's leather jacket as the man took a step toward them.

It was suddenly ripped from her hands as Michael attacked. He tackled the man like a football linebacker. He grabbed fistfuls of that glorious hair and slammed the man's head against the floor several times.

Ellie took the opportunity to rush to her grandmother's side. She felt for and, thankfully, found a pulse. She didn't want to move her, sprawled as she was. What if something was broken? What if Ellie only made it worse?

She looked up. Her heart lurched at the sight of Michael and the assailant both on their feet. How had the man gotten out from under Michael's relentless pummeling? His face was streaked with blood, his own no doubt as Michael appeared unscathed. That same wicked smile split his gorgeous face, less gorgeous now with one eye swollen shut and his teeth red with blood.

They couldn't stay here. She had to get Gran somewhere safe, somewhere they could hide if this went bad for Michael. A new wave of concern crashed over her at the idea that whatever that thing was might win this fight. Somehow she knew there was only one way for this to end.

Someone was going to die.

"You think to defeat me, tiny human?" the man asked.

Michael pulled something from his pocket. A tiny click, and a lethal-looking blade materialized. A switchblade.

Ellie felt a tiny flicker of hope. Both men were evenly matched in sheer size and bulk. But a weapon gave Michel the advantage. That is, until the stranger manifested a sword the likes of which she'd only seen in movies and medieval re-enactments.

"Don't worry," the man said. "I won't kill her right away. It will take days, maybe months, for me to get my fill of her.

Unable to hold back, Ellie screamed again when the man charged Michael with his massive sword. Michael was done for. No possible way could he defend against such a blade with his tiny, little—

She shielded her eyes, her scream cut short. A blinding light flared, but only for a few seconds. When she could see again, Ellie was stunned to find Michael's tiny switchblade had grown. In his left hand he held an equally lethal sword, but Michael's appeared a little more modern, lighter and more easily wielded. Tiny iridescent flames streaked up and down the blade. Was it the blade itself or a reflection of the afternoon sunlight coming through the window?

It didn't seem to matter. Michael had no apparent advantage over his opponent. Their blades clashed again and again, neither man seeming to tire, neither gaining the advantage. That is until Michael switched his sword to his right hand and nicked the tip across the other man's abdomen.

The shocked expression on the man's face was almost funny. He dropped his sword to press both hands to his wound. Sparks showered to the floor as the iridescent flames from Michael's sword zigzagged over the man's body. He roared at Michael with a fury like Ellie had never heard, before falling to the floor. He twisted and struggled against a series of seizures that was almost pitiful.

Michael straddled his prone, writhing body and shoved his sword into the man's chest. Haunting, hopeless groans filled the air. His flesh turned an inky black, wrinkling before her eyes. His once handsome face melted, oozing off of his skull and skimming across the floor. It disappeared beneath the cabinet under the kitchen sink like smoke out an open window until there was no sign of his existence.

She dragged her eyes away and back to where Michael stood, only slightly out of breath. There was no sign of the weapon he had used to destroy the man who'd threatened them. "She needs an ambulance," Ellie said, too stunned for anything else.

Michael pulled out his phone and made the call. After he hung up, he retrieved the man's broadsword. "Our story is that we found her like this. We must have scared her attacker off when we arrived. I'll take this," he said, indicating the broadsword, "to my uncle."

"What was that thing? What happened to him? Where did he go?" So many questions. What was the weapon Michael had used? Who were these ancestors he'd mentioned? She stared him. She thought she knew him, thought she had him figured out long ago. But obviously there was more to Michael Munro than she'd ever imagined.

He was saved from answering her by the sound of approaching sirens. He hung back as the paramedics stabilized Gran and loaded her into the ambulance.

Ellie held her frail hand until she had to step back to allow the EMTs to close the doors. She blinked back tears, wanting desperately to go with her. But the technician suggested she come later. The doctors at the hospital wouldn't even speak to her until they had treated and stabilized the victim. Besides, the police, who had already talked to Michael, waited to get a statement from her. She would talk to them, then find the damned thing that was making her and her family a target.

She went back into the house, ignoring the officers taking pictures and fingerprints. They weren't going to find anything. Somehow she knew it. Moments later, she had given the police the story Michael had suggested and ushered them on their way.

She turned away from the door to find Michael standing close behind her. "That thing called you *human*, like it was a bad thing, like *it* was something else."

Michael took a deep breath and let it out in a slow stream. "That creature was a...a...demon." He waited for her response.

It didn't take long. "Like from hell?"

He nodded, sort of. "Maybe. I've encountered them before."

"You've encountered demons before that may or may not be from hell?" She didn't try to hide the sarcasm in her voice. Did he think she was an idiot?

She searched his face, her eyes boring into his, looking for a hint that he was deranged. She only saw the Michael she had known. He was still the same. Still her friend. Still the only man she could count on.

Demons. Special powers. It was all too much to believe. Let him have his secrets. Let him feed her bullshit to keep from telling her what was really going on.

She was so tired.

He said nothing as she hugged her arms around herself and stepped close enough to lay her cheek against his chest. She closed her eyes, releasing a long pent up breath, when he wrapped his own arms around her.

"Is she going to die?" Ellie mumbled against him.

He pressed a kiss to the top of her head and pulled her tighter into his embrace. One hand idly stroked up and down her spine.

It felt so good to be in his arms. Safe. Wanted.

Loved.

Ellie swallowed at the pain of a yearning she had vowed never to feel again. She had hoped that coming back to Gran's, back to Savannah, she could capture that deep longing she had for home and family, to feel like she was part of something connected by a bond that could never be severed.

She had always had such a connection to Michael. But she didn't want it. That kind of chemistry could not be healthy. No one had ever gotten under her skin the way he did. There was hardly a day she didn't think of him, didn't crave him.

It was purely physical, she was sure, an obsession that was doomed from the start. He didn't fit her plan for her life, one infused with a low-risk of emotional trauma, but that didn't stop her from craving him with a hunger she wanted satisfied *now*. She was a grown woman. She could handle it. She shouldn't lead him on, shouldn't lick him and taste him and ride him until she was spent, and he was completely out of her system.

But damn if she didn't want to.

She unwrapped her arms from her waist and snaked them around him. Boldly, she cupped his tight ass cheeks in her hands and pressed herself against him. Holding her head back, she looked up at him. Their gazes tangled, hers inviting, his guarded. She wondered what he was thinking.

Probably what a flake she was.

With a pained expression, he grabbed her by the shoulders and pushed her to arm's length. Shaking his head, he glared at her.

"Don't Ellie. I'm not the boy I used to be."

Shooting her hands up between them, she cast his arms away and stepped out of reach. Of course he wasn't. He was a motorcycle-riding, muscle-bound killing machine, self-assured and confident in a way that men feared and women craved. He could have any woman he wanted these days. Why would he want some bossy, cold, undependable old girlfriend who'd treated him like dirt the whole time they'd known each other?

A few short hours ago, he'd had his hands and mouth all over her. Now he was pushing her away. Maybe his attraction only rose to the surface when he was in control.

Maybe he wasn't attracted to her at all but used her vulnerability to exact some measure of revenge. Hurt and embarrassed, she lashed out him, just as she always had.

"So, you're a big, bad man now? You think all those muscles allow you to be more picky about the women you fuck? Just because you aren't attracted to me anymore doesn't mean you get to play games with me."

She turned and dashed up the stairs before he could see her pain.

***

Michael watched in stunned silence as Ellie fled up the stairs. *She thinks I don't want her.* The very idea was ludicrous. So much so it struck him funny, and he almost laughed out loud. He sobered almost instantly. Ellie was not a needy woman, but she needed him now.

He bolted up the stairs two at a time. He found her in her room, viciously throwing the contents of a large, worn shopping bag onto the bed. It appeared to contain the contents of her bedroom in Atlanta that she'd brought with her a few weeks earlier. He wouldn't have noticed except that he was surprised she hadn't unpacked it and put everything neatly in its place. Her shoulders shook, but she made no sound. When the bag was empty, she tossed it aside and grabbed another, her complete disregard for order a sure sign she was upset.

Michael's heart ripped to shreds inside his chest. He couldn't ever remember her crying. The sight was almost his undoing.

He crossed the room and took her in his arms. No sooner had he touched her than she broke down, agonizing sobs wrenching her body, her knees buckling beneath her so he had to support her. He pressed his hand to the back of her head, holding her face against his chest as he rocked from side to side, making ridiculous cooing noises.

Here was his Ellie, crying out her pain in his arms, and there was nothing he could do about it. He wanted to rip someone's throat out. If only he knew who's.

The demon he killed had been a soul-stealing, expendable piece of shit. He had most certainly been doing another's bidding. No matter what it cost him, Michael would find out, and destroy it, just for the mere act of making Ellie cry—most definitely for threatening her safety hurt her grandmother.

He nearly engulfed her entire head with both hands and tilted her face up to his. Using the pads of his thumbs, he wiped her cheeks. He stared at her, remembering was it was like to be with a woman, to be with *her*. Her eyes were puffy from the effort of such forceful crying. He had never seen a woman more beautiful. Her lips, swollen and blood red, beckoned him. Ignoring all resistance, he lowered his head to hers.

When their mouths collided, it took all his strength not ravage her with the full potency of his desire. She was distraught and upset. She deserved tenderness and patience, things he was extremely low on at the moment. She needed sweet and comforting, not raw and savage, which is all he feared she would get from his right now. His cock was rock hard and painful.

Ellie rose up on her toes, slipping her tongue between his lips and probing. Her enthusiasm only chipped away at his already weakened willpower. She made him feel like a pubescent teenager again, wanting to impress her with his prowess and abundance of testosterone. He had loved this woman his whole life. He was obsessed with her, like no other woman he'd ever known. Was it too much to ask? Too much that he wanted to be the focus of her world as she had always been his?

Yet, now she knew he was a man of great darkness, an unholy creature with tainted blood. He was a man who had nothing to offer her. How could she accept him, even if he somehow convinced her they were made for each other?

All he could think of with her kissing him was stripping her clothes from her body, revealing all that glorious golden skin, those perfect nipples the color of pink sand. He wrapped his arms around her, enveloping her and pulling her flush against his body. He didn't just want to kiss her, he wanted to claim her, to brand himself on her soul. He kissed her as if his life depended on it.

She rewarded him with a moan of such contentment, his heart nearly burst. It thrilled him more than he wanted to admit that the attraction was not one-sided. Hazardous and without reason, but at least she felt it too.

Ellie reached beneath his t-shirt. Her hands fairly sizzled against his already heated skin. He flexed without thinking when she slid up and cupped the mounds of his chest. She tweaked his nipples between thumb and forefinger, sending a jolt of lust straight to his balls. He allowed her to break their kiss just long enough to shove the t-shirt over his head before he clamped his mouth to hers again.

By the gods, she tasted good. Like sex and honey and woman. It was like he had not realized he was starving until this moment, when the only sustenance he needed for survival was in his grasp.

Without breaking contact, she reached down and started fiddling with her jeans. Wanting her naked as soon as possible, Michael ripped her t-shirt right down the front. Praise Arduinna—she wasn't wearing a bra. Her breasts, sprang free from the confines of her clothes, tantalizing, irresistible. Those glorious mounds filled his hands, heavy and malleable. He kneaded them, holding her steady as she shifted from one foot to the other pushing the jeans down her legs.

He caught his breath. The woman must be a demon, eager to possess his soul. He had the power of the gods. Well, some of them, anyway. Michael thought he was strong, considered himself formidable.

He was wrong.

He was weak, easily defeated.

Ellie wasn't wearing underwear.

**

The look on Michael's face was dark, savage. He didn't say anything, just stared at her. His eyes glittered in the afternoon sunlight that shone through the bay window. That unusual gold color had always fascinated her.

She should stop now, push him as far away as possible. Once she got her pilot's license, she hoped to never let her feet touch the ground, not for long. There was no room for a husband, kids, family in such a world. She wanted to see everything, experience thrills she'd only heard or read about, seen in movies and television shows.

Ellie mentally smacked her forehead. Why was she thinking about a family and white picket fences? This was just sex, after all. Purely physical. Right now, she could think of no better way to relieve some of the anxiety that had been piled on her in the last few days. She could handle this.

But could Michael?

She knew he had feelings for her. What those feelings were, she couldn't say. He said it hurt when she left all those years ago. Could it be true? Ellie's experience with men was that sex was pretty much all about a good time. Michael was a man. He should appreciate a no-strings-attached tumble.

She didn't turn away when he bent his head to hers. She had only one thought: Michael was *more* than a man. It was like he was more than human, not in a comic book sort of way, but just...better.

Their kiss was electric. She felt it shooting through her body, igniting her most sensitive spots and fueling an inferno in her core. Ellie had certainly kissed other men in the last six years, but nothing had come close to this. She tugged him back onto the bed, her fingers laced behind his neck, her tongue tangled with his.

Michael braced himself above her. He kissed her with a passion that made her ears ring. His lips brushed back and forth across hers making her feel needy and impatient.

She splayed her hands across his shoulders, slid her palms across the plane of his back, dragged her finger tips through the ridges of the well-developed oblique muscles that led around his tight waist. When she reached the button of his jeans, he shifted his weight to one elbow and clasped both her wrists with free hand.

She whimpered when he broke the kiss. Her eyes widened when he pushed her arms over her head and pinned them to the mattress, shoving aside rumpled clothes, several pairs of shoes, and the few personal items she'd had at her mother's apartment, scattered remnants of the bags she'd brought from Atlanta three weeks ago.

He dipped his head and took one of her nipples between his teeth. Ellie arched up to meet him, sucking in a sharp breath when he stroked the tip with his tongue. He loomed over her now, one useless hand captured by each of his. He alternated back and forth between her breasts, teasing her, urging her to plead for him to end her torment.

They tousled around on the bed as Michael worked his way down, wedging his body between her thighs, dragging her hands with him over the carnage that was all her worldly possessions, until his knees came to rest on the floor. He still had her imprisoned, one hand on each side of her hips. He knelt there, staring down at her, his golden eyes drinking in every inch of her.

Ellie should have been self-conscious at the familiarity, the complete surrender of being so intimately scrutinized. She wasn't. She was turned on beyond anything she could have ever imagined. This wasn't a stare that was meant to intimidate a woman, this was meant to brand her. And it was working.

He released one hand and laid his fingers against the inside of her thigh with a gentleness that belied the fierce look in his eyes. He stroked her tender flesh with the rough pads of his fingers. He let go of her other hand and palmed his way across her hip and into the crevice between her thighs.

He glanced up at her, a look so smoldering she squirmed beneath its intensity. She shifted across the bed, a weak attempt to remind herself that she should not be doing this.

Michael took the opportunity to spread her legs further apart. He lowered his head with tormenting slowness to encircle her navel with his lips. His tongue teased the jeweled stud she wore there.

Ellie wanted to scream. If he touched her clit, she'd come, no holding back. She squeezed her thighs against the wide V of his back, shamelessly grinding her most intimate spot against his chest.

With a swiftness she never saw coming, Michael had her thighs in his hands, her knees pushed back to her head, and her pussy at his mercy.

She grappled around on the bed, searching for anything against which she could brace herself. The wall, the headboard, a pillow. Trinkets scattered beneath the onslaught as Ellie squirmed and wriggled beneath him.

Michael pushed over her. She could feel his hard cock against her thigh. When had he taken off his jeans? His met her with an open-mouthed kiss that sent her senses reeling out of control once more. The pressure of his erection against her became more and more urgent.

Clarity zipped through her mind for the briefest of seconds. "Wait," she mumbled against his lips. She pushed against the brick wall that was his chest. "Condom," she managed to breathe out.

He stared down at her, a tortured look on his face.

"Maybe there are some in Gran's room."

Michael looked horrified. "Really?"

Ellie began to wriggle beneath him. "I don't know how long it's been, but she was active before I left." He finally relented and let her push him aside "And she would have used a condom."

"It could be old."

She scooted off the bed, grabbing an old t-shirt. She was not ready to parade around completely naked in front of him. "Do they go bad?" When she stood up, something heavy clanked to the floor. She pulled the shirt over her head and bent down to pick it up.

It was indeed heavy. A piece of what appeared to be pottery or some kind of stone, shaped into what might have been a triangle if it hadn't been broken. A large chunk was missing from one side. It had a pale greenish tint and residue of gold inlay.

Michael stood as well, following her lead by pulling his jeans over his glorious ass as he did so, and joined her. He regarded the object with a wary expression. "What's that?"

She shook her head. "I've never seen it." She held it out to him.

The moment it touched him, their hands seemed to fuse together. He stumbled, grabbed his head with his other hand, and fell to one knee.

Shocked, she knelt in front of him. He trembled all over. She stared in horror as his beautiful, golden eyes started to roll back. "Michael!" She tossed the stone aside, and instantly his condition improved.

She cupped his face in her palms, her gaze darting back and forth as clarity returned to his eyes. He took a deep breath and pushed himself up enough to sit on the edge of the bed. He braced against one hand, still weakened.

"What is that?" He asked for a second time.

Ellie walked over to where it had landed on the floor.

"Don't touch it," he said, his voice dangerously low.

She ignored his warning and picked it up. When she walked back toward him, Michael sat up straighter, stiffening. Ellie wondered at the effect the object had on him and why it wasn't the same for her.

"We need to take this to my uncle," Michael said.

***

Ellie rested her forearms on Michael's thighs, her fingers laced together. Her grip was a little more relaxed than the first time she'd ridden his big monster. She hadn't died the first time, so maybe this time would be equally disaster free.

Her first reaction to his motorcycle was one of wariness and unease, fear of the unknown. She had to admit, the image Michael presented—tough, muscle-bound, biker—was hot. Too hot. And thrilled her way more than it should.

But as she found herself growing more accustomed to the open-air, the rush of pavement beneath her feet, the absence of a seatbelt, Ellie realized it was that same feeling of freedom and excitement she loved about flying. She savored the reckless exhilaration that flowed through her as they leaned to one side and then the other, zipping through the narrow streets. Her heart vibrated from the thunderous rumble of the shiny chrome engine.

They had gone to the hospital first, despite a phone conversation with a female doctor who took Ellie's call. Gran was in stable condition but had yet to regain consciousness. She had offered to call immediately if there was any change, but Ellie wanted—needed—to see Gran for herself.

As it turned out, they only let her into the ICU for a moment, a too-brief moment. But it was enough to spur Ellie forward in her determination to shield them from further danger.

Moments later, they pulled into the alley between two of the oldest streets in Savannah and stopped behind a house that faced Gaston. Her suspicions about the relation between Michael and the rich guy were confirmed when they climbed the steps, ducking beneath a growth of wisteria that threatened to overrun the entire patio, and came upon a tarnished brass plaque that read *Dresser House, circa. 1876* embedded into the exterior wall of the house. The *Palmer* half was on the other side of the duplex.

She caught her breath when the man himself opened the door just as they reached it. Looking up at him as he filled the doorway, Ellie found Lucan Munro even more impressive that she had at the diner. No wonder all the girls at Betty's had the hots for him. Black hair shadowed features that combined to create one of the most good-looking men Ellie had ever seen. His hazel eyes lit on her first, and he pressed her with a warm smile.

"Greetings, lass."

His brogue warmed her. Ellie smiled back and took the hand he offered. He guided her over the threshold and into a foyer that someone had long ago turned into a bar. A worn, cracked mirror covered one wall. The counter was covered with chipped linoleum that had faded from years of sunlight fighting its way through the wisteria to land on this side of the windows.

She would have expected a man a rich as Lucan Munro was rumored to be to hire the best designer in Savannah. Instead the place looked like its last remodel had been in the seventies.

The only hint of the owner's wealth was his collection of Scotch, a supply large enough to last years. Even she could tell it was the good stuff. How could a man who spent so much on expensive suits and the finest Scotch ignore the rundown state of his million-dollar house? Was he one of those men who hoarded all his money, a miser who binged on irrational pleasures?

She and Michael followed him through to the sitting room where he poured some of the rich amber liquid from a decanter into three tumblers and handed one to each of them. By all outward appearances, he looked to be close to thirty, but his manner and something about his eyes made him seem much older.

Ellie took a sip. The fiery amber burned across her tongue and down her throat. She could actually feel it moving through her body to her stomach. She breathed deep, grateful she hadn't broken into coughing fits. "I'm sorry I was a no-show yesterday," she wheezed. "I—"

"I ken yer troubles, lass," Lucan interrupted her. He took a deep pull from his drink.

"Of course you do," she mumbled into her glass, taking another sip of her drink. This one went down much easier. She noted the subtle richness that lingered on her tongue.

Still, her voice came out raspy and breathless. "How did you know my mother? Why were you protecting her?

"Later." Without elaborating, he turned to Michael. "What do ye have?"

Michael laid the sword on a sideboard so old and battered, Ellie wondered that it could hold the extra weight. The two men stood over it, mumbling in low tones. When Michael turned it over, Lucan stood straight, his expression dire.

"That's the Comyn crest."

Ellie moved closer to peer around them. "Who are the Comyns?" she asked.

Michael made room and pointed out the gold shield fixed to the cross piece. Emblazoned on its surface was a lion reared up on its hind legs. "An old Highland clan. Enemies of Clan Munro."

"The spawn of Lucifer," Lucan added.

Ellie wanted to laugh. "You buy into this whole demon story?" She couldn't believe it. Lucan Munro was educated, worldly. Ellie immediately regretted her flippant tone. Lucan turned those hazel eyes back to her, but this time they held anything but warmth.

She stepped away from the sideboard, putting some distance between herself and Michael's uncle. He obviously rode the same insane train Michael did. Maybe it ran in the family.

Lucan turned to Michael, his face a stone wall, void of any tell-tale signs that would reveal his feelings.

Michael seemed to need no such signs. He shrugged and somehow managed to look contrite and defiant at the same time. "She's seen things that needed explaining."

Lucan glared at him. "Just remember. My secrets aren't yers to tell," he said. Lucan dragged his attention from Michael and focused it on her. He stared at her until she began to fidget. Michael moved over to stand between them, as if he wanted to her protect her.

Lucan took a step closer. "What d'ye have in yer pocket?"

Michael looked like he wanted to bolt when she pressed her fingers where the stone throbbed against her hip. What had it done to him? She'd seen how it weakened him, but it was more than that. It had affected him emotionally. He almost seemed…afraid. She dug in the front pocket of her jeans and pulled out the stone. Lucan came closer, his hand reaching out to take it from her.

"Don't touch it," Michael warned.

Lucan rolled his eyes but didn't say anything. The moment his fingers curled around stone, they began to dry into an ashy color that proceeded to spread up his arm. His eyes turned inky black, the same hollow voids as the creature that had attacked Gran, and the roar of a thousand demons burst from his mouth.

CHAPTER SEVEN

Michael ran to Lucan's side, but he knew there was nothing he could do. The stone hadn't affected him this way, but he'd been weakened. If not for Ellie, what might it have done to him? He stood helplessly as she tried to pry Lucan's fingers apart to get to the stone, but it was no use.

"It's like wood," she said, speaking through gritted teeth. "It's clamped in so hard, I can't get to it." Her struggle became more and more frantic. "Help me, Michael. We're losing him."

He moved around behind his uncle, grasping his arm just above where the ashy-gray was moving towards his shoulder. It did seem to be turning his arm to wood and would soon reach his chest.

Suddenly, a green fluorescent light filled the room. Michael was knocked back onto his ass. He spread his arms wide to cushion his fall, but he still hit the floor hard. When the light faded, a woman had taken his place next to Lucan. Her skin had a greenish tint so faint one would barely notice it. Her long, wavy hair was the color of emeralds.

He had never seen her before, but Michael knew this was the goddess, Arduinna. He rolled up to one knee. "My lady," he said.

She didn't look up, didn't acknowledge him in any way. She took Lucan's hand in hers and began stroking his arm from the elbow down. After several long, tense moments, his skin began to return to its normal color as the wood receded. Before Lucan's fingers would have unfurled, depositing the stone into her lap, she moved aside. It hit the floor with a loud *thunk*.

With no hesitation, Ellie retrieved it and put it back in her pocket. Wide-eyed, she stared at the goddess but remained silent. Michael stood and moved to her side, offering whatever support he could as she faced this new reality.

Arduinna cradled Lucan's head in her lap. She bent close, her luxuriant hair spilling around him in a verdant cascade. Her pale, dainty hand rested on his chest. Her full lips moved but Michael could make out no sound.

He breathed a sigh of relief when Lucan's eyes snapped open, *his* eyes, guarded and ageless and hazel in color. Lucan reached up with a trembling hand and brushed a finger down the goddess' cheek.

"Sirona." Lucan's voice was barely more than a ragged whisper.

Before their eyes, his uncle and the goddess disappeared.

Ellie jumped.

"Where did they go? Who was that?"

"That was the goddess we serve, Arduinna. My guess is she's taken Lucan to his cousin, Sirona. She's a healer."

"Is she a goddess, too?"

Michael didn't miss the sarcasm in her voice, and natural reaction to a seemingly ridiculous explanation that would only get better. He shook his head. "Actually, Sirona is an angel of mercy, a guardian."

Ellie nodded, as if he was reporting the weather forecast.

"Do you want some coffee?" he asked.

Ellie picked up her tumbler from where she'd set it when she went to Lucan's aid. Tossing her head back, she drained its contents. Her jaw tightened, but she swallowed with little more than a grimace. She lifted her chin towards the decanter. "I'd like another one of those," she said.

While he poured her another dram, Ellie used his phone to call the hospital. She paced around the sitting room while she talked, inspecting the faded wallpaper, fiddling with ripped and torn upholstery, rubbing her finger over the woodwork. Looking for dust?

She wouldn't find any. Lucan may not have done anything to fix the place up, but it was spotlessly clean.

She disconnected the call and handed Michael back his phone. "That was the medical assistant. A doctor is in with Gran right now. She hasn't regained consciousness yet. There are no injuries that they can find, no obvious signs of trauma, so they have no idea what's wrong with her." She sighed and sat on the sofa, one of only a couple pieces of furniture that still had stuffing in the cushions. "They're running tests," she said, taking the tumbler he handed her.

She took a pull and closed her eyes. The look on her face made his heart clench. He wanted to take away her pain and worry. He wanted to whisk her grandmother off to South America so Sirona could heal her, as well. Frustration ate at him that he didn't know how to help her.

She pulled the stone out of her pocket and inspected it closer. Using her thumbnail, she chipped away at the corrosion that had formed on parts of the surface. "It's like an arrow head," she said. The more she cleaned it, the greater urgency Michael felt to move away.

She glanced up when she noticed his discomfort. "Do you feel something when you're this close to it?"

Did he? Michael couldn't pinpoint anything exactly. "C'mon. I'll show you where Lucan's computer is."

Her eyes widened. "You can read minds?"

He shook his head. "I had a vision of you looking for that thing on the internet." That seemed to relieve her a little. She stood and followed him.

A closed door bisected one wall of the dining room. Michael opened it and led her inside. This was the only room in the entire house Lucan had decorated. Most of the furniture was from Scotland, antiques he had been lugging around for hundreds of years.

Ellie's mouth gapped open as she stared at the ornate room. The big mahogany desk took up most of the space. There was even a comfy sofa his uncle slept on most nights. While Michael fired up the computer, she paused to admire the extensive library of ancient texts.

He had an internet browser open by the time she joined him. She seemed reluctant to sit in the master's colossal leather chair, but curiosity overcame her hesitation. She set the stone on the desk between her and the keyboard and started typing.

She read for a long time, clicking back and forth between web sites, asking him questions from time to time, but making little progress.

"Who is the woman?"

Michael looked up from where he lounged on the sofa. "What woman?" Ellie waved one hand towards the array of photographs propped on the corners of the desk. "Oh." He wondered how much he should tell her. "That's Neala. Lucan's wife."

She looked away from the screen for the first time since she'd sat down. "He's married?"

"Not at the moment. She is only nineteen right now, and he has to wait until she's twenty-five."

She screwed up her face. "Your uncle's dating a girl who is only nineteen? Isn't she a little young for him?"

How much more could Ellie take before she reported him to the authorities, before she tried to have him locked away in a mental hospital? "He's not what he seems, my uncle."

She turned back to the computer screen with an all-knowing arch to one eyebrow. "Why am I not surprised?"

She needed to know that what they were dealing with was not of this world. Making up his mind, he decided to ignore Lucan's warning that his secrets were his own. "Her age doesn't really matter. He's immortal...so..."

She looked surprised, but not for reasons he would have thought. "He's not one of those demons, is he?"

"Oh, no," Michael was quick to assure her. "He's...well, he's a god, of the ancient Gaulish pantheon." Even he realized how silly it sounded when spoken out loud. "She is fated to be his wife, but he's forbidden to have any contact with her before she's twenty-five. It's a long story," he said when she would have interrupted him to ask questions. "Neala has a powerful soul, so much so that some demon or another is always after it. Lucan has—people who look after her."

"So he's not dating her. He's stalking her."

Michael almost laughed. "Just enough to protect her soul. Neala is mortal. She will die peacefully in her bed somewhere around the age of ninety. At least that's what usually happens."

"How do you know? I thought your visions were only fleeting and that you could only see things that are about to happen in the next few minutes."

"This isn't a vision. It's a covenant Lucan made with the true God. When she dies, Neala is reincarnated." He waited, letting her take in what he had just told her, before continuing. "Lucan ages by all appearances. After his beloved passes away, with her husband at her side, Lucan spends the next days or weeks getting his affairs in order, then fakes his own death. He then begins tracking down the location of her soul's rebirth. When he finds her, he sets about restoring his empire while he waits for her twenty-fifth birthday. Only then can he make contact with her."

Ellie had stopped looking at the computer screen. Michael had her full attention. "Does she know who he is?"

He shook his head. "He has to make her fall in love with him all over again."

Her shoulders collapsed a notch. "What about their children?"

"Oh no, no children. Neala cannot have children. It's mainly the reason he's made it his mission to save as many of them as he can. Even if she could kids of her own, the almighty God would never allow a child to spawn from the union of a pagan god and a child of Christ."

"A child of Christ? You mean, she's descended from—" Ellie expelled a deep breath and sat back in the chair. She scrubbed both hands over her face. "Is anything I ever thought about the world true?"

Michael chuckled, relieved at how well she was taking it all.

She pulled her hands away from her face, and grinned at him. "It's very romantic, though."

Michael was warmed all over by her smile. When had Ellie King ever had a notion about romance? She was smart, funny, brave. But romantic? Yes, he admitted, she was all of those things and more. Michael had accepted his obsession with Ellie way back in high school. But now things were different. This was far worse.

He *liked* her.

***

Ellie could feel a smile lingering on her lips. When was the last time she smiled? *He* did that to her. She was beginning to admit he was everything that was good and solid in her life. She was happiest when she was with him. She hadn't realized that until now. Or maybe she had but fervently blocked it out to protect her heart. Even in the darkest times, he lifted her up. He made her feel he would follow her anywhere, always the rock that kept her grounded.

It was that fragile dependence that frightened her to death. How would she cope if that rock crumbled leaving her alone and heartbroken, yearning for the return of someone who was never coming back?

She couldn't go through that again. She'd been a child when Mama had left her with Gran. Children were resilient. She'd gotten over it, or at least she told herself she had. Ellie was no longer a child. Now that she knew demons were real, she feared what might happen to her if she allowed herself to believe in something as implausible as love. If she exposed herself to the whim of another and was rejected once again, would she be at the mercy of the nightmares she'd only heard about during mass? Would the sentinels of hell claim her weakened soul, damning her to eternal suffering?

Michael watched her from across the room, his gaze intense and filled with yearning. She felt it too, that pull, that need to lose herself in him, to let the rest of the world fall away until it was only the two of them. How easy it would be.

But then what? Real life would take over. They would struggle to get by week after week, for surely this 'job' with his uncle wouldn't last forever. She had no skills to speak of and would probably end up being a waitress for the rest of her life. She imagined dirty, barefoot children in the back yard, some kind of instant hamburger casserole from a box every night, Michael coming home later and later until finally he didn't come home at all.

No, that was wrong. He'd probably take the kids, too, leaving her completely alone.

It was just a fantasy. One she'd cooked up to stymie the pain of not giving in to her desires. To silence the voice that told her Michael wasn't that kind of man, that she should take a chance. She wanted desperately to believe that he would never leave her. As she sat there across from him, she realized she *did* believe it. But what if she was wrong? Fear of utter disappointment kept her from letting him in.

It wasn't a risk she was willing to take. Better to keep her distance. She was going to learn to fly jets one way or another. Gran would recover. She had to. Otherwise how could Ellie make up for being such an unruly teenager, for not being more appreciative of Gran's sacrifice? She blamed herself for what had happened. Her mother had made her own bed, but if Ellie hadn't abandoned Gran, had stayed with her instead of running off at the first crook of her mother's finger, Gran would not have been in any danger. She wouldn't be lying in the hospital fighting for more than her life. Gran was fighting for her soul.

Ellie wasn't going to let sappy stories of a centuries-old love turn her to mush and drag her focus from what she needed to do. At least Michael hadn't made love to her, not completely. How could she ever turn away again if she let it get that far?

Ellie pressed the power button on the monitor, dousing the room in darkness. When had it become night? Michael switched on a lamp. The light bathed him in a soft glow that made her truly believe he was descended from gods. She wanted to curl up with him on the big sofa and forget all the bad things in the world. Demons. Lucifer. These monsters had been used forever to frighten children and adults alike into being obedient. How could they be real?

Yet there was no denying what she'd seen. That thing had literally been sucking Gran's soul from her body, right there on the kitchen floor. The green woman had *disappeared* with Lucan before her very eyes.

"Did you find anything?" Michael's deep voice broke the silence.

"Nothing." She picked up the artifact and stood, stretching her legs. She stared down at it as she walked around the enormous desk. It looked like a dozen other arrow heads in shape and material, some kind of flint maybe. It had the same indentations where the stone had been chipped away. The edge opposite the side that was broken was sharp, despite its age. Ellie had caught herself from inflicting a nasty cut more than once. But it was too big, about the size of her hand with her fingers pressed together, minus the missing piece. And she hadn't found a single picture or other reference to one with gold inlay. "Maybe we should call the police."

"No need." He stood up, keeping his distance from the stone, and pulled his cell phone from the pocket of his jeans. "They're about to call you." He handed it to her.

No sooner had she taken it than the phone vibrated in her hands. She jumped and nearly dropped it. Swiping her finger over the green button, she glared at him. "Stop doing that," she whispered. "Hello?"

"Miss King? Detective Blackburn. The coroner has finished your mother's autopsy." He took a deep breath and let it out in a loud rush.

Ellie shoved the stone into her pocket and sat down on the couch. She wasn't sure she could take any more bad news. She pushed the speaker button so Michael could hear. "And?"

"Ellie, your mother died of organ failure."

"Which organ?"

"All of them." He sounded surprised. "There is no evidence of poison, strangulation, blunt force, just a complete shutdown of her whole system. The coroner could find no reason for it. He can't even rule it a homicide. Ellie, I'm sorry."

"You're not done with your investigation?"

"There's nothing to investigate. Cause of death is medical malfunction."

"And my stolen vehicle?"

"Our team has completed its investigation. They went over every inch of the SUV. There's no connection. You can file a claim with your insurance company if you determine anything has been stolen, but otherwise, it's ready to be picked up along with your mother's remains."

"What about those two men you found dead?"

"Definitely homicide. Their throats were ripped out."

***

Near midnight, Ellie wanted to scream. Michael hadn't done anything to invoke such a reaction, but invoke her he had. He'd been a perfect Southern gentleman, sitting there on the settee in his ass-hugging jeans. Chest, arms, and shoulders about to bust right out of that black t-shirt like some comic book hero. He hadn't made any move what-so-ever to take up where they'd left off when they found the spear head.

It was exactly what she wanted.

And exactly what was driving her mad.

Instead of being satisfied by their brief tumble, she was eager for more. All these years she told herself she was over him. Michael was part of her past. But it had taken very little for her to crave him in such a way, she wondered how she ever did without him.

She knew he was worried, but he seemed so calm. Gone was the hot-headed boy that left his feelings visible for the world to see. This man kept a tight rein on his emotions and acted with deliberate intentions, carefully weighing the options first.

Ellie had almost broken that control earlier. Just thinking about it made her catch her breath, drawing his attention.

He wanted to kiss her. She didn't need special powers to know that. Her lips tingled, remembering how it felt having his mouth against hers, his tongue tangled with hers.

Instead of being startled, Ellie groaned in frustration when Arduinna's green light filled the room.

While Lucan was standing on his own two feet, Ellie could tell it was difficult for him to do so. The goddess settled him on the sofa, shooing Michael out of the way and sending him to fetch a dram of Scotch.

He did as the goddess commanded. "You look better," Michael said, handing Lucan the tumbler of Scotch.

"I feart I was gone. Now I just feel like my body's been ripped to tiny pieces and nailed back together."

Ellie tried to reconcile what she thought she knew about the world with the beautiful woman standing before her. Michael had told her Arduinna could change the color of that thick mass of hair with a thought. Wouldn't that be a nice power to have? The goddess was at least six feet tall, athletic, like a volleyball player. She had large breasts and long legs that were sure to bring the strongest of men to his knees.

She caught Ellie ogling and stared down her slender nose at her. Ellie cleared her throat and glanced away.

"Let me see that thing." Arduinna said.

"My lady—" Lucan reached for her hand, but she brushed him off and took a cautious step forward.

Ellie pulled it from her pocket and held it out, cradled in her palm.

Arduinna tilted her head back and forth but did not come closer. "Turn it over," she said.

Ellie did as she was told. "I searched the internet but couldn't find out anything about it."

The goddess looked at her then, her piercing green eyes drinking Ellie in from head to toe. "Perhaps I will have better luck," she said.

Despite her cool demeanor, Arduinna's voice had a soothing lilt that relieved some of Ellie's anxiety. All the tension in her body just floated away. Arduinna turned back to Lucan and squeezed his hand before disappearing in a shower of green sparks.

At least Ellie wasn't startled out of her skin this time.

Lucan finished his drink and stood. He kept a safe distance from Ellie's still outstretched hand, but inspected the object much as the goddess had done only a moment before. "This is made for a spear," he said. "Verra dangerous in the wrong hands." He indicated for her to put it away.

He crossed to the sideboard and hefted the sword they had left lying there, all but forgotten. He was perfectly at ease handling the heavy weapon, like he'd been born with one in his hand. Ellie didn't have much of an interest in history, but she had a clear image of Lucan brandishing such a weapon, the Highlands rising behind him, a cold wind whipping his thick hair about and lifting the corners of his kilt just enough to tease a woman.

"'Tis no' a coincidence that the demon was carrying a Comyn sword. We havna seen the last of those bastards." He laid the sword back on the sideboard and came to stand before her. "Ye ken it was this demon that killed yer ma? I'm sorry, lass."

Ellie swallowed hard but held back the tears that stung behind her eyes. "If Michael hadn't destroyed him, he would have taken Gran." She turned a warm smile to him. "I'll always be grateful for that."

Lucan drew her back to the conversation. "I sent Sirona to the hospital. Your grandmother's soul needs time to rest. She'll recover soon enough." He looked back and forth between Ellie and Michel. "I have to fly to Atlanta tomorrow. The two of ye can ride along." His teasing gaze landed on Ellie. "Perhaps get that flying lesson ye missed."

Ellie didn't question how he knew she needed to go to Atlanta. Nor did she doubt that Lucan knew what she had learned from the police detective. She thought her heart was going to burst right out of her chest. "Really?"

"Aye. On one condition." He nodded at Michael. "The lad here doesna leave yer side."

Ellie could think of worse things than having Michael underfoot. More concerning was how she would keep her hands off of him. Still, the Dresser-Palmer House was such a monstrosity she should have no problem keeping her distance.

"Deal." She was barely able to contain her excitement. Tomorrow she would be in the cockpit of Lucan's private jet. *I wonder what model it is.* "Where do I sleep?"

The two men exchanged looks. "Ye canna stay here," Lucan said.

Michael clarified. "The house isn't set up for company. There's no furniture in any of the rooms except these." He indicated Lucan's study in addition to the sitting room they were standing in.

It dawned on her that Lucan was waiting to bring his bride home before making any changes to the house. He would leave it to her remodel and redecorate like she wanted it. They would share their life in this house. *Great. More romantic mush to fill my head.* "We can't go back to my house," she said.

"You'll stay with me."

Until that moment, she hadn't thought about where Michael lived. If she had, she would have guessed he lived here, with his uncle. He was full of surprises. "Which is where?"

"Moon River Marina."

She imagined a single room studio, tucked away in the far corner of the barn where boats were stored in the winter. But he surprised her further.

"I keep my boat there."

Even better. Some ancient vessel that could hardly be called seaworthy. Cold. Damp. Cramped. They would probably have to sleep in hammocks tied in such close quarters, she wouldn't get any rest at all. Better to stay here and sleep on the ratted sofa.

Then there was their host himself. Lucan may be pining away for his beloved, but that didn't mean he'd been celibate all these years. Ellie imagined a god would certainly have the power to seduce a woman, even against her will. She looked at him with new interest. Was he capable of such a thing?

By appearances alone, he was a dark and sinister man. Better to take her chances with the devil she knew.

Plus, she was looking forward to getting back on Michael's Harley.

CHAPTER EIGHT

Michael secured his bike in the marina's parking lot and led Ellie toward the dock. He kept a close eye on the shrubbery. The landscaping was beautiful, but it provided an ideal hiding place for bad guys. Someone was after a spearhead powerful enough to take down a god. His guess was that it was a pretty bad guy.

He wasn't taking any chances with Ellie's safety. He might be vulnerable to that weapon she carried, but damned if he couldn't take down anything that came after it. He was in much more danger from Ellie herself. She was the only woman who had the power to rip his heart to shreds, a near fatal wound he didn't think he could survive again. The closer she got, the more time they spent together, the weaker he became. He found it harder and harder to resist. And Ellie didn't seem inclined to make it any easier for him.

He opened his mind, blocking out the scent of her shampoo, the night time glow of her skin. Was the tingle up the back of his neck a testosterone induced reaction to her proximity, or was it something else?

Michael allowed the visions to flow through his thoughts. He saw a big splash on the surface of the river, probably a cobia or bluefish passing by on its northern migration. A BMW zipped into the lot. A young couple, late teens, jumped out and rushed to a yacht that most likely belonged to the father of one of them. One of his neighbors came out and took a leak off the bow of his boat.

Before they got half way down the dock, all of these things had come to pass. The fish was gone. The teenagers were hidden safely away on daddy's boat.

Michael called out to his neighbor as they passed. "You don't stop polluting the water, someone's liable to throw you overboard."

"A man has a right to piss outside," the man called back.

He's drunk, Michael thought. *Again*. Michael wouldn't be at all surprised if the booze head *fell* overboard.

Ellie didn't say anything as they passed one yacht after another. When they reached the end, he stopped and turned expectantly, anticipating her reaction. His Cobalt wasn't large enough that he need a crew to take it out, but he had plenty of room for guests. He hated that it was so important to him that she was impressed.

He need not have worried. The look on her face made him want to puff out his chest and strut around like a cock in a hen yard. What had she expected? That he lived in a hovel?

"Happy Tracks?" She read the name painted across the stern.

"Bad luck to change the name of a boat." He jumped on board and held out his hand to her. "It fits. I've made many happy tracks on this boat."

Even in the dark, he could see the color flush her face. If he didn't know better, he'd think she was jealous. His heart jumped to his throat at the thought.

Michael gritted his teeth. For the love of Arduinna, he was a doomed fool.

Ellie took his hand, squeezing tighter as she stepped across the empty space between the dock and the diving platform.

Michael took the opportunity to pull her into his arms. She didn't resist, but that could be because she was so completely enamored of his boat. She fit perfectly against him, like the second of a two-piece puzzle. How could she not see it? How could he make her?

Oblivious to the turmoil going on inside him, Ellie gaped up the ladder that led to the flybridge. The delight and anticipation on her face was too much to resist. Reluctantly, he let her go.

"Make yourself at home," he said.

With a little squeak of excitement, she grabbed the rungs and took off.

Michael followed her up the ladder, his mouth watering at the sight of her round ass cheeks just above his face. Her jeans cupped her from side to side as she lifted one foot and then the other. By the time he reached the top, he was hard enough to cut glass.

Ellie ran to the bridge, grasping the wheel with one hand and the throttle with the other. She smiled out over the water, drenched in moonlight, no doubt dreaming of flying. She did a lot of that these days.

Walking up behind her, he tried to see what she saw. The freedom and excitement. All he'd ever seen was a future without her in it. Dare he hope for a different view?

He reached around her, crowding her, and tilted open the front window. He burned from the heat of her body against his. The breeze that blew in off the water did little to cool his urge to be inside her. Ellie's hair lifted on it, swirling around and teasing him with silky caresses that made him want to shove those jeans to her ankles and fuck her right there on the bridge.

She turned suddenly to face him, that smile he'd seen more and more of curling her lips. He wanted to kiss her, but he didn't. Instead he just watched them move while she spoke.

"It's beautiful, Michael. How long have you had this?"

Dragging his gaze from her mouth, he stepped back, giving her some space and distancing himself from temptation. "A few months." His voice came out rough and quiet. He cleared his throat. "Want to see below deck?" he asked, trying to keep his voice light.

She seemed reluctant to leave the bridge, but curiosity got the better of her. With eyes downcast, Ellie squeezed between him and the captain's chair. Her thigh brushed across his pulsing cock. When she froze and snapped her eyes to his, Michael's resolve melted. Gone was the eternal irritation, the certainty of disappointment, the eagerness to be anywhere but here.

Before he could make up his mind what he really saw there, she pressed on by and carefully made her way back down the ladder. There was another steering wheel downstairs, but the view from there didn't have the same effect on her. Michael unlocked and slid back the glass door, leading the way inside and down three more steps into the cabin. He grabbed two bottles of water from the fridge and handed her one.

Ellie thanked him and sat down at the table. Michael sat across from her, both of them silent for a time, lost in their own thoughts. Michael tried to think of anything that would take his mind off the fact that Ellie King was on his boat. His Ellie was here, where he lived. If he reached out, he could touch her. He thought of icebergs, snow skiing, an ice-cold spring.

"I've been thinking," she said.

So have I. Michael wanted to tell her *what* he'd been thinking but she'd seemed distant, uncomfortable since their near miss in her bedroom. If she knew the erotic desires plaguing his thoughts, she might decide he was a deranged pervert and take off. That wouldn't do, for now that she was here, he never wanted her to leave.

***

Ellie watched the play of emotions cross Michael's face, his parted lips, his flushed skin, the glittering shine of those eyes. His undisguised passion for her always made her own body react in kind, yearning for him despite the danger she'd found herself in. He made her feel things she hadn't felt since high school, things only he had made her feel even back then.

She focused instead on his features. The color of his eyes was so stunning, his other, savagely masculine attributes were often overlooked. Ellie wondered how that was possible. He was too stunningly gorgeous for any woman's piece of mind. Full, sensuous lips, dark, furrowed brows, bone structure a model would kill for. A close-trimmed beard dusted his perfect jaw that she could easily believe was molded by the gods.

He was her very darkest fantasies come to life.

And there *were* those eyes, the very color that had drawn humans since the beginning of time, caused them to risk everything. Who was she to resist? She got lost in them for a moment. They were hypnotic, intoxicating, and filled with...determination? Was it possible that despite his efforts to get her naked, Michael was trying just as hard to resist her?

Damn it! Back to emotions again. Couldn't she just keep it physical? She was perfectly capable of a physical relationship. She'd had two other *friends-with-benefits* since Michael, but she had mostly just been interested in the "benefits" part. Michael was so much more.

If only she could satisfy this craving she had to nibble on that perfect jaw, to lick him all over, to feel his cock pumping into her until she came hard enough to last her a good long time, without risking her heart. With a sinking feeling and big chunk torn from her resolve, Ellie admitted she was falling for him.

As if she'd ever gotten up after the last time.

"Maybe it's from the spear they used to kill Jesus on the cross." She'd heard some fantastical tales today, many of them difficult to explain any other way, and read theory after theory on the internet. Was it such a reach to consider the possibility? This she knew—Jesus was a man. He had lived on Earth and died at the hands of the Romans. It was a *fact*.

There was no denying the spear head had unnatural power. Ellie pulled it from her pocket and set it carefully on the table. "It could be, right?"

Michael didn't get up or move away, but she could tell he didn't like having it so close.

"Do you feel anything when you get close to it?"

"No, only the one time I touched it." He narrowed his eyes. "I didn't see that coming. Nor did I anticipate its effect on Lucan."

"You warned him."

"Only because of personal experience. I had no premonition of what it would do to him."

She picked it up, amazed that she could do so the way it had taken down Michael and Lucan, and examined it more closely. "What *did* it do to him?" she asked.

Michael let out a haggard, incredulous breath. "If not for you, it would have killed him. I suspect that was the reason for its creation."

She put it away and looked up to meet his gaze.

"To kill a god," he said.

"Jesus was the *son* of God. Would that count?" He nodded. "I wish I had put that into the search engine," she said. She drained the remaining water from the bottle. "It's all too much," she admitted, spinning the empty bottle on the table. "Gran, my mom, demons...*gods* for crying out loud. Where does it all end? When will everything be normal again?"

"Don't count on normal, Ellie. That part of your life is over."

He was right. She could never go back to a time of ignorant bliss. The sooner she could get this relic somewhere safe, or better yet destroy it, the sooner she could get back to something that could at least pass for normal. She didn't want demons chasing her for the rest of her life. How would she protect herself when Michael was gone?

Her heart ached at the thought. It was distressing to realize how much she needed—no—wanted him around.

"What is that weapon you used on the demon?" she asked, hoping to shift her thoughts to anything besides a day without him.

Michael pulled out his switchblade and clicked it open. "Lucan created it. An insignificant weapon, easy to conceal, that turns into something between a claymore and a lightsaber. It'll destroy a demon with nothing more than a nick." He put it away. "Of course it's equally lethal against my kind."

His kind. It was inconceivable that Michael was a different *kind* of person, that he carried the blood of ancient, pagan gods. She had always believed him to be a man without purpose, a man with no drive. She had been so wrong. His immortal ancestor was on a mission to rescue every abused child in Savannah, and Michael worked tirelessly to make that possible. She had misjudged him again and again. He was so much more than a moody, pigheaded, deadbeat.

He was fascinating.

Ellie felt all jumbled up inside. Part of her wanted to get as far away from him as possible, while the other part wanted to lay claim to him in such a way that he would never consider another woman. She couldn't balance her feelings, and it made her edgy and strained.

She didn't like it.

She looked around at Michael's latest surprise. He lived on a *yacht*. Maybe not the biggest one in the marina, but *Happy Tracks* was exotic and richly detailed, from the rich leather beneath her ass to the polished wood trim. And she just knew that standing up top while skimming across the water would be much like flying.

The cabin was cozy, intimate, but had every convenience. Fridge, oven, two-burner stove. There was even a dishwasher. The door to the bathroom, or *head* according the sign, stood open, and she could see how roomy it was on the inside. The separate enclosed shower was more than large enough for a man of Michael's build.

Saving the world must pay a lot more than working at Betty Bombers.

The spear head was uncomfortable in her pocket. She wanted to be rid of it. She was curious. How could she not be? But more than anything, she wanted to be through with all of this. She should just turn the artifact over the police. If she no longer had it in her possession, the demons would have no reason to come looking. And maybe she and Gran could pick up where they left off.

She thought about riding in the cockpit of Lucan's jet. Just a few hours from now.

No way was she missing out on that again.

Tomorrow, after she'd flown the jet, retrieved Mama and Gran's SUV, she would give it to Detective Blackburn. He could find a museum to put it in, and Ellie could get her life back on track.

After she flew the jet.

Michael got up and threw the empty water bottles in a tiny trash can marked 'plastic'.

"You can sleep in the main cabin. There are still a few hours before Lucan picks us up."

"Where will you sleep?"

"There's a guest bunk, but I think it's better if I keep an eye out tonight. You, though. You need your rest. You're flying jets tomorrow." He waggled his eyebrows at her.

Ellie grinned at him. "I'm so excited, I don't think I'll be able to sleep," she said, a thrill coursing through her body.

"Still, you've got a big day. I can always catch up on the flight."

She gawked at him. "Which is what? Twenty minutes?"

He laughed. "My uncle can be a little eccentric sometimes."

Ellie joined him, chuckling softly until their gazes clashed. For a long moment, neither of them said a word. The look he gave her was raw, aching. He tried to hide it from her, but she knew him. He was vulnerable.

"It's probably better if you get some shut-eye," he said, his voice as strained as the protective wall he'd built around himself.

He was right. She needed to rest. The coming days were bound to take a lot out of her. Still, she stood there.

"Probably," she finally said, her gaze locked on his.

His dazzling eyes, so tortured and mesmerizing, stared back at her. Why was she still standing there?

Because she didn't want to leave. She wanted to hold him, to wrap her arms around him and soothe the pain he had lived with for so long. To feel the demand of his lips, the sizzle of his bare skin against hers.

Ellie's heart nearly exploded when he took two steps and crossed the space between them, never taking his eyes off her face. He reached out and cupped her cheek with his hand.

She caught her breath, warmed all over by his hand on her face and the gentleness in his golden eyes. The loneliness and pain she felt from him broke her heart. She covered his hand with hers and gave him a soft smile. Unable to resist, she pushed to her tiptoes and kissed him.

She was completely unprepared for his reaction. In one swift motion, he pulled her against him, lifted her off her toes, and pushed her backwards through to the forward cabin. The room was small, not that she could pay much attention with his mouth latched to hers. A queen-sized bed took up most of the cabin.

Michael laid her back on the bed, never letting his mouth leave hers, holding her with a hot, demanding kiss that left her breathless and weak. The soft slap of waves against the side of the boat reached her. They swayed gently in the slip, bumping the dock occasionally on one side or the other. His long, hard body lay between her legs. His erection pressed against the center of her body. Her own body burned to feel him naked.

The delicious scent of him tore through her, exciting her in ways Ellie never dreamed possible. Tiny pinpoints of light pricked behind her eyes. She ran her hands over his shoulders, down his back and wrapped her arms around his back, holding him to her.

The way he kissed her was raw and uncivilized. It made a squeal bubble in Ellie's throat. Heat flushed her spine, making her break out in a hot sheen that made her even more anxious to be out of her clothes.

Michael ran his tongue along her bottom lip, pulling it into his mouth and sucking gently. He nibbled her, teasing her until she felt like little more than a puddle. He was hot and exciting. Delectable.

He thrilled her beyond human imagining. How easy it would be to lose herself. To throw caution aside, to open her heart and take a risk.

The idea terrified her.

Michael seemed to sense that in her. "Let yourself go, baby," he mumbled against her lips. "You don't have to be in control all the time." He trailed kisses from her mouth, along her jaw, to capture her ear lobe between his lips. "Gods, Ellie. I can't get enough of you."

His words, whispered so close to her ear, made her shiver. His breath was warm on her neck.

"Michael?"

"Hmm?"

She didn't want him getting any ideas about that white picket fence and naked babies running around in the backyard. "You know this is all I can give you."

Michael stiffened. His kisses along her sensitive skin froze. He pushed himself up, lifting off of her and staring down with a scowl. "Did I ask for more?" His voice was low, dangerous.

"No, but I don't want to give you the wrong idea. I'm trying to be honest."

He rolled off of her and shoved to his feet. "Well, you achieved that," he said. "Brutally." He adjusted his clothes and stepped out of the room. "Get some sleep, Ellie." He closed the door so hard, the flat screen at the foot of the bed threatened to fall off the wall.

CHAPTER NINE

Michael sat in the plush leather seat of his uncle's Falcon as they cruised at an altitude of seven thousand feet, or so Captain Ellie had announced. He could see her in the cockpit, the real pilot pointing at various instruments as he explained what each one did. Michael narrowed his eyes at the man when he touched Ellie's arm. For his sake, that had better be what he was explaining to her.

He tried to imagine what she was feeling. Flying wasn't Michael's favorite thing, but he understood the adrenaline rush she got from it. He felt the same way on his bike, cruising the open road, the wind in his face. It was a freedom he felt nowhere else. Except, maybe on his boat.

Ellie hadn't had that passion for flying when they were younger. It was a thrill she'd developed later. When she talked about the experience that sparked that dream, her whole body lit up. If only he could make her light up like that.

He thought he had. Her internal furnace had been burning pretty bright last night. His had been a raging inferno. Until she doused him with words that deflated him like a balloon escaping before a knot could be tied in the end. Her words had jolted him out of his passion. He'd been hurt—angry dammit. Never once in the entire time he'd known her had he made any demands, not on her freedom, her future, nothing. He'd been happy just to be part of her world.

That had changed. Now he definitely wanted more, but she didn't know that. She may have sensed it. After all, he wasn't very good at hiding his feelings. But he hadn't made mention of his yearnings. She didn't have to marry him, but for Arduinna's sake, couldn't they at least *go steady*?

He watched her in the pilot's seat as Lucan's voice droned on beside him. She was animated as she talked to the pilot, and he seemed to be equally enthralled with her. In his mind, Michael saw the man lean over, as if that was necessary in the tight confines of the cockpit, and rest his arm behind her. He reached across to the control panel with his other arm, brushing her breast as he did so. Michael couldn't read feelings, so the man's touch could be accidental. Intentional or not, he envisioned Ellie stiffening, pulling away from the pilot in awkward discomfort.

Michael was unbuckled and out of his seat in an instant. He was entirely sure Ellie could take care of the man herself, but he didn't want the bastard ruining this experience for her. He reached the door just as the pilot started to lean in her direction.

"How's it going in here, Captain?" Michael's frame filled the door, not difficult as even the pilot probably had to turn sideways to enter.

The pilot jumped and repositioned himself in his own seat. Michael swallowed the urge to grab him by the throat and throw him out the back door.

"Just fine, Mr. Munro," he said, clearing his throat first.

Mmm-hmm. "I wasn't talking to you," Michael said.

Ellie looked over her shoulder at him with eyes that were brighter than the sky in which they were suspended. It seemed her smile outshone the sun. The sheer pleasure on her face was infectious, and Michael found himself smiling back despite the hurt and anger he still felt.

"Are you having fun?" he asked.

She looked back out the tiny window. "There's nothing like it, Michael. This is so much better than that other time."

Michael clenched his jaw, recalling what she'd told him about the last pilot she'd flown with. He, too, had tried to take advantage of her. Michael was glad he could be here to ensure this experience was everything she dreamed of and stop some other asshole from convincing her that all men were pigs.

Michael looked down at the pilot who kept his gaze carefully locked on the horizon. "Good. I'm watching you back here," he said, confident the man got the message. "Don't get cocky and try any high-flying acrobatics or anything."

Ellie laughed, the tinkling laugh of a girl who been presented with her first pony. "I won't."

He stood there for another long moment. He admired her determination, her drive. She had decided she wanted to fly jets and nothing was going to prevent her from doing just that. He wished he had the same fortitude. He wanted Ellie King for his own, his partner, his life mate, but he had no idea how to make that happen. With a silent sigh of hopelessness, he turned and made his way back to his seat.

Lucan sat on the couch that took up one side of the plane. He raised one eyebrow as Michael walked back from the cockpit. "Everything all right?"

"Just making sure everyone knows the ground rules," he said.

Lucan regarded him as he sipped from the tumbler of Scotch that seemed to be ever present in his hand. "Ye're fond of her," he observed. "'Tis not like ye to be hung up on a single lass."

Michael continued to watch Ellie. Oh yes, he liked her. Too much. He suddenly realized just how empty his life was. Before Lucan had found him, he'd considered suicide on more than one occasion. He'd been shunned and rejected as long as he could remember, and after Ellie left, he accepted that he was unworthy of love, that no one would ever care about him, that he'd be alone for the rest of his life.

Add to that the increasing regularity of his visions and the debilitating headaches brought on by them, and Michael had difficulty finding a reason to go on.

Then Lucan Munro had walked into his life. Literally. He'd sauntered out of the shadows and slaughtered a half dozen men, all powered by the blood of demons, and revealed a world that defied logic. Michael had readily accepted his heritage. In truth, he would have believed anything, so relieved was he to learn the source of his visions and the tremendous strength and fighting skills he had been born with. His uncle had saved him in more ways than one.

If not for Lucan, he might not have been around that day when he'd looked up from his breakfast and seen her. Her appearance was all the more startling because he hadn't seen it coming. It had been such a shock, at first he hadn't believed it. All the longing he'd had for her and everything she represented came back to him in a flash.

He was seventeen again. And just as foolishly smitten has he had always been.

"She's okay," he said, trying to make light of an attraction that was hard to hide from a human, much less one of the most post powerful Celtic gods roaming the earth.

***

Ellie stared out the window of the restaurant. After they picked up the SUV from the police yard and collected her mother's remains, Michael had suggested they stop for a late lunch before heading back to Savannah. Ellie was more than happy to comply. She wasn't looking forward to that drive—again. It seemed like she'd been back and forth more in the last weeks than she had her entire life. She had fished out her cell phone and left it charging in the Durango, but it wasn't the most valuable thing she'd lost when the vehicle was stolen. She'd check first that the envelope with her teenage mementos of high school—okay of Michael in high school—were there.

Right in the top of the box where she'd put them. She stuffed it to the bottom on the off chance that he might see it. She didn't want him to get the wrong idea.

As was becoming his habit, Michael surprised her by directing her to the hotel they'd stayed in—had it only been two nights ago? Ellie felt like she'd aged ten years since this all started. Her life was spinning out of control, and she was powerless to stop it.

The Sundial restaurant, seventy-three floors above the city, rotated at a snail's pace, giving her an ever-changing view. The sky was as blue as a jay, accented here and there by big, fluffy, white clouds. If she looked down, she could see straight to the street below, a breath-taking sight that made her head spin. She could hardly pull her gaze away long enough to enjoy what was by far the most delicious meal she had ever eaten.

"Have you been here before?" she asked, a weak attempt to keep from moaning as she swallowed her Blackened Georgia Trout.

Michael nodded and took a sip of water. Ellie tried not to notice the way his throat moved when he swallowed. Or the way his tongue slid out and swirled around his lips.

She took a big gulp from her own water glass.

"Lucan likes this place, and I've been along for the ride a few times."

"So your uncle is a god. How is he different from you?"

"Well besides being about a million times more powerful, he has skills I don't, talents I don't even know about." He took a bite of his steak. "Plus, he's immortal."

"But you…"

He shook his head.

"And do people still worship these gods?"

"There are still people who perform rituals and maintain alters in honor of the ancient ones." He shrugged. "What's a god to do?" No sooner had he finished off his steak and laid his napkin on the table, a server whisked his empty plate away. "He was just like me, once. There were four of them. They grew up together. But one way or another, their godliness was bestowed on them, and they became immortal. Lucan's cousin, Camulus, is the god of war. He's in the army. The other two are brother and sister. But they went in different directions. Tanis is an angel of the one God, and his twin, Sirona, is a guardian angel, a healer."

Ellie remembered the goddess had taken Lucan to Sirona when he was near death from his contact with the spear head. When he returned, he said Sirona had visited Gran. Ellie could hope these stories were true.

She shook her head. "I wish I'd paid more attention in Vacation Bible School instead of making sure everyone glued their macaroni on right." He chuckled at her joke, making her heart trip. She suddenly found herself wanting to know all about him, to dig deep and discover things she thought she'd never cared about before.

"Do you remember your mother?"

His gold eyes darkened to a rich, amber color. He took a deep breath before answering. "Flashes. Her smile, the way I felt when she hugged me. I can't see her face anymore, though." He looked out the window. The sky had grown darker, the clouds more ominous. "It wasn't long after she died I started having visions. A hodge-podge of pictures flashing through my head. I couldn't make any sense of them, but I knew when something bad was about to happen. It scared me. Some of my fosters thought I was possessed."

"Humph—seems like that was a real possibility."

"Anything's possible. Most times my visions come soon enough that I can beat the bad guys. But you can't always win."

She recalled his earlier elusion to not acting in time. She'd wondered then what he meant. Now she could tell by the regret in his eyes that he must have failed somehow. "What happened?"

He didn't say anything for a long moment. When he did, his voice was tight, strangled by emotion. "I had only been with Lucan for a couple of months. He was still teaching me how to channel my powers. I was already pretty decent in a fight, and he was able to show me how to focus my visions so I could make sense of them, see them more clearly, and see details that would lead me to a culprit or anticipate my opponent's next moves.

"Late one night, I woke up, aware that a grave injustice was about to take place in the Starland District. A teenager, black kid, was in the wrong place at the wrong time, walking down a dark street with his hoodie over his head. Neighborhood watch guy blew him away before I could get there. Poor kid had no weapon, wasn't doing anything except taking a shortcut home through the wrong neighborhood." He stopped suddenly and stared out the window.

She could see him clenching his jaw. His throat worked as he tried to swallow, and Ellie knew he was trying hard to contain his emotions. Her heart melted. Michael was a good man with a good heart. A lifetime of rejection and isolation hadn't spoiled that, and she was grateful. Like a thunderbolt, she was hit with the realization she could love Michael Munro, deeply and eternally. Whether she wanted to or not.

She reached out and squeezed his hand.

Those golden eyes shot back to hers. They remained silent, staring at each other as the restaurant continued its unhurried rotation. A sudden flash of lightning outside the window startled her, drawing her away from Michael's intense stare. Ellie frowned at the sky that had been so blue just a few minutes ago. Now it was dark, menacing.

Michael pulled his hand from hers and clutched his water glass. Downing its contents, he continued his story. "I failed to save the boy. And to make matters worse, the son-of-a-bitch got off scot free." He looked back at her with a sneer he probably intended as a smile. He failed.

"Arduinna is also a goddess of justice, and I served her well after the man had his *fair* trial. There was nothing left of him for anyone to find. Rumor is he was so ostracized by the community he was forced to leave town."

Ellie couldn't bring herself to feel bad for the bastard. While Michael's form of justice was well-served, there was too much vigilante police work needed these days. "I'm glad you're with me," she said. She almost caved at the hope on his face. But she didn't want to lead him on, to drag him into the chaos of her life, the confusion of her own emotional state. She hesitated. "There's no one I feel safer with." The disappointment that flared pinched her heart.

Before she could comment further, all signs of disappointment vanished. Instead Michael jerked as if someone had slapped him, growled a word that should never be uttered in such a refined place, and flipped their dining table onto one side, shoving it against the window with enough force to shatter the glass.

He barreled into her, knocking Ellie to the floor and half crawled, half dragged her to the center of the room.

Struggling to breathe, she tried to wriggle away from him. "What the hell?"

The words still lingered on her lips when thunder clapped so loud, the building shook. She was momentarily blinded by a sudden flash of light that filled the room.

"We have to get out of here," Michael yelled, pulling her to her feet and hauling her through the smoke-filled restaurant. Looking back, Ellie caught a glimpse of the smoldering spot where their table had been. A gaping hole let smoke escape into the Atlanta sky.

***

Before the other diners and employees could get their bearings, Michael had led her to the stairs, shielding her as they ran through smoke that soon activated the overhead sprinklers. Ellie covered her ears against the deafening blare of the alarm. Michael's premonition had saved their lives and allowed them to surge through the chaos while everyone else was still trying to figure out which way to go.

Her heart pounded. She had visions of 9/11 and the collapse of the twin towers. What if that happened to this building? Fear choked her, but she kept running. They had already descended two flights when people above them started pouring into the stairwell. More and more filed in below them, employees trying to usher hotel guests to safety. Before long, the stairs were clogged, and it was impossible to hurry. They were forced to slow down and follow along like cattle through a shoot.

"We have to get out of here," Michael said. He held her hand in a vice grip.

Ellie ignored the pain, grateful to have him to hang onto, and followed Michael blindly. He surged through the crowd and burst through the door onto the sixty-second floor. It was deserted. Michael rushed over and pushed every available button for the elevator.

"We can't take that," Ellie said. "Everyone knows you can't use the elevator if there's a fire."

"There is no fire." He darted back and forth from one side of the hallway to the other, punching the elevator buttons again and again in his impatience.

"Maybe they're not running," she suggested.

"As long as there's power in the building, they'll run." As evidence, one of the doors slid open. "C'mon." He grabbed her hand and pulled her inside, then pressed the button for the parking garage.

It was a long ride down. They stood silently, watching the numbers light up in descending order. Sixty-one. Sixty. Fifty-nine. Michael tapped his foot.

Ellie wanted to scream. The wait was torture. "How do you know there's no fire?"

"A lightning strike on the exact spot where we were sitting can't have been a coincidence. I think we...one of us...was deliberately attacked."

Ellie swallowed hard, remembering the handsome demon who had tried to drain Gran's soul. She stared at the elevator panel. Forty-two. Forty-one. Forty. Would they ever reach the ground? "Do you have your magic knife?"

He grinned at her. "Never leave home without it."

Suddenly, his grin disappeared, replaced by a curse so foul it made Ellie's ears ring. He crowded her into one corner, wrapping his hard body around hers. Before she could react, his mouth was on hers in a hot, desperate kiss. Ellie forgot to be afraid. The sensation of Michael's lips on hers was enough to distract a virgin bride-to-be in the middle of her first lap dance.

He pulled back, looking at her with a need that set her heart to racing from something more than fear. "Head down," he said in a voice that was far too calm. He pressed her head to his chest, completely shielding her with his body.

With a deafening bang, something landed on top of the elevator car. The entire box jerked and seemed to free fall for a few long seconds as the cables strained against whatever was up there. She peered around Michael at the panel. Sixteen. Fifteen. Fourteen.

Hurry. Hurry. Hurry.

They were under full attack by now. Someone, or something, on top of the car was attempting to punch its way through the ceiling. It was leaving deep fist marks in the steel overhead.

Nine. Eight. Seven.

They were never going to make it.

The elevator jerked to a halt on the fourth floor. Michael let go of her to punch the buttons, but to no avail.

"We can't stay in here." He pushed his fingers between the doors and strained to pry them open. Just as he made space enough for her to squeeze through, the thing above them tore a jagged gash in the ceiling of the elevator car and dropped down to land in crouch.

It was a man, or at least he looked like one. Instinctively, Ellie knew he was not of this world. Before he could rise to his feet, Michael kicked him in the face and shoved Ellie through the opening.

"Run!"

"I'm not leaving you," she cried.

The man rose slowly, his evil gaze darting back and forth between the two of them. He grinned revealing blood covered teeth from where Michael had kicked him. "How sweet." His voice was gravelly with a hint of the same Scottish accent as Lucan. "The lass doesna want to leave ye."

With a cruel laugh, he held out one hand as if to grab her even though she was well out of reach. Ellie couldn't breathe. It was if he held her by the throat and cut off her air supply. She clawed at her throat, struggling to draw a breath. Her eyes widened as her feet lifted off the floor. She tried to scream, but no sound could make it past her choked windpipe.

Michael attacked, rushing the man and slamming him against the back wall of the elevator.

Ellie hit the floor hard. Ignoring the pain of her abrupt landing, she crawled off to one side, looking around for something to use as a weapon. Pushing tenderly to her feet, she rushed over to the fire extinguisher and broke the glass. Racing back to help, she screamed at the sight of blood covering Michael's shirt. It was the split second distraction she needed. Ellie swung the fire extinguisher against the man's head as hard a she could.

He dropped to his knees.

Michael took the extinguisher from her and pounded the man until he stayed down. Breathing heavily, he stood over him, making sure he didn't move, then threw the extinguisher down, grabbed her hand, and took off for the stairs.

The stairwell was still clogged, but this time Michael shoved people aside dragging Ellie along with him. They burst through the door to the parking garage.

"Give me the keys," he said as they ran.

Ellie fished them from her pocket and tossed them to him just as they reached the SUV. She jumped in, pulling the door closed as Michael squealed away. They zipped through the garage, following the exit signs round and round and down the ramp toward the street.

The attendant booth was in sight. The guard rail was down, but Ellie knew that wasn't going to stop Michael. Just as the ramp straightened out, their attacker suddenly appeared directly in front of them.

Michael floored the SUV and hit the man dead on. He slammed against the windshield and flipped up onto the roof.

Ellie looked back. There was no sign of him. She soon learned why.

She screamed when her window shattered, raining glass all over her. Michael jerked the steering wheel from side to side, trying to shake him off. When he reached inside the window and grabbed her by the hair, Michael barreled into a pillar, sideswiping the concrete and successfully scraping the man off the side of the SUV. Ellie could see him tumbling away behind them.

"Are you okay?" Michael shouted.

"Yes. Go, go, go."

Tires squealed as they tore out onto the street. Ellie continued to watch out the rear window, but there was no sign of their attacker. Michael sped through the city, putting distance between them and what must surely be a demon from hell.

CHAPTER TEN

Michael parked Ellie's SUV in the marina's lot. The sun had set, but its soft rays bathed the sky in a calliope of reds, oranges, and yellows. On any other evening, it would be very romantic, a certain aide in getting his date out of her pants.

Not tonight. Getting into the pants of the woman he'd brought home was the furthest thing from his mind. He'd almost lost her, his Ellie, in a way that he could never get her back. He couldn't imagine a world without her in it. It wasn't a world he wanted to live in.

Gripping the wheel with both hands, he glanced over at her. She stared across the Wilmington River, watching the brilliant colors of the sky fade into twilight. She was so beautiful, he had to remind himself to breathe.

"Won't he find us here?" Ellie's voice was soft, low.

Michael shook his head. "I don't think he knows me. It's you he's after. He knows you have the spearhead, and he wants it."

"He's a demon like the other one, isn't he?"

"I sensed more power from this one. He's not your average, everyday demon."

Ellie sighed. "Why is this happening to me? Where did my mom get that thing?"

"My guess is the pilot hid it in your room, probably intending to retrieve it later. The demon probably went there looking for it, and your mother encountered him."

She turned her head to look at him. Tears sparkled on her lashes, shattering his heart into a million pieces. "Do you think she suffered?"

Of course she had, but he wouldn't tell her that. "No. She probably just drifted away, imagining she was being kissed very deeply by a handsome man."

One corner of her mouth tilted up. "She would have liked to go that way."

She stared into his eyes for a long moment, then reached for the door handle. "You got anything to eat on that yacht?"

"I've been known to scrounge a morsel or two." As they walked down the dock to his slip, both of them continued to glance around. Nothing seemed out of the ordinary, but Michael vowed to pay more attention to the visions flashing through his head. He couldn't afford to be caught off-guard again. If he lost Ellie...

He jumped onto the deck and reached out to help her aboard. She stepped into the circle of his arms and wrapped her own around his waist. Michael held her, resting his cheek against her soft brown hair. The apple scent swept him with a sense of nostalgia that he wanted to hold onto, to lose himself in. If only he had the power to make her love him.

Pulling away, he led her down into the cabin. No one would mistake his thirty-two foot Cobalt for a yacht, but he was proud that Ellie considered it as such, even if she had only been trying to lighten the mood.

He started opening and closing cabinets, pulling out crackers, peanut butter. "I hope you're hungry," he joked. In the mini fridge he found some cheese and deli meat. As he bent over to retrieve them, she came right up behind him and pressed her hips against backside.

Michael froze, instantly hard. Did she have any idea what she did to him?

Ellie curled her body over his. "What if I'm hungry for something else?"

He stood slowly, savoring the feel of her soft curves pressed against his back. He almost came undone when she reached around him and squeezed his erection through his jeans. He turned to face her, raking her hair back from her face with both hands.

"You don't have to do this, Ellie."

"Do what?" Her question was all innocence. Her hands were anything but. She reached down and unbuttoned the fly of his jeans, releasing some of the pressure on his painful hard-on.

He'd never known this feeling, not in his entire life. The love he had for this woman was so deeply imbedded in him it frightened him. Now that she was back in his life, he would be hard pressed to let her go again. He would die before he let that happen.

When she reached into his jeans and cupped his erection through his boxers, Michael ran a hand down her arm, smiling at the goose bumps that arose on her flushed skin. He stared into those deep brown eyes that had held him in her power for so long and covered her hand with his much larger one, urging her on.

She pulled away and pushed his t-shirt up to his shoulders. With a wicked grin, she leaned forward and flicked her pink tongue over his nipple. He growled at the surge of excitement that overloaded all his most sensitive areas. He held his breath as she trailed kisses down his stomach.

She fell to her knees and looked up at him with a smile that melted his heart. Michael sucked in a sharp breath when she pushed his jeans and boxers to his ankles in one move.

Ellie nipped at his hipbone, teasing the sensitive skin and sending chills scattering over his entire body. Laughing, she stroked the crisp hairs at the center of his body and dragged one finger down the length of his cock. Pulling back, she examined him, teasing the tip with the pad of her thumb and letting his moisture coat her. She slipped her thumb into her mouth and tasted him.

Michael had never seen anything so erotic. He watched in silence as she explored the length of him, stroking, kissing, licking all the way down his shaft. She licked his sac, making his balls churn and tightened until he thought he couldn't stand it any longer.

He nearly exploded when she took the swollen head between her lips. His body jerked in response, and a loud groan escaped his lips. He stroked her hair as she gently tongued him from hilt to tip. The feel of her lips, her tongue was like nothing he'd ever felt before. She had laid claim to him in a way no other woman ever had. What was it about her that made him willing to accept whatever tidbit or morsel she offered?

This was more than a morsel. This was his Ellie, making love to him with her mouth and pleasuring him in a way that he had never thought possible. It was more like his last meal, and he intended to get his fill.

He held her shoulders and groaned with each nibble, lick and suckle she gave him. She gripped his hips as she tortured him with wicked delight. She was completely shameless, and he loved it.

He looked down at her. He couldn't believe she was real. He had dreamed about her so many times, he feared this would also turn out to be a cruel dream, and he would wake up at the last moment to find himself alone.

"Ellie—" His voice sounded strange, foreign even to his own ears, a choking, husking growl. "If you keep this up, I won't be any good to you the rest of the night." It wasn't true. He would be hard and ready for her every single day and night until the end of time. But he gave her one last opportunity to back out, to stop before it was too late.

For her.

It was already too late for him.

***

Ellie stood and peeled off her clothes. She stood there in the tiny living room-slash-kitchen completely naked. The ravenous look in Michael's eyes reached deep inside her, made her feel things she didn't want to feel. All she wanted right now was to forget the thing that was chasing her, to waste away the hours with the sexiest man she had ever known, to lose herself in the erotic playground before her.

Grabbing the tail of his shirt, she pushed it up over his washboard stomach, then his bulging chest, taking her time and savoring the reveal. He kicked his way out of his jeans and boxers, and by the time his head cleared the t-shirt, he was as naked as she.

Ellie grinned. "You are gorgeous," she said.

Michael pulled her forcefully against him. The heat of his skin sizzled against hers. The look he gave her was hot, wicked. He ran his tongue up the column of her throat, stopping to nibble the tender skin at her hair line and suckle her earlobe. His warm breath made her shiver. He grasped her ass cheeks in both hands and lifted her off her feet.

The feel of his cock pressed against the wiry hairs at the juncture of her thighs made moisture pool between her legs. Ellie wrapped them around his hips, her arms around his broad shoulders, and held on for the ride.

His lips still attached to her ear, he crossed the few steps to the forward berth. As he laid her back on the captain's bed, he trailed nibbling bites down the column of her throat, laving his velvety tongue over her feverish skin and pushing her thighs apart. Michael's weight pressed down on her, a welcome heaviness that only made her more eager to have him inside her.

He moved over her sinuously, all grace and power and man, continuing his trek down her body. The masculine scent of him, the rugged texture of his skin against hers excited her beyond anything she'd ever imagined.

He made his way torturously to the center of her body and pushed her thighs further apart. He pressed both thumbs into her opening, exposing her clit. He coated one with moisture from her pussy and stroked her with the slick pad. Then repeated with the other. Back and forth. Back and forth until she thought she would faint from the sheer pleasure of it. When he leaned closer and blew gently on the throbbing nub, it sent her over the edge.

Just as she began to slide, he touched his lips to her, setting off an explosion of fireworks that could prelude the end of the world. And Ellie wouldn't have cared. He swirled his tongue around, tantalizing and maddening, before sucking her clit between his lips and drawing an orgasm from her that went on and on, leaving her drained and panting.

But not quite sated. Her body still sizzled with desire. If he could do that with his mouth, what could he do with his cock?

She couldn't wait to find out.

She arched her back as Michael pushed over her. She couldn't get close enough. Only when his was buried inside her, when they were as close as two people could be, maybe then she could scratch that itch and finally get him out of her system.

Reaching over her head, Michael slid open the door to a tiny compartment in the headboard and pulled out a condom. Ellie pressed one hand to his chest and pushed to a sitting position. She took the package from him and ripped off one side.

She cupped his balls with one had as she rolled the condom down the length of him with the other. She squeezed them gently. Well—mostly.

Michael dropped forward, supporting himself with both hands against the headboard, elbows locked, and a pained expression on his beautiful face. He hypnotized her with those eyes, wild like a tiger's. She'd never seen anyone with eyes that color. So rich, so…alluring.

He let out a sigh as he pressed his forehead to hers. His labored breathing was steady, controlled. She held his cock in an easy grip and guided him to her. She moaned when the tip split her lips apart.

"Ellie—" His voice cracked with emotion.

Her chest tightened at the raw feelings he couldn't hide. "Shhh. Just don't talk, Michael."

Still gripping the headboard, he entered her. She was so wet, he slid to the hilt, filling her and making her shout with pleasure. He captured her cry with his mouth, sealing his lips to hers.

Her muscles contracted around him. He groaned but remained buried up to his balls inside her. Ellie wriggled, rubbing her clit against him. How could she be so aroused? Only moments before, he had given her an orgasm like nothing she'd ever known. Now she was on the brink of another, just as mind-blowing.

He didn't move, just kissed her, tangling his hot tongue with hers and tasting every corner of her mouth until she was whimpering and begging him to move.

Finally, he began to circle his hips, leisurely rubbing his cock deep inside her. He ground into her before pulling out with aching slowness until the tip tickled the outer lips at her opening. He kept kissing her while he prodded her pussy lips apart with the thick head of his cock, tiny nudges that rubbed against her swollen clit and threatened to send her off into oblivion.

Without warning, he plunged into her, once, twice— three times before she let go. The cabin seemed to go black. All sound became silent. All she heard was Michael crying out her name as he threw his head back and slammed into her one final time, his whole body going tight.

Ellie eyes actually teared up the sight of his climax. It was as if he was being ripped apart.

He collapsed on top of her and breathed her name again. The sound of it coming from his lips made her heart twitter. It didn't make sense, the feelings she had for him. She'd fought as long as she could remember.

It didn't matter. Not when he was inside her, gasping her name and giving himself in a way she instinctively knew he hadn't with any other woman. He loved her. Ellie had always known it. She didn't know whether to be thrilled or scared.

Tonight, it didn't matter.

***

Much later, Ellie lay next to Michael on the queen-sized bed. His scent was all over her. She savored this intimate moment, his naked body wrapped around hers. She didn't want to think about the jumbled mass of emotions roiling around inside her. She just wanted to enjoy this and forget about everything else.

Not an easy thing to do, especially when he cupped her cheek in one palm and gave her the sweetest, most gentle kiss in the history of kissing.

He smiled down at her. "Thank you," he said.

She frowned. "What for?" She hadn't been doing *him* any favors.

He brushed strands of her hair away from her face, the touch of his finger a soothing sensation that made her want to close her eyes and let out a big sigh. She wouldn't think about how unnerved she should feel.

"For not reminding me that this is all I'm going to get." He reached down between them, splaying his hand over her chest, letting her taut nipple tease his palm. "And for being so...incredible."

She rolled over slightly so she could see him better. "You're welcome." She smirked at him, arching one brow and fixing him with a teasing expression. "You weren't too bad, either."

He stretched onto his back and slanted his gaze at her. "Watch out, Ellie. That was almost a compliment."

She laughed and leaned over to nibble along his rib cage. "I can give a compliment," she mumbled against the goosebumps that rose on his skin.

He urged her back down on the bed. "You'd better get some sleep. Who knows what surprises we have in store for tomorrow."

"You don't have to do this, you know. I can take the spearhead to a museum. If I no longer have it, there's no reason for that demon to come after me."

"I'm not leaving you on your own."

"I just want to be clear that you don't have to feel obligated, to put yourself in danger—"

"Ellie, stop talking." He grunted in frustration. "You just don't get it, do you?"

She peered up at him. He had one arm slung across his eyes but still looked absolutely gorgeous in the shadows. "Get what?"

He was quiet. Ellie could only guess at his thoughts. He was going to tell her he loved her, she could sense that he wanted to. But what did she want? How would she respond? She wasn't going to say it back. She didn't love him.

Did she?

She was so confused. No matter how she fought it, if she wasn't already in love with Michael Munro, she would be soon.

"That relic has enough power to destroy a god. My family. I can't allow it to get into the wrong hands."

Disappointment flooded her. Maybe he didn't love her. Maybe it was all a misguided fantasy of hers that had no basis in reality. Could she have been so arrogant? So superior to assume—

She heaved out a big sigh. What a fool she was. She had imagined him pining away for her all these years. With skills like his, he had obviously had a lot of practice since the night they'd given up their virginity. Either that or he'd read way too many how-to manuals.

Okay, not *too* many, because he really was incredible.

A sudden thought rocked her. What if he'd been disappointed? He said it was—well, he could say anything, couldn't he? And he probably did, to all the women he fucked. *Oh yeah,* she ranted silently, *it's so easy for you, isn't it? With your rockin', hot body and* Miami Vice *boat. You probably have those condoms stashed all over this thing.*

His breathing slowed, and she wondered if he had fallen asleep. How could he sleep when she was in such turmoil?

Ellie was suddenly angry, and she didn't know why. That wasn't true. She knew exactly why. Jealousy. It was an ugly thing. She had no right. She had been the one to leave. She'd had no intention of ever coming back. But somehow, in a far off corner of her mind, in a secret nook where she locked away all the things she wanted to think about later, she had always expected him to be waiting for her.

It wasn't realistic or even fair, but it was her fantasy. She didn't have to be fair. She wanted him for her own, and may his gods help any woman who thought to lay claim on what she had always thought of as hers.

So why did she resist? Why couldn't she just admit it?

"What's wrong?"

Ellie jumped at the sound of Michael's voice. He must have sensed the change in her mood.

She inched away from him on the bed. Maybe if she put a little distance between them, she could clear her head of all the sappy romantic notions that were a threat to her sanity. "Nothing," she said.

She felt him turn his head to look at her. "You sure? You seem a little edgy."

"I said it was nothing," she snapped.

"Well, you don't—"

"Look. I've got a lot on my mind. I'm worried about Gran. I'm being hunted by a demon. Why do you take everything so personal? The world doesn't revolve around you, you know." She didn't look at him, didn't want to see the pain her words caused.

"You forget, I know you pretty well, Ellie. I can tell when you're mad at me."

"Maybe you don't know me as well as you think," she said. *Maybe if you'd just tell me how you feel so I wouldn't have to guess—*

Michael climbed from the bed.

"Where are you going?"

He turned to face her before stepping through the narrow portal. He looked like a god himself, standing there in all his naked glory, bronze skin poured over sculpted muscle. He was so gorgeous, it hurt to look at him. So masculine and solid, it was all she could not to beg him to come back to bed.

"Does it matter?" he asked.

Yes! her mind screamed. *But I'm afraid.* She shrugged. "Do what you like. It's your boat."

She turned away from him, frustration and self-loathing twisting inside her. Hot tears stung her eyes. Damn it. She wanted to follow him and apologize for her bitchy attitude. But she couldn't bring herself to admit that she was falling hard for Michael Munro and feared she was losing herself in the process.

CHAPTER ELEVEN

Ellie woke hours later to the smell of bacon. Nothing could get her out of bed faster. She tossed back the covers and sat up, careful not to crack her head on the low ceiling. The narrow door was closed, but she could hear Michael moving around on the other side.

Her jeans lay on the foot of the bed along with a clean t-shirt that would be way too big for her. She checked to be sure the spearhead was still in her pocket, then maneuvered into the clothes as best she could in the tight confines of the cabin, tying the shirt at her waist and wishing for a mirror.

"There's another bathroom through that door in the corner."

Ellie jumped. He must have envisioned her emerging from the bedroom, a horrendous mess. She found the door and stepped inside what could hardly be called a bathroom. It was more like a tiny shower stall with a sink and a toilet.

A glance in the mirror reminded her she had been silly. Insecurity didn't suit her. Her hair was a little mussed. And she could do with a touch of lipstick. But she didn't look half bad considering the circumstances. She was determined to have a shower today, in her own bathroom, and dress in her own clothes.

With a shyness she hadn't felt in her entire life, Ellie reached for the door. A bat had fallen across it, so she propped it in the corner, wondering when Michael had ever played baseball. The door didn't have a knob or latch of any kind. Instead she had to push on it, and when she did, it popped open with a jolt. She practically fell out into the living area.

Michael caught her before she stumbled. She landed against what appeared to be a brick wall but turned out be his chest. His scent swept over her. He smelled of Irish Spring and some very manly shampoo.

"I hope you slept okay?"

"Yes, thanks." She pulled away and sat at the table. Michael turned back to the stove, allowing her a moment to admire him. He wore only a pair of jeans. Tight, butt-hugging jeans. No shoes. No shirt. No, sir. That would be too much to ask. Instead she drank him in like he was a crystal pool in the middle of the desert.

She nearly choked when he turned suddenly and set a plate in front of her.

"Baby, you keep staring at me like that, and I'll fuck you right here on the floor."

Ellie sat up, pulling her shoulders back. As tempting as that sounded, she was struck by a more disturbing thought that kept niggling at her. "Do you have visions about me? You know what I'm about to do...before I know?"

Michael sat across from her. "I have glimpses." He nodded at the plate he'd put on the table. "I knew exactly when to have your breakfast ready."

She looked down at the food for the first time. Before her was a plate piled high with her favorite breakfast of eggs, grits, toast, and bacon. Lots and lots of bacon. She took the knife and fork he handed her. "You made this?" she asked.

"I wanted to watch the show without distraction." He seared her with a look so hot she was speechless.

It was a day of firsts.

Gathering her wits, she dove into the food. "You're in a good mood this morning," she said, just before she took her first heavenly bite.

Michael watched her lips close on the tines of her fork. He seemed hypnotized by her mouth. Ellie savored a rush of excitement to realize the power she had over him.

He dragged his gaze from her mouth to her eyes, holding her in that hungry look and almost making her forget her breakfast.

"You've been getting mad at me for no reason since first grade. I've had to learn to rebound faster and faster."

She occupied herself eating so she wouldn't have to respond. Guilt assailed her that she hadn't been more fair to him. He deserved better. He was the most loyal friend she had ever had. He loved her unconditionally, with all her faults.

Still, she couldn't reconcile herself with being the Susie-Homemaker she'd tried to convince herself he wanted. She had plans, goals. She wanted to see the world, make something of her life. She didn't fit into the picture of domestic bliss. She couldn't cook or keep house, and she didn't want to. Of course, if her eggs and grits were any indication, Michael was an excellent cook.

She glanced around. The boat was pretty clean, too.

Who was she kidding? Michael didn't want a maid. He wanted a partner, someone to share life with, someone he cared about who cared about him in return.

"In answer to your question," he continued.

What question? She had already forgotten.

"I don't usually see private, intimate things. Just general actions and reactions of things that are about to occur."

"So no…mind-reading or anything like that."

He smiled. "The ability to read *your* mind would be more prized than immortality. But no. I can't read minds."

She finished off her breakfast and leaned back on the bench. Precognition. Mind-reading. Immortality. It was surreal. To learn the world was nothing like she thought. There were people who possessed other-worldly powers and lived forever. Some of them were good people. Some pure evil. Then there were those who weren't people at all. Gods. Demons.

She'd begun questioning her Catholic upbringing about the same time she hit puberty. She was skeptical by nature. But Ellie would never have considered herself a non-believer.

Now she didn't know what to believe.

It was frightening in many ways. And for someone who was not easily frightened or otherwise intimidated, the discovery was unsettling. Ellie let the enormity of her situation, the indomitable danger that threatened her, sink in. She had kept those thoughts at bay, unwilling to face this new reality, but an overwhelming sense of distress broke through. She felt choked with fear. She nearly panicked, her insides twisted into knots.

She didn't know how to fight this.

But then, she didn't have to. For the first time in her life, Ellie was forced to let someone else take control, to let someone besides her be in charge. Someone much more knowing and capable than she.

"Thank you," she said. "For saving Gran, for putting yourself in danger." She stared into those eyes, wishing things were different. That they were just two regular people with regular problems like other people had. "For staying with me all this time."

He would think she meant these last few days, but in her own heart, Ellie knew—she was grateful to him for a lifetime of loyalty, for being the only other person in the world besides her grandmother who had always been there for her, no matter that she was a selfish bitch who didn't deserve such devotion.

Michael reached across the table and took her hands in his. "I'll never leave you, Ellie. As long as you want me around, I'll be right here." He stroked his thumb back and forth across her skin, sending jolts of pleasure up her arms.

How she longed to spend a leisurely day cruising up and down the river, with a handsome man who sent her senses reeling, enjoying the beautiful sights that were Savannah. She hadn't appreciated the city before, as with so many other things.

She vowed to correct that starting right now.

With a sigh, Michael leaned back and fished his phone from his pocket. "I hope this is good news."

Seconds later, the phone rang.

***

Cael Comyn waited in the ante room of the Prehistoric Preservation Department.

He hated waiting.

He had been waiting for nearly six hundred years, and finally success was in his grasp. He could feel the spear's power. It was near. Hidden somewhere in this boring town. If only that incompetent servant he'd honored with the task had retrieved the spearhead and killed the woman as commanded, the world would be his by now. Instead he'd held the artifact hostage in demand for more...more of something. Cael didn't even know what. Nor did he care. Greedy human bastard. They were never satisfied. He'd taken great pleasure in ripping out the throats of Jonathan James and his companions. After one of his brethren had disappeared, Cael had realized he would have to do the job himself.

The lass was the key.

He almost had her in Atlanta, if not for the lad. Cael still chafed that the whelp had gotten the best of him. If his father heard about that, hell wouldn't be deep enough for Cael to hide from the humiliation.

He had tracked her here, to Savannah-Fucking-Georgia, but had not yet pinpointed her location. Her dwelling had been unoccupied for days, and while he sensed the lingering power of the relic, he knew it was not there. It *had* been, however, and that pleased him.

She was nearby. When he found her, he would take great pleasure in procuring the spearhead from her.

He watched as one young female student after another paraded past him. Savannah's College of Art and Design was home to more than twelve thousand students, most of them women. Dr. Perkins, head of the Preservation Department had a steady supply of pussy. Lucky bastard. Cael used his powers to envision them naked, parading past him wearing nothing but shoes and a backpack, completely oblivious of how he saw them.

They ignored him, staring straight ahead and hurrying by without making eye contact. Cael wasn't as lucky with women as he could be. He was handsome enough, he didn't age, and he was well built thanks to the power surging through him. Perhaps it was his penchant for seeing them suffer, hearing their pleas for mercy. The women he fucked seldom survived the ordeal. Even women who at first displayed interest, quickly sensed the evil in him and shied away.

Of course, by then it was too late.

He stood when Dr. Perkins' door opened. Cael almost failed to mask his surprise when Neala emerged from his office. The scent of her divine blood made his mouth water.

He hadn't seen his uncle's wife in at least a hundred years. Ever since the bloody Munro had kidnapped her from Inverwick Castle, the Comyns had been trying to steal her back. He'd tracked her, usually through the Munro, from one lifetime to another. Elusive as a snow leopard, she remained just out of reach. Frustration had fed his hatred for centuries. Not only was Neala's soul one of the most powerful on the planet, but a Highlander did not let such an insult pass without repercussion.

Neala took one look at Cael and stopped dead in her tracks. She didn't know him, of course, yet recognition flared in those earth colored eyes.

And fear.

Cael's cock sprang to life. He smiled at her, nodded his head in greeting, but she looked away quickly and darted past him.

Insolent bitch. He glared at her retreating back. *Soon*, he thought.

"Ah, Mr. Comyn," Perkins greeted him from the doorway. "Come in please, and close the door."

Dr. Perkins' welcoming demeanor vanished when Cael closed the door behind him. "Do you have it?"

Cael didn't care for the other man's air of self-importance. He would take pleasure in killing him when this was done. He busied himself reading the professor's *I*

Love Me wall. There were a number of awards and various diplomas, one from The Sorbonne, hanging strategically. "The lass who just left your office. What name does she go by?" He straightened a frame that was only slightly crooked.

"Um, Lindsey. Smith. She's a student here."

"I'll need a copy of her schedule," Cael said, continuing his perusal of the room.

Dr. Perkins stuttered. "I-I can't give you that," he said.

Cael turned and gave the man such a look, he actually seemed to wilt. "Aye, ye can. Ye're bein' compensated well enough." He glanced at the computer monitor on the professor's desk then looked back at him. "I doona like to ask twice."

Resigned, Dr. Perkins sat at his desk. His fingers twittered across the keyboard. A second later, the printer whirred to life.

Cael retrieved the sheet himself, folded it, and put it in the pocket of his lapel. "I ken the location of the spearhead and will have it in my possession verra soon." He sat in one of the two leather captain's chairs positioned in front of the big wooden desk. "What have ye found out?"

Perkins tapped more keys and stared at the computer screen. "The spear was created by the One God eons before the time of man," he read aloud. "It's touch is lethal to those who were cast from Heaven. Equally deadly to the Heavenly Host." He looked up hopefully. "You'll need someone to handle it for you."

Cael stood and walked to the door. "I'll let ye know," was all he said as he left.

He passed through the ante room before pulling Neala's schedule from his pocket. Lindsey Smith. Her name was always common, a piss-poor effort to hide her, as were all his efforts to shield the lass from her *family*. Eventually, their paths always crossed.

This time, he would have her. And Lucan Munro would know suffering that would bring him to his knees.

***

When they arrived at Lucan's house, the goddess was already there. Michael wondered briefly about the relationship between Lucan and Arduinna. She was known for her voracious sexual appetite, but Lucan had been solely dedicated to Neala since he found her tied to a bed at the Comyns' Highland stronghold six hundred years ago. He had rescued her on the spot and remained her loyal champion for centuries, honoring his covenant with the One God through each of Neala's reincarnations. Michael didn't believe even a goddess could turn his uncle's head.

Still, twenty-five years was a long time to wait.

Would he be as steadfast if he were immortal and Ellie was reincarnated again and again? Would he have the stamina to track her down at the end of each lifetime, wait a quarter of a century for her to come of age, then make her fall in love with him all over again?

Without question. Michael would suffer any hardship to spend eternity with his Ellie.

He doubted she could make the same claim, and it hurt more than he wanted to admit.

They settled themselves in the salon. Arduinna turned her emerald eyes to Ellie. "Do you have the relic?" she asked in her lilting voice. It reminded Michael of a birdsong.

Ellie nodded and reached into the pocket of her jeans.

The goddess stopped her. "No. Keep it hidden. Its touch is lethal, and I'm not sure it isn't dangerous even *without* touching it." She crossed the room and cupped Ellie's cheek in one hand. "It is a terrible task you have been given, *mon connil.*"

Ellie glanced at Michael, who stood before the fire place, before responding. He cringed at the fear and uncertainty in her eyes, wanting nothing so much as to relive her concerns but finding it increasingly impossible to do so.

"What task?" she asked.

Michael moved to sit beside her on the sofa. He took her hand, and she let him, lacing her fingers in his and holding their joined hands in her lap. His heart surged at the trust she put in him. That was how it started, right? Trust then love?

Maybe....

He didn't dare to hope. He knew Ellie cared for him, as much as she could care for anyone who didn't fit into her plan. But would she ever *love* him? And would it be enough to make her stay with him? In a sad effort to protect his weak emotional state, he hardened his heart, or at least he tried to convince himself of it. His heart was so far gone, he no longer had any say in the matter. Ellie owned his heart.

He pushed such sappy thoughts away. Right now, Ellie was in danger. And his petty feelings were of little consequence by comparison.

Arduinna sat in one of the faded chairs across from them while Lucan poured himself a Scotch. "The spearhead cannot be destroyed," she explained to them. "It was created by YHWH and only He can destroy it. It is a terrible weapon." She fixed Ellie with a pointed look.

"The one who wields it is capable of commanding all the forces of this world."

Ellie stiffened beside him. "So this demon that's chasing me wants to take over the world?"

The goddess shook her head. "Cael is only Lucifer's henchman. If he can secure the relic for his master, his place among hell's elite will be assured."

Lucan nearly choked on his drink. "Cael?" He crossed the room and stood next to Arduinna. "Not of the Comyn clan?"

She looked up at him with an air of seduction that made Michael wonder how Lucan resisted. "The very same," she said. "Lucifer's blood runs through Cael's veins, and he will stop at nothing to become the favored son."

"Or use it to destroy Lucifer and claim himself lord of hell." Lucan tossed back the rest of his Scotch. "That canna be allowed to happen."

Michael recalled the story. Cael had been nephew to Neala's husband, laird of Clan Comyn. Lucan had killed Cael's uncle and father in his bid to become her savior. Cael had been seeking revenge ever since.

That he was descended from the lord of darkness himself was news Michael had not anticipated. They had been lucky to escape such a powerful being. Would they be so lucky next time?

"Agreed," Arduinna said. She turned those piercing green eyes back to Ellie. "You must find the missing piece and return it to the true Got to be used in his service."

"How am I supposed to do that?"

"We must trust that you will know what do to when the time comes."

Ellie wanted to refuse. "Why me?" she asked.

"You are the only one of us who can handle it, *mon connil*," she said. "As a human, you are not affected by the mere touch of the spearhead. You would have to actually be stabbed—as with any other."

"Yes, but can't I just give this to a priest and let him return it to God?"

The goddess smiled, as heart-lifting gesture that seemed to light up the whole room. "If only it were that simple," she said. "If Lucifer takes possession of this weapon, the world as you know it will no longer exist. I fear his henchman will take it from you before we can find another to do what needs to be done."

Ellie turned her soulful eyes to him. Michael wanted to comfort her, but he doubted there was any way to take away her trepidation. The goddess was right. It was a terrible position to be in, to hold the fate of the world in your hands.

"What do we have to do?" Michael asked without looking away.

Ellie gave him a tentative smile.

She was the bravest woman he had ever known.

CHAPTER TWELVE

Ellie was determined to go to the hospital. According to the doctor who had called to update her, Gran had regained consciousness but was still groggy from the medication she was being given. Ellie was relieved that Gran was coming around and would soon be on the mend. She was at least be awake enough that Ellie could talk to her.

She thought back to that phone call and shivered. What had left her so unsettled wasn't the gentle voice of the female doctor on the other end, nor the hope that her grandmother would be okay, nor even the dangerous situation Ellie was in. No.

What had her quaking in her shoes was the man she currently her thighs around.

Michael had pulled her into Lucan's bare kitchen without a word, pinned her against the counter, and kissed her as if it was the last kiss he would ever get. Ellie had welcomed it, craved it from the moment they left the god and goddess in the other room. She opened her mouth, drinking in as much of his as she could get. He tasted so good. He was like a savory meal after a long fast.

Moments later, her cell phone vibrated. He had known it was coming, that phone call. And he had used the wait time to make her forget the danger she faced and entice her body to new heights of anticipation.

What power!

That Michael could see the immediate future already made him super-human, but what he did to her body...that was beyond all reckoning.

Now, she squeezed tighter, molding her legs to his. She hugged her arms around his waist. The rich scent of leather wafted back to her on the wind. Every now and then her helmet would bump against his when he slowed suddenly or came to a stop. At first she would call out a muffled apology, but he didn't seem to mind and after a while, she just took it as part of the motorcycle experience.

Bumping helmets.

She and Michael made it to the hospital well before visiting hours ended at nine. Gran was in the intensive care unit, so Michael wasn't allowed in to see her. Ellie left him pacing in the waiting room, missing his presence by her side more than she wanted to.

Gran's keen eyes turned to her as soon as she entered. "Ellie-lamb," she whispered. Her smile was faint, and she closed her eyes for a second from the exertion.

Heart in tatters, Ellie rushed to her bedside and lifted her hand from the mattress. "Hey, Gran." She blinked back tears. "H—how do you like your room?"

She tugged on Ellie's hand, urging her closer. "Where are we?"

Ellie took a deep breath. "This is the hospital, Gran."

She gripped Ellie's hand, a faint squeeze that was proof of the danger she still faced. "No nursing home."

Ellie shook her head. "No, Gran. I'll take care of everything."

She nodded slightly.

Ellie swallowed hard, trying to keep her voice from quaking. "Do you feel better? Do you remember anything?"

She smiled again. "Good medicine." She didn't speak again, and Ellie waited until she'd fallen asleep before slipping from the room.

Michael was right outside. "How is she?" He handed her a cup of coffee.

Grateful, Ellie held the warm Styrofoam cup between her palms and took a sip. It was just like she liked it, semi-sweet and creamy. "She was awake but heavily medicated. She doesn't remember anything."

"That's good."

She looked up, leaning into and taking strength from him, that was the only thing keeping her on her feet. "It is?"

He circled one beefy arm around her. "Sure. She's recovering. That's all that matters. And if she doesn't suffer the memories of a demon trying to suck out her soul, even better." He led her to a couch.

She ignored his attempt at humor. "I have to speak to her doctor."

Michael pushed her gently down and sat beside her. "I spoke to the nurse at the desk. She'll be here shortly."

Ellie took another sip of her coffee, and sure enough, they were soon approached by a beautiful African-American woman in a starch white lab coat. She reached out to shake Ellie's hand.

"Ms. King. I'm Dr. Baker. We spoke on the phone."

The doctor's grip was firm, but her skin was soft and smooth. Ellie was glad such nice hands were taking care of Gran. "She doesn't remember what happened," she said, not really wanting an answer to the most obvious question. *Is she going to be okay?*

"It was you who found her?" She glanced from Ellie to Michael.

"We had just returned from Atlanta," Michael said. "When we arrived and found her lying on the floor, we assumed there had been an intruder..."

Dr. Baker shook her head and turned back to address Ellie. "There don't appear to be any signs of trauma that would suggest that. I believe she suffered a mild heart attack due to the shut-down of her major organs. It's understandable that she doesn't remember the moments before."

"Should I stay here?" Ellie was hopeful. Surely she was safer here than at home.

"She'll most likely sleep until morning. If she remains stable overnight, we'll move her out of ICU and into a regular room tomorrow. I want to keep her a few days for observation or in case of another attack."

Ellie thanked her and bid her goodnight with a promise to return tomorrow. It took them nearly an hour to get to Gran's house on Oglethorpe. Michael avoided Truman Highway and maneuvered through the back roads, changing directions often and keeping a watchful eye on the side mirrors for anyone who might be following.

He pulled right up onto the sidewalk, nudged the gate open with the front tire and parked behind the house. Ellie didn't let him get more than an arm's length away as he secured the gate and entered the house through the back door. He made a thorough sweep, not speaking until he was sure they were safe.

"I can't stay here," she said.

Michael barely looked up from where he was checking the locks on the front door. "Of course not," he said. "You're staying with me."

Part of her railed at his he-man tone, not used to being told what to do by anyone, much less a man who was acting all *superior*. The other half felt warm and tingling in response to his brawny attitude, the confidence that he could keep her safe and would stop at nothing to do so.

She hated how he left her torn and uncertain. Ellie thrived on being self-assured, taking charge of her circumstances. These random feelings of helplessness were bad enough, made far worse by her attraction to the cave man who made her feel giddy just by taking on the role of hero.

He turned his full attention on her then. Those mesmerizing eyes that made her legs tremble. His full, sensuous lips parted, then curled into a delicious smile. "Unless you'd rather not," he drawled.

Ellie snapped her gaze to his eyes. "Rather not what?"

"Stay with me." He crossed the landing to where she stood next to the stairs. He circled his hands around her waist and pulled her to him. Reaching up with one hand, he brushed her hair over her forehead, trailed it down her cheek and across her jaw bone.

Lucky for Ellie, he had wrapped his other arm around her waist and now supported her. Otherwise, she might have hit the floor. "N—no," she stammered. "I'll stay with you." She didn't resist when he slipped a finger between her lips. She held it with her teeth, sliding her tongue around the tip.

Michael sucked in air through clenched teeth. He planted a quick kiss on her lips, then stepped away and turned her toward the stairs. "Go take a shower. I know you want to. Make it a good one."

She grabbed his hand. "You'll stay right outside?" She didn't let the note of fear in her voice keep her from asking.

"Nothing could drag me away."

With a girlish giggle, Ellie bounded up the stairs. She couldn't wait to wash away two days of fear and distress...and sex.

She knew what would happen if she stayed with Michael on his boat, but she didn't care. She was a grown woman. She could handle a physical relationship and walk away when it was over.

So why did that thought make her so sad?

***

Michael set two plates of three-cheese tortellini swimming in pesto cream sauce and a basket of warm, crusty bread on the table. It was his favorite dish and one he could whip up in fifteen minutes. They had returned to his boat without incident, and after ensuring every door and porthole was locked tight, he had fixed them the quickest meal in his repertoire.

Ellie gaped at the food then up at him as he slid into the seat across from her. "You're full of surprises," she said before picking up her fork and digging in. She popped one of the tiny cheese-filled pastas into her mouth and closed her eyes as she savored it. When she opened them, her pleasure shone bright, a beautiful change from the worry and anxiety he'd been seeing there. "Wow, that's good," she said. "Where did you learn to cook?"

He shrugged. "When you live on the street, you learn early to fend for yourself."

"You didn't live on the street."

"Well, I spent a lot of time there." Michael shoveled food into his mouth. It seemed they hadn't eaten in days, and he was starving. "It was either make food or go hungry."

"It was the same with my mom. If I didn't scrounge something, there would be nothing." She stabbed a tortellini with her fork. "I never had to do either of those things when I lived with Gran. She always took care of me, even when I was being a royal brat."

"I'm sure you weren't a brat all the time." *Yeah, you probably were.* Dammit. Even her flaws were endearing to him.

"I didn't appreciate what I had," Ellie said. "I was always so angry that my mom had abandoned me, I took it out on everyone, especially Gran." Her eyes shown with unshed tears.

Michael wanted to comfort her, but he wasn't sure how. It wasn't easy to admit your short-comings. He loved her all the more for the strength she constantly displayed.

"She was so good to me," Ellie continued. "Even when I didn't deserve it."

"You deserved it. Every child deserves to be loved and cared for." He gave her a lopsided smile. "Even the angry ones."

"I should have treated her better."

"You will," he said.

"I remember that last foster family you stayed with. They didn't seem so bad."

"Some of the families were okay, but I never stayed with anyone who was actually interested in helping kids. Most were looking for a little supplement to their already meager income. Others had more perverted motivations."

He stared down at his plate. "Not many members of that last group around anymore," he said.

Ellie ripped a piece of bread in half and swirled it in the sauce on her plate. "Do you ever feel...guilty...about taking the law into your own hands?"

"Never," he said without hesitation. "The law is always given a chance to do the right thing. I wait and step in when the law doesn't work."

She popped another tortellini in her luscious mouth. "And does that happen often?"

"More often than you think."

They were silent a while as they finished eating. Michael listened intently for any unusual sounds from outside. He'd had no precognitive images that would alert him to any danger, but that didn't mean danger wasn't lurking nearby. Since Lucan had rescued him from that alley last year, Michael had learned much about cataloguing his visions, but he had no control over when they appeared. Nor could he seek out specific things he was looking for.

He thought back to that night. He had been ready to die, had accepted his fate, and welcomed a more pleasant after-life than the hell he had been living. He hadn't been afraid. Only disappointed that life had dealt him such a shitty hand and that the whole of his existence had amounted to very little.

He had set out to change that. He may not be recognized as a hero, but Michael had saved many children from a frightful existence. For those he'd been unable to save, revenge was a sweet reward.

But nothing had prepared him for the constant worry that he would be unable to protect his Ellie. The demon they had encountered in Atlanta wasn't like the others. He was stronger, more lethal. He had powers Michael wasn't sure how to combat. Lucan had recognized the name, and Michael could tell from his reaction that they needed to be concerned. At least Cael Comyn didn't know where they were.

He glanced up at Ellie. Her safety and well-being meant everything to him. If anything happened to her...

He needed to turn off his emotions, needed to distance himself so he could think clearly. His visions weren't coming as fast as he wanted, something he would normally have welcomed. But keeping Ellie safe weighed heavily on him. He had to utilize all his powers if he was going to protect her while she fulfilled the quest she had unfairly been saddled with.

"I'm sorry about leaving the way I did." Ellie's voice broke into his thoughts.

He stared at her, but didn't say anything. What could he say?

"I mean, just leaving like that without saying anything."

He shrugged, trying to make light of it but failing miserably. It had hurt when she left, a pain he had never gotten over, as much as he hated to admit it. "You didn't owe me anything," he lied.

She reached over and took his hand. "You were my friend, Michael. My only friend. I should have told you I was leaving."

"It was a long time ago, Ellie."

"I know, but...."

"I only went to school for one reason. I went that day, even though I knew before I got there that you were gone. I had to see for myself. I knew how badly you wanted to live with your mother. It wasn't a surprise." *It just hurt like fuck.*

"I should have said goodbye, but I knew you'd try to talk me out of it. You were so intense, so serious. I was afraid I would be trapped here forever, so when my mom called out of blue...well, I bolted." She stood up and put their dirty dishes in the sink. "I always thought it was about her, that I would have done anything to live with her, for us to be a family again." She sat back down and fixed him with a wary look. "I think I was running away from you."

Michael swallowed. For six years he had worked to convince himself that her leaving had nothing to do with him, that it wasn't personal. Now here she was, on his boat, telling him that he was *the* reason she left. His heart hurt all over again.

"I was young and stupid, Michael. I didn't know what I wanted."

"But now you do?"

She took a deep breath and let it out. "I thought I did."

They stared at each other. Michael's heart pounded. He wanted her to love him, to stay with him. He wanted to build a life with her, have a family. *Be* a family.

By the goddess, he was a pussy. He was more powerful that most mortals, as strong as ten men, descended from an ancient god. Yet he was as mushy and sappy as a fourteen-year-old girl.

If only he could cut off those feelings. Let her go like she'd done him all those years ago.

But she hadn't let go, not completely. She was here.

And damned if he wasn't going to fight like hell to keep her.

***

Cael Comyn stood in the shadows next to the boat house. He'd had little difficulty tracking the cocksure lad to this marina just outside of town. He could see the tiny vessel from his vantage point, a speck bobbing on the water at the end of a line of sail boats. The tall masts rose into the night sky. Rigging clanged against them, echoing in the quiet of early evening, drawing attention away from the small cruiser at the end of the dock.

Perhaps that worked for some.

Despite the distance, Cael's demon powers allowed him to see the lad's boat as clearly as if he stood just next to it. Curtains were secured over the narrow windows, but he could see shadows moving around inside. He could make out the lass' curvaceous silhouette. If he listened hard enough, he might even be able to hear their conversation, but just watching was enough.

For now.

Let them get comfortable. Let them relax. It would be an easy enough task to dispatch the lad and take care of the girl. For her sake, Cael hoped she had the spearhead with her.

He grinned in the darkness. No, he didn't. Not really. Because getting her to tell him where it was would be half the fun.

His body hardened. He would take his time with her, whether she had the artifact on her or no'. Maybe he would let the lad live long enough to watch a master at work, instead of killing him right away. Cael had performed before an audience before and found it added a certain element of pride that only increased the pleasure he took from his victim.

When he was ruler of hell, he would institute the regular exploitation of these humans for the pleasure of the demons who would worship him. He would feed their endless hunger for human souls in a way Lucifer had never allowed. While the dark prince permitted individuals to torture God's favored creatures, he did little to rally his followers as a group. A mistake Cael would correct when he became prince.

He puffed out his chest. Prince of Hell. He would change that to *King*. The title suited him. His Uncle Angus had always told him the Comyns were destined for greatness. Cael was determined to fulfill that destiny.

After the hated Munros had killed his father and uncle, Cael had sworn allegiance to the dark prince, and Lucifer had welcomed him. Cael was one of the few remaining descendants of the Nephilim, the race of monsters spawned in the early days after the creation of Terra. Lucifer and his fallen angels had been banished to the newly formed planet. Some repented. They were forgiven, though not allowed back into heaven. Groups of them had laid claim to various parts of the world and settled down to make the most of eternity. As an unexpected bonus, humans began to worship them as gods so exile wasn't too bad.

The others, those who had instigated the rebellion, had immediately set about seducing the females they found here. The spawn of those unions was the greatest evil ever known to mankind. The One God had sent a flood to wipe them out, but a small few survived. It was this ancient bloodline that flowed through Cael's human body and gave him the strength and immortality of a god.

And soon, when he'd defeated all those who stood in his way, he would be the most powerful being in existence.

CHAPTER THIRTEEN

Ellie finished clearing the dishes off the table. Michael had been quiet for a while, and now he had his eyes closed. Had he drifted off to sleep? Unlikely. Was he in some sort of trance? Is this what normally happened when he had one of his visions?

She thought back to the times she had witnessed his powers. He'd warned her of phone calls, both from the police and Gran's doctor. He had reacted just in time to save their lives at the restaurant in Atlanta. But she didn't recall him acting like this. At the restaurant, his premonition had come on so suddenly, she hadn't known anything was wrong until he dragged her to the floor seconds before lightning struck their table.

Not sure what to do now, she stood in the center of the kitchen area and whispered his name. Michael cocked his head but otherwise made no response. She took advantage of his stupor and studied his face. Even with those striking eyes closed, he was exceptionally handsome. Jet black hair framed his masculine features. Every moment she spent with him melted the iciness of her entire existence. What had happened to the self-assured, over-achiever who took charge of her circumstances? She felt like a damsel in distress.

Was Michael her knight in shining armor?

He jumped when Ellie rested her hand on his shoulder but gave no other indication that he even remembered she was there. She ignored her irritation at *that* idea. When she said his name again, slightly louder, he pressed one finger to his lips.

"Listen," he said.

She did. Ellie held her breath, listening for any sound from outside. The water made a soft slapping noise against the side of Michael's boat. Gulls shrieked in the distance. Ropes and other hardware clanged against the tall masts of the sailboats nearby. But otherwise, there was nothing.

"I don't hear anything," she whispered.

"Shhhh."

With a smirk, she slid back into the seat across from him.

Her butt had barely hit the leather when Michael jumped up. His sudden action startled her. "What is it?" Her heart pounded, his reaction setting off warning bells and making her want to find a place to hide.

"I need to have a look around," he said.

"What? No. Why? Did you see something?" She was growing frantic now. She couldn't explain the heavy feeling in her gut, but she did *not* want him to go out there.

Michael shook his head. "Something's not right. I can feel it."

"Did you have a vision?"

The look on his face did nothing to comfort her. "I haven't seen anything. *Anything.* That's not right. Usually my visions come so fast and close together, I have trouble making sense of them. I have to sort them and try to see them individually, more clearly, before they make any sense. But right now…nothing."

Ellie reached down and fingered the artifact in her pocket. "Do you think it's the spearhead?"

He paced in the tight space of the boat's interior. "Could be. But it hasn't really hampered my powers so far, except when I touched it."

He had only touched it the one time, when they first found it among her things at Gran's house. She shuddered. When Michael had nearly passed out, her heart had lurched to her throat. Her concern for him had been instant and devastating. What if something happened to him? She had known him most of her life. He had been her first, and only, love. She could admit that now, at least to herself if not to him. She had always known she could come back, that he would be there.

What if he went outside and didn't come back? Her heart squeezed. She couldn't lose him. He was her rock, the one constant in her life she knew she could always count on.

She stood up and clutched his arm. "Don't go out there. What if he's around somewhere? Maybe that's the reason your powers are weakened."

"I have to see, Ellie. We can't sit here like a blind target waiting for him to attack."

"At least let me go with you."

To his credit, he didn't laugh. "I'm not sure you could help, baby, and you'd really be more of a hindrance. I can't fight if I'm worried about you."

Ellie wrapped her arms around herself. "I don't want to stay here alone. What if something happens? I'll be a sitting duck." She wished she could say what she really wanted to tell him. That she was worried about *him*. That she couldn't imagine a world without him in it. That she didn't want to live in that world or any other.

Not without him.

She kept her gaze locked on his. The concern and affection he felt for her was clearly evident, making her feel warm all over. He pulled her close, wrapping his big body around hers.

"I'll be fine, baby. And back before you know it."

Ellie ran her palms up and down his muscular back. How she wished none of this had happened, that that spearhead had never been hidden among her things. Damn that pilot. If not for him, she and Michael could have simply picked up where they left off.

Well, their reunion might not have been simple, but at least they wouldn't be in fear for their lives. That sort of thing tended to put a damper on a person's libido.

Or maybe not, she thought when his cock stirred against her stomach. She reached between them, grasping him through his jeans. "You better come back to me, Michael Munro. I'm not done with you yet."

He growled softly, weaving his fingers in her hair and cupping her cheek against his palm. "The only thing that's going to be the death of me, is you." He lowered his mouth and kissed her.

The touch of his lips triggered prickles of delight that shot right down to her toes. Ellie grabbed him and held on tight. She didn't want to let go, and she kissed him back with a desperation she hated. It made her feel weak, out of control.

But desperate she was. Desperate for him to stay safe. Desperate for a life she never thought she wanted.

He pulled away from her too abruptly and stepped back. His muscled chest rose and fell with deep breaths as he stood there, filling the small space and staring at her with equal consternation.

He turned suddenly and climbed the three steps to the deck. Ducking down, he peered back inside. "Stay here. Don't open the door for anyone but me." He slid the door home then and was gone.

Ellie had never felt so alone in her whole life. Her heart pounded with fear and worry. She wanted to run after him. What if he needed her? She listened for his steps across the deck. Then the boat rocked gently when he jumped to the dock.

After that, she heard nothing.

***

Michael turned and looked back at the boat before heading down the dock. Maybe he should take her with him. She would probably get into trouble on her own. By Arduinna, the woman had always been stubborn. Although, he had to admit that she'd come down off of her high horse quite a bit. The supportive, reliable woman she was on the inside was finally emerging. He had known she was hidden in there somewhere. Her strength and courage had always given him confidence. Any man would be lucky to have Ellie King as an ally.

And the look she'd given him before he left…she was worried about him. His chest pinched a little at the thought. When had she started caring?

He took a step back in Ellie's direction, but then stopped himself. He couldn't let his emotions drive him. He had to keep a clear head.

Yeah, right.

He hadn't been lying when he'd told her she would be a distraction. He couldn't think when she was around. The demon they'd encountered in Atlanta was much stronger than anything he'd encountered before. It would take more than Michael's meager power to defeat him. He'd need all his wits about him.

Reluctantly, he turned away. He scanned the shoreline as he walked, his keen eyesight allowing him to peer into darkened hedges and murky shadows. He paid close attention to the few images swirling around in his head: a frog jumping across his path, the arrival of a pick-up truck carrying three fishermen, the muffled sound of an argument aboard one of the boats he would soon pass. Nothing extraordinary.

He swept the grounds of the marina with determined strides, methodically but with a sense of urgency that drove him to greater and greater frustration that he found nothing on which to pin his sense that something was wrong.

As he made the long trek back down the dock, he kept his ears tuned to every sound, his thoughts on the lookout for any hint of an impending ambush.

Nothing.

Happy Tracks bobbed gently on the surface of the river, just as he'd left her.

Except the sliding glass door stood open.

Michael leapt across the open water and landed on deck, crouched like a cat and ready to fight to the death. He grabbed the overhang and swung down into the cabin.

Ellie was gone.

It took little more than a quick glance to see that she wasn't there. Fear churned in his gut. And guilt. He should never have left her. What if the Cael Comyn had her, and Michael couldn't track them?

In that instant, he realized he could never go back to a life without her.

He thought of all the other times he'd fucked up, mistakes he'd made, close calls that had almost cost him his life. And now he'd put Ellie's life in jeopardy.

Unacceptable.

He reached behind the door of the forward berth and grabbed the bat he kept there. When he turned back, he froze.

Ellie's delicious ass was making its way down the steps. When she reached the bottom, she seemed relieved to find him there. "Oh, thank God. Are you all right?" She half turned and waved back up the steps. "I went to look for—"

Michael crossed the distance between them in two strides and dragged her against him. He crushed his mouth to hers so hard, his teeth cut into the inside of his lip. Prying her mouth open, he delved into her with such urgency, he didn't even bother to breathe.

Ellie clung to him, relief for his safe return evident in the way she sagged against his body, letting her curves mold against him. She clutched his shoulders and allowed him full access to her luscious mouth. If she was surprised by his kiss, she didn't let that stop her from getting her fill of him.

And fill her he would.

Without taking his mouth from hers, he lifted her in his arms and carried her to his bed. He let go long enough for them to get naked, then crawled over her on the bed and settled himself between her thighs. He latched his lips to one of her pert nipples and suckled softly, flicking the tip of his tongue over the hardened nub until she moaned with pleasure.

Michael longed for the leisure to make love to her properly. He wanted to taste her for hours, wanted to forget the rest of the world existed, that it was only the two of them, now and forever. One or two nights weren't going to be enough. He wanted Ellie King for eternity.

He pulled away and stared down at her. It was dark inside the cabin, but the soft light from the other room illuminated her beautiful face.

"Ellie," he croaked out.

She reached up and stroked his cheek. "What's wrong?"

He pressed his forehead to hers, finding it difficult to speak past the lump in his throat. "I thought you were gone."

Ellie stretched up and pressed her mouth to his. She slid her palms down his sides, leaving goosebumps in their wake, and let her hands come to rest on his hips. She entwined her long legs around his, reached between them and guided his cock to the warm opening of her body. "I'm not leaving," she whispered.

Michael slid into her with a sigh. *Home*, he thought. This was home. Not this boat or this town, but this woman. Home was wherever she was.

Breath hissed between his teeth as he rocked into her with slow, languid strokes. The pleasure was so excruciating, it was almost painful. Raw heat lanced through him, driving him to greater and greater speed. But he forced himself to go slow, not wanting it to be over too quickly, wanting it to last forever.

"Let go, Michael," she said. "Give it all to me."

He made a choking sound, a husky, growl that sounded more animal than human. "Spread your legs," he demanded. Since when did he *demand* anything from Ellie King? It was a new sensation, but one that felt good. "Wider. Lift them around my hips."

She obeyed. Another first.

"Lock your ankles around me."

Ellie shivered and did as he asked. She whimpered and wriggled beneath him, trying to take more of him.

Not this time. He was in control, and for once, he intended to stay there. He moved in and out of her with a sweet friction that he couldn't maintain much longer, no matter how hard he might try. Her muscles were bearing down on him, making it impossible for him to keep a clear head.

Fisting a hand in her hair, he pulled her head back, slanting his mouth over hers, taking her in a deep, soul-searing kiss, fierce, possessive.

She didn't resist, but instead opened wider for him. She pulled her knees up and back, giving him full and complete access to her.

Michael drove himself inside her with one, deep penetration after another, methodically pumping into her with deliberate strokes, grinding and nudging the swollen bud of her clitoris with friction that sent her over the edge.

She clasped him to her then, screaming his name into his mouth and bucking wildly against him. Her muscles clenched on him, squeezing, shuddering.

It was more than he could stand. He let out a roar of pleasure so intense he feared they'd hear him all across the marina, but at the moment he didn't care. He tried to slow down, to back off. He wasn't ready to come yet.

His whole body tightened, and he exploded inside her.

***

Ellie snuggled back against Michael as he wrapped his big body around hers. They lay there in the silence, the gentle rock of the boat making every effort to lull them to sleep. It was late by now, and Ellie felt like she hadn't really slept in days. She let her eyes fall closed and took pleasure in the feel of Michael's heat against her back.

It seemed like weeks since her mother's murder, and Ellie was exhausted from the strain of losing her. She swallowed the ever-present knot in her throat. She'd not had time to properly mourn, having been on the run ever since. She needed a good wailing cry, to get out all the anguish and disappointment. Maybe then she could start to move on. She had no choice now except to face a life without her mother, a devastating loss despite the past six years.

From a young age, Ellie had dreamed of their reunion, a fantasy that had sustained her through her childhood and early teens. The reality of that reunion had been a sad disappointment, but now there was nothing. Not even the fantasy.

She gripped Michael's arm where he'd wrapped it protectively around her. It was heavy with muscle and made it difficult for her to breathe, but she hugged him tighter to her, savoring the discomfort that made her feel safe, protected.

Loved.

That he loved her came as no surprise. Ellie had always known it. But it seemed so much more real now, so much more important. Perhaps it was because she loved him back.

Ellie gave a little jerk. Her eyes popped open and stared off into the darkness. Her heart seemed to stop for a moment, then pounded so hard it almost took her breath. She was overcome with heat that seemed to ignite at the back of her neck and spread through her like wildfire.

She loved him?

No—she didn't. She was simply caught up in everything that was going on. She had erected barriers, kept her distance, hardened her heart. She had run away, dammit. She wouldn't let it happen. Falling for her high school sweetheart was one thing. But a demi-god? With supernatural powers? This had disaster written all over it.

If she was honest with herself, she would admit that she'd fallen for him long ago. They'd been friends as children, allies nearly as long as she could remember. She had missed him every day for the six years she'd been away.

What a fool she had been.

She wanted this to last. *This*. Motorcycle rides along Georgia's beautiful back roads. Sunny days spent aboard Michael's boat cruising up and down the river. Trips to the city to enjoy fancy hotels and fine dining. Slow, languid lovemaking without the urgency or danger that hung over them now.

No, I do not, she reminded herself. Ellie wanted to spread her wings and experience more than the tiny world to which she'd been born. She wanted to fly. She wanted independence, pride in knowing she didn't need anyone to take care of her. Someone had been taking care of Ellie her whole life. Now it was her turn.

The last thing she needed was the added burden of a romantic relationship, especially one with a man who took *everything* personally. Michael's observations were dark and heavy. She'd recognized that even before she'd known he had visions. She couldn't count the times she'd caught him deep in thought, and wondered what devastation he assumed was headed his way. Was it any wonder he was so ready to accept a negative outcome? Expect the worst and be spared disappointment?

His demeanor was oftentimes so serious, she wanted to smack him out of it. Such a bleak mood was bound to affect her, draining her energy and bringing her down. If she let herself be concerned with emotions, she'd be constantly worried about hurting his feelings. She didn't have time for that.

If only he weren't so fascinating.

Even without his godly powers, Michael wasn't like any man she'd ever known. Yes, he could be broody and fatalistic, but he was also loyal to a fault, wholly devoted once he gave his heart to a cause. It bothered her at times that he could so easily discern what made her tick, but that ability to see beneath the surface was a trait Ellie admired.

He could make her skin tingle with little more than a glance. His smile flashed between practically non-existent and too-frequent to ever be taken seriously. When he really smiled, something she suspected was reserved only for her, it seemed to light up her whole world, and make her feel that anything was possible. Those rare smiles quickly faded, leaving her uncertain and insecure.

That was what she had been missing for so long, that extra boost of confidence, the firm belief and reassurance that she could do anything, and no matter her failings or short-comings, she would still be loved.

What a fool, she thought again. She'd had it all along.

She didn't want to think about it. There was no need for speculation about any future she and Michael might share. That would drive her crazy. So many things could happen, so many things could go wrong. What if Michael couldn't protect her? What if the demon got hold of the spearhead and presented it to Lucifer? Or worse, used it against him. Was Cael Comyn more of a threat than

Lucifer himself? Did it matter which of them used the ancient artifact to take over the world?

There was a sobering thought. Whoever possessed the spear would be all-powerful. He would bring about pestilence and death, the sun would be blotted out and darkness would cover the earth.

She gave a deep, weighted sigh. If the demon won, the world would become a completely different place. All the more reason to savor the here and now.

Which she did for the next few hours.

CHAPTER FOURTEEN

Ellie sprinted to the SUV. The sky had opened up and was dumping rain in great sheets that made it difficult to see very far. Michael, running right behind her, used the key remote to unlock the doors, and they were able to use the headlights as a guide. They jumped into the front seats at the same time, slamming the doors and breathing in great gulps of air.

Ellie looked up at Michael and burst into fits of giggles. He was drenched, and the laughter that bubbled from within her made her feel better than she had in days. They were going to see Gran, and Ellie was hopeful that she was in better spirits today.

Michael smiled back at her, making her heart do a little flip-flop. It amazed her that he could still lighten her heart despite the constant anguish of their situation. She took a deep breath and settled back as they pulled out of the parking lot.

They drove to the hospital in relative silence. Lucan had repaired the busted window with a wave of his hand, and Ellie gazed of it now, drinking in the beauty of the city. It was still early, so morning traffic, slowed by the weather, was at a standstill in many places. Michael maneuvered them through one side street after another, constantly checking the side and rearview mirrors for anyone who might be following them.

Ellie noticed the stern look of concentration on his face that she figured had nothing to do with the traffic and everything to do with his concern that his visions were not coming fast enough. She kept watch on the road, then back to his face, wishing she had the power to read minds so she could know his thoughts without breaking into them.

She found herself lost in her own thoughts, as well. Last night had been the most thrilling, exhausting, satisfying experience she had ever known. Michael made her feel things she had tried to avoid most of her life but now craved like a flower craves the sun. She wondered if Michael had always been her greatest source of energy, but in her misguided need for independence she had shut him out when she should have been drawing him in and holding on for dear life.

Her thoughts were interrupted when they pulled into the hospital complex. The rain had stopped, leaving the asphalt shiny and slippery and a fresh, clean scent to the air. He took her hand as they walked inside, and for once, she let him. Instead of pulling away, Ellie laced her fingers in his, relishing the warmth that spread up her arm and the growing feeling of security he brought on.

The nurse at the ICU desk informed Ellie that her grandmother had been moved to a regular room. Relief swept over her at the news, giving her a sense of hope she hadn't felt in days. Maybe everything would be all right after all.

Ellie recognized Gran's voice as soon as they stepped out of the elevator. She could hear her shouting from down the hall, something Ellie didn't remember ever hearing before. Gran was always calm and mild-mannered. She seldom raised her voice.

Heart pounding, Ellie rushed toward the sound. She came to a skidding halt outside the room and pushed through the half-open door.

"What's wrong?" Ellie asked upon entering.

Gran looked away from the nurse who was trying to calm her down. The look of relief on her face spoke volumes.

Ellie rushed to her side. "Gran, what is it?"

Gran reached out and took Ellie's hand. "Oh thank goodness. I couldn't remember your phone number, and my phone is not here." She glared at the nurse. "They don't even have a number on file for you."

He smirked at her, but spoke in a gentle voice. "I'll check back in on you in a little while, Mrs. King."

When he had gone, Ellie sat on the edge of the bed. Michael stood by the door, a sentinel who would give his life to protect them. Ellie's heart swelled inside her chest, but she ignored it and focused all her attention on Gran.

"Are you feeling better?" she asked.

Gran waved her question away. "I'll be fine," she said. "I'm more worried about you." She took both of Ellie's hands in hers. "I fear you are in great danger, Ellie-lamb."

She wondered how much Gran remembered about the night she was attacked. "What do you mean?" She didn't want to reveal too much about what she'd learned. Best if Gran remained in the dark as much as possible.

Gran glanced over at Michael, seeming to notice him for the first time. "It's good to see you again, Michael."

He nodded in her direction. "You too, ma'am."

Looking back at Ellie, she lowered her voice. "I need to speak to you alone," she said in a quiet voice.

Without a word, Michael stepped outside and closed the door. She knew without checking that he would be standing right outside. She tried to relax, knowing no one was getting through that door without going through a Celtic demi-god. That made her feel a little better. She gave Gran her full attention, anxious to find out what she knew.

"The night I fell ill, it wasn't a medical emergency. I was attacked."

Ellie sat up straighter. She knew this of course, but she had hoped Gran wouldn't remember the horror of that night. "Did you know the person?"

She shook her head. "He seemed familiar, but I'm sure I've never seen him before."

"What do you mean familiar?"

"Something about his manner, the way he moved. His accent was one I didn't recognize and he had a strange scent about him."

"What did he say?"

She stared at Ellie for a moment before answering. "He was looking for you. I don't even know how he got into the house without my hearing him. I was at the kitchen counter, and when I turned around, he was just there. He asked about you, where your mother's room was, and then he…"

She trailed off, looking decidedly uncomfortable. She glanced away, looking down at where their hands were still joined on top of the bedding. "Then he…uh…kissed me."

Ellie almost laughed at the look on Gran's face. If the situation had not been so serious, she would have teased her about the blush that rose from beneath the neck of her hospital gown and spread to her graying hair line. "Did you kiss him back?"

"I don't rightly know. I remember thinking that it had been a long time since a young handsome man kissed me, but after that, I don't remember anything until yesterday when I woke up. They moved me here a few hours ago, and I've been trying to get in touch with you ever since."

Ellie hugged her. "Oh, Gran. I'm so sorry. I should have stayed here last night, but the doctor assured us you would sleep through the night."

Gran patted her on the back and sat back against the pillows. "I just wanted to be sure you were safe. You have to find somewhere else to stay until the police find the man who did this."

Ellie hesitated. She couldn't tell Gran about the demon who attacked her, but she didn't want to tell her the police were not looking for him, either. "I've been staying...with Michael." She waited for Gran's reaction, only slightly surprised to see relief.

"Good. That's good. Promise me you won't go back to the house. Not yet."

"I can't promise that, Gran. I need to look for something." She squeezed her hand when Gran would have protested. "It'll be okay. Michael will be with me. He won't let anything happen to me."

Ellie realized for the first time, that she truly believed that. She had to believe it. But something Gran had said resonated with her. Was it in her blood to be attracted to the wrong men?

"I need to look through mom's things, the stuff she left when she ran off before I was born."

* * *

Michael knew the moment before Ellie was about to step out of her grandmother's hospital room. Waiting right outside, he opened the door just as she would have reached for the handle. She cocked an eyebrow at him, but didn't speak.

She turned back and gave a little wave. "I'll check in later, Gran, and let you know what we find out." Her voice projected confidence and a light-heartedness, he wondered how she pulled off.

When she stepped from the room, Ellie had a look of consternation about her face that made him realize she was struggling to keep it together. He wanted to comfort her, offer her his strength, but when he reached for her hand, she pulled away.

They waited in silence at the elevator. When the silver doors closed behind them, isolating them inside the rectangle, he tried again.

He reached out. She stepped away.

"Is she okay? What did she say?"

Ellie hugged her arms around waist. "She'll be fine. She remembers him, that he kissed her." She gave a little snort of disgust. "Is that some kind of rogue gene in my family. The women get the hots for the wrong men?"

Smack.

His shock and hurt must have been evident on his face, for she immediately rolled her eyes, and huffed out a frustrated breath. "That's not what I meant. You take everything so personally."

Michael ground his teeth until his temple started to throb. "What *did* you mean?" he finally ground out.

With jerky movements, she scrubbed her hands over her face. "I don't know." They came to the ground floor, and Ellie was out of the elevator like a shot.

Confident she wasn't going anywhere without him since he had the keys, Michael took his time following her.

He drove to her house in brooding silence. Her ability to go from relatively pleasant to bitchy in the span of minutes had always baffled him. And now that he was grown man, it really pissed him off.

When they arrived, she climbed the stairs without another word, stomping up to the second floor, then further into the attic. Wanting little more than to wring her neck, he decided to scrounge around in the kitchen. Maybe he would find a clue in there, or at least something to eat.

He stormed through the living room to the back of the house. They hadn't been back since the night the demon had intruded, the night Ellie had found the artifact that had left Michael weakened and brought a god to his knees.

He stood in the doorway. It was there they'd found her grandmother, sprawled out on the floor with a demon calmly sucking out her soul. The very idea made Michael's blood boil. If he hadn't had the weapon Lucan had given him, would he have been able to defeat the creature?

A treasure hunt through the food stores produced a container of pimento cheese and half a loaf of stale Texas toast. No problem. He could throw it on a griddle. It'd be fine. A quick whiff in the tea pitcher revealed a foul, sour smell that had him screwing up his face and dumping it down the drain. He set a pot of water on to boil while he scrubbed the pitcher and fetched more tea bags from the pantry.

He hated to think of the damage to Ellie's mental state if she had lost her grandmother on the heels of her mother. He well knew the pain, having lost his own mother at an age when he remembered the bite of her death. He'd never known his father. Hadn't known anything about him until Lucan had found him and revealed a heritage he could never have imagined. His mother's passing had left a hole in his life, deepened by his subsequent journey from one house to another. He was only a boy, but he had to grow up fast. It was bad enough to be so thoroughly orphaned, so quickly and carelessly thrust into *the system*.

Further isolation brought on by his brooding and detachment had only been eased by the presence of one girl, now a woman and still able to rock the very ground he walked on. Only she accepted him into her world.

Then she had taken that world away.

He'd learned a lot since then, about how to blend, how to fit in, and move about unnoticed. It wasn't hard. Most people saw what they expected to see, so it was easy for him to keep a low profile. He'd made it through the last six years without her. He could do it again.

But he sure as hell didn't want to. The pain of her abrupt departure still stung. The hole she'd ripped in his heart had never quite mended. He couldn't take the hurt of her leaving, not again.

From this point on, he would keep his hands off. As soon as the danger had passed, he was out of there. This time *he* would leave, go far away and never come back. All he needed to do was weigh anchor and set off down the river.

Easy-peasy.

Who was he kidding? First, there was no way he was keeping his hands off her. She had the most luscious body he'd ever seen on a woman, curves a man could hold on to, skin that made his fingertips sizzle. Second, he wasn't sure he was strong enough to sever himself from her of

his own free will. Demons he could fight. Ancient gods—
no problem. But Ellie King? Michael was afraid he would
hang on to the last thread of hope until it snapped, hurling
him into the abyss.

Easy my ass. Nothing with Ellie was ever easy.

Why was that? Why couldn't she be less
temperamental and easier to get along with?

Because then she wouldn't be Ellie. By the goddess.
She was enough to drive a man to drink. He could hear
her rummaging around upstairs. Before they left the
hospital, she said her grandmother had packed her mom's
room, storing all her belongings in the attic, and then set
about turning the bedroom into a wonderland any little
girl would love.

Ellie had hated it, she'd admitted with tears in her
voice. She felt guilty, he knew, for not appreciating her
grandmother more, for leaving her with little more than a
goodbye. She'd vowed more than once to make it up to
her.

Why didn't she feel equally guilty about leaving him?
He could use a little making up to. She knew how he felt
about her. She wasn't naive enough to not recognize that
he'd loved her, even if was the first love of a teen-age
boy. She was a teenager, too. Lots of teenagers
experienced intense, profound love the first time out. She
knew he'd be hurt, but she'd left anyway. She was self-
centered, uncaring. She was always right. She knew it and
was happy to let everyone else know, too. Why would a
man love a woman like that?

He snatched the pot of boiling water from the stove
and dropped in the tea bags.

She set his soul on fire, that's why. Ellie was dynamic
in a way that drew him like the sun and made him want

more from life than mere existence. He wanted to live, to experience joy in things most people took for granted. Summer nights grilling in the back yard. Weekend rides to new places. The laughter of his own children.

But what if neither of them had the choice? What if he couldn't protect her? He stiffened as cold dread snaked down his spine. He shook it off. For once in his life, he would make the future his. He would determine the outcome. It wouldn't be over until *he* said so.

This time, he wouldn't be resigned to the whim of the fates. Those bitches could go fuck themselves.

***

Ellie plopped down in a worn chair at the dining room table. They had already gone through the stuff Ellie had retrieved from Atlanta, even though Michael had assured there was nothing there, so she'd gone straight up to the attic when they arrived. She been glad at first that Michael had let her go alone. She needed the time to get her thoughts together. But within moments, she'd begun to miss him. Not just the security he brought, but the companionship, the conversation. The thrill of having him near.

She should be more grateful for it.

She'd forced her thoughts to the task at hand. She had to find the missing piece before taking it to the priest. What would he do with it? Destroy it? Vanquish it to some other realm? Anything was possible.

The stone had been warm against her hip. It radiated a power that energized her despite the strain of rifling through her mother's things. It was too much to hope that she'd find the missing piece, but she'd hoped find a clue.

There had only been a few boxes in the attic that belonged to her mother, but going through them had been emotionally exhausting. It seemed like every item she found brought up memories even though Ellie had been only five when Gran packed all those things away. An unwelcome sense of nostalgia grew with every box she opened, every item she pulled out and set on the floor. There were clothes that still smelled like Mama. Mementos from her teenage years before Ellie was born. Things she'd never seen but still reminded Ellie of her mom.

Her heart ached. Her face and eyes felt puffy and swollen from constantly fighting back tears. The ever present lump in her throat felt like it was the size of an apple and threatened to suffocate her. She swallowed hard, but nothing was going to make it go away except a good, long cry.

She didn't have time for that now.

Michael emerged from the kitchen with a plate and a glass of iced tea. He was no longer pouting, but hurt was still evident behind those mesmerizing eyes. Guilt assaulted her once again. Why did she always hurt the people she should be the nicest to? He was the only person in the world besides her grandmother who cared about her. She should guard those feelings like they were the most valuable things in her life.

What was wrong with her that she felt the need to keep everyone at a distance? Okay, so her mother had abandoned her at a young age. Lots of kids were raised by a grandparent or other family member. Had she imagined that she'd been popular? She hadn't had real friends, but who's fault was that? She had no one to blame but herself. It wasn't that she didn't have people who cared about her. She hadn't let them care.

Her emotions lately ping back and forth, wreaking havoc with ability to stay focused and stick to a single path. Michael was like a relentless bull forever trying to capture that elusive red cape. He didn't give up. He kept coming and kept coming regardless of her constant efforts to keep him at bay.

She couldn't think about that now. There was too much at stake for her to be worrying about hurting the feelings of one man, even if that man was the most important in the world. Or at least in her world.

With a mumbled thanks, she took a bite. She actually moaned as she chewed then swallowed the delicious, gooey bite. This was far more than a mere grilled cheese. A sip of the ice tea took her straight back to happier times. She hadn't had a decent glass of tea since she left Savannah six years ago.

Ellie didn't apologize for her earlier behavior, although it was on the tip of her tongue to do so. Michael didn't appear to expect one, so she supposed it worked out. She would make it up to him later. When all this was over, when they weren't being chased by demons. She refused to think that she might not get the chance.

"This is great. What did you to do it?"

Michael shrugged. "There was no butter, so I had to spread the bread with mayo before putting it on the griddle." He fingered the few things she brought down from upstairs. "Did you find anything?"

She pushed one of the journals she'd found toward him. "Nothing that made me stand up and take notice."

He flipped through the journal, his gold eyes scanning the pages for clues. Every now and then he would stop and read a section, but then move on.

Ellie watched him. Everything about him intrigued her. When had he become so irresistible? When had she begun to watch his every movement, hang on his every word, yearn for a glance or touch from him? The whole world was spinning out of control. Her traitorous feelings threatened to override her brain at every turn. She found it increasingly difficult to keep them contained. She needed to slow down, to take the time to analyze those feelings, to expose her vulnerabilities at a snail's pace, one she could easily rein in and lock away again if she needed to.

Before she was too far gone.

She caught her breath when he looked back up at her.

Too late. She'd passed the *too far gone* marker miles back.

"I don't see anything," he said.

Reaching over, she flipped to the back of the journal, where a slip of paper was tucked between the last couple of blank pages. It was note, not in her mother's handwriting, but in the scrawl of a man. It was a handwriting she didn't recognize.

"It's the only thing I found even remotely out of the ordinary."

Michael tilted the paper toward the light coming through the French doors and squinted to read the faded ink. When he'd finished, he flipped it over to see if there was more on the back. She had done exactly the same thing. "What does it mean?" he asked.

Ellie had no idea. The note was addressed to her followed by the words, *your sins are the abyss between you and what you seek*. A tingle snaked up the back of her neck, no less chilling than when she'd read it the first time. She gave him a look that said just how thrilled she was about the next leg of their quest. "There's only one way to find out," she said. "I have to go to confession."

CHAPTER FIFTEEN

"Forgive me, Father, for I have sinned. My last confession was—a long time ago."

Ellie peered through the screen at the priest on the other side. She had found no other clue as to what she would find here. Was the man across from her really even a priest? Had he been expecting her? Was this the priest Arduinna had instructed her to deliver the spearhead to? Did he hold a clue to the whereabouts of the missing piece? He waited in silence, so she continued. "I haven't been nice to my grandmother even though she sacrificed so many years raising me and giving me a home."

She waited. Still nothing.

"I had sex last night." She started to get a little miffed when the priest still made no response. Gran had made her go to confession often as a child, until Ellie was old enough to refuse to go to mass at all. She expected the priest to comment, nod, grunt...something. "With a man. And also the night before." Was he sleeping over there? Instead of rattling the screen like she wanted to do, she opened her mouth to speak again, but this time, he interrupted her.

"I knew your father, Ellie." His voice was barely more than a whisper.

Had she heard right? Shocked into speechlessness, she sat back on her heels. Her knees had begun to ache from kneeling, but the discomfort was forgotten in an instant with those words.

My father? Ellie had not thought of her father in years. Gran would never speak of him, and all Mama would tell her was that he had been her guardian angel, and now he was gone.

"How? How did you know him?"

"I've been waiting for you to come. He said you would come." He bowed his head for a moment, the fingers of one hand pressed to his mouth, like he was trying to decide what to say.

"He was here," the priest finally whispered. "He came to St. John's as a young priest. It was just a few days later that he met your mother. She was tempting for any man, but your father was lost from the first time he saw her. I tried often, but couldn't sway him from spending time with her."

Ellie had to strain to hear him, especially over the loud roar that had started in her ears. "Where is he now?"

"Gone."

Wanting to scream in frustration, she grasped the wicker screen that separated them, ready to rip it out of the frame if necessary. "What do you mean? Gone where?"

"Shhh. Not so loud. Late one night, I caught him sneaking out of the rectory. Thinking they were running off together, I tried to talk him out of it, but he was frantic with worry. He claimed your mother was in danger. That he was the only one who could save her.

"She came to see me a few days later. Her pregnancy had begun to show, and she was leaving town. She wouldn't say anything about your father, but she said you would come looking for answers one day, and I was to give you this."

He slipped a scrap of paper beneath the screen. Even in the dim light of the confessional, she could see was yellowed by time. Ellie snatched it up, handling it more gently when she realized how worn and fragile it was. With shaking hands, she lifted back the folds and stared down at the same scrawl that had been on the note she'd found in the journal. It was written by the same man.

Her father?

She ran her fingers over the writing. Had her father written it? When she finally focused on the words, she realized it was an address. Cold dread spread up the back of her neck. The location was one everyone who lived in Savannah knew.

She dropped the note, fully expecting it to burst into flames, and covered her mouth with shaking hands.

When she glanced back through the screen, the priest was gone.

***

Ellie had to walk fast to keep up with Michael. The rain had left a fresh scent to the air. Clouds still blocked the late afternoon sun, and the occasional shot of lightning flashed in the distance. The dreariness of the day only fueled the sense of doom that had settled over her.

"We are not going there," he said again. He turned abruptly and strode back the way he had just come, scrubbing one hand over the back of his neck and mumbling to himself.

Ellie nearly stumbled trying to follow him. "We have to," she argued. "What if the missing piece is in there?" She had come out of the church in a flurry and shown him the note she'd gotten from the priest. He'd taken one look at it and declared that there was no way they were going to the address that was written there. His agitation only served to increase her own uneasiness at the prospect.

Michael continued pacing in front of the cathedral, his long strides eating up the pavement. "Ellie, anyone who's lived here for five minutes knows that's the most haunted place in Savannah."

Of course she knew that, but right now, the devil himself couldn't keep her out of that house. She felt a throb of irritation at his reluctance. She stopped with a frustrated huff. "They're just stories told to make the ghost tours more interesting. They're not real."

He stopped, turned back to where she waited, and glared at her. "Not real? Everything is real. Haven't you figured that out?"

That was slowly beginning to dawn on her, but Ellie wouldn't be deterred. She would go alone if she had to. But she knew Michael would never allow that. He would follow her to hell if she insisted on going.

She let her gaze bore into his. "I've walked past Calhoun Square a million times." Legend claimed that more than a thousand slaves were buried beneath Calhoun Square, not to mention the murders and suicides that were rumored to have taken place inside the house on Abercorn. People, locals and tourists alike, had reported seeing ghosts for years. Not the friendly, mischievous kind, but terrifying apparitions that had earned the house the title of Most Haunted House in Savannah. Most of the stories weren't true, but that didn't stop tourists from flocking to it. Nor did it stop the ghost tour companies from embellishing them to drum up more business. "I've never seen a ghost, or felt one's energy, or had my camera go wacky. Nothing."

"That doesn't mean the threat isn't real," he said.

"What threat? Even if there are ghosts, all they do is scare tourists. Ghosts can't hurt you. Right?" She tried to sound confident, but it was hard with her heart pounding in her throat and the sense of dread that had her shaking with nervous anticipation.

"Wrong."

Ellie's confidence deflated. "Wrong?" It was too much to hope for. Of course he was right. If she had learned nothing else, it was that there were many things about the world she would never have accepted a few days ago. Gods, angels, and demons roaming the earth, blending with humanity, wreaking havoc or saving the world while people went about their daily lives, oblivious to the supernatural world in which they lived. And now she was faced with having to go into a house most long-time residents of Savannah avoided like the plague.

For the first time in her life, Ellie wished she was less controlling, less determined to take charge and see the task done. She wanted to relinquish the sense of responsibility she had nurtured as long as she could remember, and let someone else be in charge. She was tired of being brave, tired of being strong all the time. For once, she wanted someone to be strong for her.

Michael moved then to stand in front of her and took her by the shoulders. A tingle spread down her arms that had nothing to do with ghosts. "Are you sure you want to go there? We could go through your mom's things again. I'll help you look."

His willingness to help look for the missing piece spoke volumes. He'd nearly been incapacitated by the artifact, yet he'd risk that rather than follow her demand. There was nothing she would love more than a reason not to go to the house at Calhoun Square. But she knew without a doubt that it was their next stop. Call it a gut feeling, intuition.

Ellie shook her head. She'd been through every box, every manila envelope, every item that her mother had left behind. There was no mention of the artifact, or her father, or anything else that would guide them on their quest. There wasn't even anything about her pregnancy. She had left before Ellie was born and had only returned the one time.

To relinquish custody of her five-year-old daughter. Old memories surfaced, but for once, the pain of abandonment did not accompany them.

"What about that priest," Michael continued. "I bet I can get more information out of him."

She cocked one eyebrow at him. "I thought you couldn't go in there." She nodded her head at the massive doors of St. John's Cathedral. When they'd first arrived, Michael walked right up to those doors, but stopped short of entering. After a few uncomfortable seconds, he decided it was best for him to wait outside. Ellie had gone in alone.

He huffed. "I'd sooner take my chances in the house of the Almighty than in *that* house." He pointed to the slip of paper in her hand.

"You're scared." She let amusement lace her words, but instead of easing the prospect they faced, it brought her own fear to the surface.

"Hell, yes I'm scared. You should be, too."

"What choice do we have?" It was the only lead they had gotten, and they couldn't ignore the possibility that the missing piece of the spearhead was located there. Not only had they been tasked by the goddess to track it down, but now there was the added intrigue that included her father. A priest! Was he one of the ghosts who haunted the house on Abercorn? What if he wasn't a ghost at all, but was still alive and living nearby? The possibilities were too captivating to ignore.

Michael started walking again, so Ellie rushed to catch up. Calhoun Square was only a few blocks from the cathedral. At least they would get there, and hopefully out again, before it got dark.

Before they reached the square, Michael turned off and headed down Lincoln. "Wait," she said, reaching out to grab his arm. "We're not going through the back, are we?"

Michael took her hand, and she let him. He didn't slow his strides but continued his determined walk, weaving through throngs of tourists exploring the beautiful squares and other sites of Old Town Savannah. "We're not going alone," he said. "Not when we have a god we can take along for added protection."

***

Cael watched the house across the street with a fevered stare. He had followed Ellie and Michael from the church, having been unable to get close enough to find out what the lass had learned when she went inside. He could mask his presence from her companion, but the closer he got, the more he risked detection. He wanted to more about the young bastard. He sensed a familiar power that intrigued him. Instead he'd hidden in the shadows, again, like a weak, frightened animal then followed at a safe distance.

He curled his lip in disgust. Humans were the weaklings. Humans and all those who treasured them. He hated them all, forcing him to live like this. Lurking in dark hideaways, feared and despised by everyone. One day, he would make them pay, make them suffer. Soon, even the Almighty would have no control over him. Once the spear was in his possession, he would blight out his enemies and take his place as a true prince. All of humanity would bow before him. And he would smile as he watched them suffer under his heel.

Once he'd secured the weapon, and taken his rightful place as hell's heir, he would focus on more personal goals.

Revenge. Atonement.

Since yesterday's good fortune had brought Neala to him, he had thought of little else. He'd dedicated his life to ensuring that the Munro pay for his sins. Now that he'd found Neala, her protector wouldn't be far. It was Cael's first sighting of either of them in over one hundred and fifty years. All he needed to do now was wait, and soon enough Lucan Munro would reveal himself.

He ground his teeth. More waiting, watching, hiding. He was damned tired of hiding. He'd left the Highlands, his home, centuries ago and had very little contact with others of his clan since then. He went back every generation, seeking out others whose dormant powers had begun to reveal themselves, if not to the human, to him. Cael could sniff out a descendent of the Nephilim like a bloodhound to a fox.

Thus far, there had been few. Most of those were unable to resist the temptation that drove them to ruin. Seduction was the most addictive of these powers. The ability to seduce a human's mind and body to commit sins that cost them their souls. It was so easy. For Cael, the adrenaline rush at taking away another's control was intoxicating. Taking possession of that human's soul was better than any drug and far more addictive. Only the strongest could control their appetites. Lucifer, his followers, and all who carried their blood were still bound by the code of seven. Lust was not something they could abuse. An overdose, even one achieved over time, left the progeny a shadow without substance, a wraith doomed to spend eternity in agony and desolation. A demon in the truest sense.

He squared his shoulders, taking up a stiff posture, when the door opened. Three people emerged from the house, forcing him to duck behind a tree. This street, like so many others in this town, was overhung with a moss entangled canopy held up by trunks with girths larger than most men's.

All that nature sickened him. Chlorophyll clogged the air. Warm sunlight sparkled through the leaves above his head. Birdsong pierced his ears and made him want to crush the little fucker beneath his boot. Was it a wonder he preferred larger cities? Not only was it easier to hide in plain sight, but Arduinna's realm had been all but obliterated by high-rise buildings, a dense population, and the sheer sprawl of concrete.

Her foothold in these smaller towns and rural areas was infuriating, and more and more she was able to influence powerful humans toward conservation. When he had the spear, that bitch would be one of the first to die.

He looked past it with cold, flat eyes, and focused his gaze on the lass. She had a sway to her walk that made his balls tingle. He would enjoy plowing those hips, his grip bruising her flesh as he emptied into her. Cael was more than willing to spread his demon seed as Lucifer commanded.

He grinned. Some command. He would have done so anyway. He only hoped the lad was still alive to see it. Any amount of suffering or angst made his own pleasure that much greater. The little bastard had been a thorn in his side. He'd foolishly thought that once he found the human who was hiding the spear, retrieving it would a simple matter.

Few things were so simple. Even for a demon. There would always be obstacles to overcome. The lad was just another of those.

Cael started and jerked back behind the tree when he recognized the third human. Not *human*, but…his breath quickened. He stood stock still, his muscles as rigid as the trunk behind which he hid. How could he have let himself be caught unaware? He must be slipping in his old age. He should have recognized the laird of Clan Munro the instant he emerged from the house.

First Neala, now the whoreson who claimed to be her savior. Could this get any better?

Lucan Munro had murdered Cael's father. A sennight later, he killed Uncle Angus and kidnapped his wife. Cael had sworn on the devil's blood that ran through his veins to avenge his family. Six hundred years he'd been waiting.

He was so close.

When Cael had run into Neala at the college, he'd known Lucan would have taken up residence nearby. The last he knew of their whereabouts, Neala had been born to a wealthy French family during the reign of terror. He'd almost had them then, but Lucan had rescued her from Madame Guillotine at the last minute. Cael had not been able to find them since.

Until now.

Now, he knew where the bastard lived.

He followed them, keeping enough distance so as not to draw their attention. The Highlander could smell him. Several times he looked over his shoulder in Cael's direction. Once, Cael had barely stepped into the shadows before the Munro spotted him.

He wasn't surprised when they stopped before the gray house. This was going to be easier than he'd hoped. Cael had visited the house earlier. He knew what she would find there. The *Liath Mòr* had been gone for years, whisking his treasures off to an as yet undiscovered location. The unguarded souls of the dead that he'd left behind lingered, though, and they were hungry for human flesh.

Yes, he knew what she would find there. He knew where it would lead them. He need only arrive first and lie in wait.

But he needed to pick up something first.

CHAPTER SIXTEEN

Ellie found herself trembling despite the warm, muggy weather. The sun was near setting, but the temperature stayed high. She had kept silent as she followed Michael and Lucan. Their longer strides made it more and more difficult to keep up, especially since she was in no hurry to reach their destination.

She always considered herself brave, but the very thought of what she was about to do was enough to make her drag her feet. It was surreal. It couldn't be happening. Surely something would change their course between here and there. Something much more pleasant. Something a lot less terrifying.

That something never came to pass. Before she knew it, they were there.

The gray, three-story house that took up one side of Calhoun Square was not noteworthy. It was surrounded by more opulent homes that would have made it even less noticeable except that it was a stop on every ghost tour in Savannah. It had a reputation that made even the most skeptical avoid it like the plague. As a teenager, Ellie had forgone the tradition of trying to sneak inside to get some definitive evidence of the ghostly apparitions that were said to dwell there. She had never felt that pull nor the adrenaline rush like other people her age. Horror movies had never appealed to her, neither the psychological ones nor the typical slasher movies that most teenagers loved.

She stood behind Michael and Lucan, a wall of muscle, strength, and power that would be their best defense, their only defense, against whatever they found in there.

The men were quiet. Neither had ever been inside the house so no one knew exactly what to expect. Lucan had tried to get more information about the home's previous tenants, but there was little to be learned other than the stories that had been bandied about over the years, most of which were entirely untrue.

The first hauntings were said to have been by the young girl who had been forced to sit, tied to a chair, and watch the poor kids from the school next door play outside her window. Her father thought it fit punishment for a defiant child who insisted on playing with children far below her station. Rumor had it that the girl had died of dehydration, a story that couldn't be further from the truth. Emily Wilson had escaped her father's brutality, grown up, and moved away.

There were plenty more stories to feed humanity's hunger for the macabre. Stories of murder, torture, suffering, that would leave any house in a state of unrest. Whether any of those stories were true or not, Ellie couldn't say. But as they studied the house, she decided it didn't matter. True or not, the house was every bit as spooky as the tour guides made it out to be.

They stood in the center of Calhoun Square, ignoring the people moving around them. It was going to be a clear night. Ellie was grateful for that. Michael watched the house with particular intent. His eyes roamed slowly over the exterior, seemingly brick by brick. Every few seconds he would stop, close his eyes, then peel them open again and continue his survey. She wished she could see what he did. Did he have a sense of what awaited them? She was about to ask when Lucan spoke instead.

"'Tis only getting darker the longer we stand here."

His words jolted Ellie to her core. She was terrified of going in there. Full body tremors now wracked her from head to toe. She grabbed Michael's arm in a tight grip and pressed her torso against him.

He tore his intense gaze away from the house and brought his face close to hers. "You don't have to go," he said.

"Yes, she does," Lucan argued. "If the missing piece is in there, she is the only one of us who can carry it out."

She slid her hand down to Michael's and laced their fingers together. She nodded, clutching his arm with her other hand. She intended to stay molded to him as if they were one person. "I'm fine," she lied.

He kissed her, quick and urgent, drawing a ragged breath from her lips. "Stay close to me," he whispered.

He wouldn't have to tell her that twice, she thought as they climbed the steps to the front porch. She stared at the weathered door. Were they really just going to walk in the front door? She turned and looked over her shoulder, then caught her breath.

A thick fog had settled around the square, blocking out the trees, the tourists, even the street itself. *What a surprise*, she thought with a sense of dread that almost sent her running back down the steps. She didn't need any precognitive powers to know that this was not going to be easy.

She had so hoped that they could get in and out before dark. Was that to be just the first of many disappointments this night might bring? Even without the fog, the sun had set, bringing the darkness she'd hoped to beat. The street lamps were nothing but a faint glow that added to the eerie atmosphere and did absolutely nothing to shed light on the most frightening situation she'd ever found herself in.

Lucan looked at Michael. "You have your weapon?" At Michael's nod, he waved his hand over the handle, and the door creaked open.

Every hair on the back of her neck stood on end. They stared into the darkness beyond the threshold until Lucan manifested a flashlight and cast the beam inside. Ellie was so scared she didn't even blink at the magic she would have scorned only a few days ago.

The door opened further, allowing them access. Lucan went in first waving the beam of light from side to side. Reluctantly, Ellie followed Michael, still clinging to him as if their skin had been fused together.

They all jumped when a door to their right slammed shut, then another to their left. Ellie clamped her lips shut on a primal scream that welled up inside her, whipping her head around in search for their attackers. Every muscle in her body was tense. The sound of her own heartbeat thrashed in her ears. From what she could see, they were alone in what appeared to be a sitting room or foyer. There was a single piece of furniture in the room. A chair covered with a dusty white sheet.

"They're corralling us in," Lucan said.

"They?" Michael asked the question Ellie wasn't sure she wanted to hear the answer to.

Instead of answering, Lucan lifted his chin in Michael's direction, a subtle directive that had Michael retrieving the unassuming knife from his waistband.

Behind them the front door closed with a soft click, raising Ellie's hackles even further. She didn't know which was worse, the startling slam that rattled the walls or the more ominous snick of the latch that closed off the outside world, trapping them inside a house of horrors they may not get out of alive.

**

Michael ignored the tingling sensation in his fingers. He would gladly take a little breach in his circulation in exchange for the grip Ellie had on his arm. Even if she hadn't been holding on so tight, her touch would have caused no end of tingling sensations across his body. One of her breasts pressed against his bicep, soft and soothing in the midst of evil the likes of which he'd never encountered before.

Ellie's touch was the only good thing he felt amongst the suffering and death he sensed all around them. Screams of the dead and dying echoed in his head. He saw visions, not of the future but of the past. Atrocities and carnage that made him want to lean against the wall and heave. Her bruising grip on his arm kept him upright and pressing forward when that was the last thing he wanted to do.

He wanted to believe her clinginess stemmed from the feelings she had for *him*, and not merely her rampant fear. Her confidence in his ability to get them out of this alive rallied his own courage. Funny, he'd never thought of courage before. With so little to live for, what did he have to fear? But if he failed this time, he risked losing the only thing he'd ever cared about. The added strength of Lucan Munro certainly gave the outcome a little better chance of falling in their favor.

They crept through the sitting room, listening to the moans echo softly around them. It was as if the walls themselves were alive and in pain and torment. Where only hours ago, he'd struggled to envision anything that might help them in their quest through the haunted house, now his head was filled with image after image that came so fast and furious, he could barely make out anything at all.

He tried to focus his efforts on the images that seemed most threatening. Many of the spirits inhabiting the house were able to do little more than shriek at them. That alone was enough to make Ellie jump and clutch at him with even more gusto.

Soon enough, one of the images became more animated in his mind, triggering a reaction that had him slicing at the creature before it even reached them while trying to hold onto Ellie with his other hand. The weapon Lucan had created for him, a sword that seemed as ancient as the gods themselves, made quick work of the creature. With a screech that faded with the sparks it burst into, the creature opened the door to more of its kind.

Immediately, a whole raft of dark, disfigured creatures emerged from the woodwork. Shadows seeped from beneath the baseboards and through the planks of the wood floor. They came from everywhere, howling and brandishing weaponry never seen by human eyes.

His premonition of the attack gave him the advantage and signaled Lucan of danger at the same time. The Highland god threw up a protective shield against their attackers, but he was a fraction of a second too slow. He threw back as many of their attackers as he could, but it wasn't enough. A handful broke through, coming fast and furious. Within seconds they were on him. Lucan staggered back, stricken.

He dropped to one knee. Michael turned so he could drive the creatures away long enough for Lucan to recompose himself. Soon they were so embroiled in battle, he realized he wielded his sword with both hands leaving Ellie unaccounted for.

Swallowing the panic that rose up inside him, he called for her, never taking his eyes off the creatures he fought.

"Ellie, where are you?" The acrid scent of sulfur burned his throat, stealing his breath and overwhelming him with wracking coughs.

"I'm here."

He heard her faint voice behind him, but the sound did little to relieve his panic. They were highly outnumbered. When Lucan had dropped to one knee, Michael thought the intent was to make himself a smaller target. But he realized now his uncle was injured.

How could that be? These creatures hardly had substance. How could even so many take down a god? Lucan was back on his feet, but it was obvious he was hurt. He flung back the attackers who had broken through his shield like they were straw men, but the effort cost him.

The remaining creatures staggered back, none of them eager to stand his ground against the dark Highlander, even if he was injured. One of them, braver than the rest, rushed him.

Michael had compartmentalized the images in his head and managed to anticipate the creatures' movements. He made quick work of the half dozen before him, then turned his attention to Lucan who had squared off against this much more dangerous entity. Michael rushed it from behind and raised his sword, prepared to split the creature's skull and send it back to hell.

To his utter surprise, he saw no hint that the creature was aware of his presence until it turned suddenly and blasted him with a force so strong, it sent him flying across the sitting room and crashing into the wall. He slid to the floor, struggling to draw breath.

His first thought was that he if he was incapacitated, he couldn't protect Ellie. She was all that mattered. He shifted to all fours, trying desperately to breathe. Through his haze of pain, he saw the creature approaching Lucan. His uncle was on his knees again, and this time, he didn't look like he'd be getting back up. His heart stopped when he realized Ellie had positioned herself in front of Lucan, as if she would be any defense against such a being.

Through sheer determination, Michael pushed to his knees and planted one foot on the floor. He pushed against his thigh, but the effort did little more than make the room spin. Tiny sparks exploded behind his eyes, blinding him. He squeezed them closed. One second was all he needed. One second to catch his breath.

But Ellie didn't have that long.

Peeling them open again, he found her fumbling in her pocket as the creature advanced on her. With every ounce of strength he could muster, he pushed to his feet, grabbing the wall to steady himself just as she pulled the spearhead from her jeans. She held it in a tight fist, facing what had to be the most frightening thing she'd ever seen like a warrior. She showed no fear in the face of such evil, but stood her ground and prepared to battle to the death.

Michael's pride soon evaporated when a vision of her fate filled his head. The creature would consume her soul, devour her flesh, and she would roam this hated house for eternity, wreaking equal torment on others who were foolish enough to enter.

He rallied his power. He need only distract the creature, draw its attention away from her, and she would have time to escape. They were mere steps from the front door. With luck, she would see the opportunity and take it.

It wouldn't be the first time.

With a wild cry, he attacked, brandishing his sword and rushing the creature from an angle sure to give Ellie a clear path to the door. His tactic worked. The creature turned on him with a snarl.

But Ellie did not run. Instead, she followed the creature on silent feet, raising the broken artifact overhead. Just as the creature would have reached him, she brought the spearhead down with a strength fueled by adrenaline, burying it between the creature's shoulders.

She screamed at the thing as she wrenched the weapon from its withered body. Black slime oozed from the tip of the spearhead, dripping onto her shoe. She stood there, heaving in deep breaths watching the dark shadows that approached, daring them to come near her.

The moans and cries of the dead muffled into a somber tone as the creature faded into black mist and seeped between the floorboards.

Minimizing his sword, Michael hurried over to her, his own strength rejuvenated enough to hold her when she swayed against him. He ran his hands over her, looking for injuries. "Are you hurt?" He made no effort to hide the concern in his voice.

She shook her head. "But your uncle—"

Dizziness washed through him as they knelt beside Lucan. He kept one arm looped around Ellie's. No way was he letting go of her again. Lucan looked like death. His skin was pale and had a grayish tint to it. Blood oozed from a wound in his chest. Michael pulled his t-shirt over his head and pressed it against the wound, trying to staunch the flow of blood.

He was engaged in that effort when the priest appeared.

**

"Pagan," he hissed at Lucan.

The clothes that identified the man as a priest were impeccable. Black robe that fell to the floor. Starched collar so white it nearly glowed. A stark contrast to the rest of him. Bloodied, skeletal hands gripped a worn rosary that hung from around his neck. His gaunt face was little more than ragged bits of skin that hung from exposed bones. Veins and tissue oozed fluids.

Michael helped Lucan push to a sitting position, propping him against the wall. "Ye would attack a man when he's down?" His uncle's strong voice held no hint of the injury he suffered.

"I would escort you to hell where you belong," the priest said.

Michael stood, pulling Ellie up with him. He kept his eyes on the priest, his back to the door, and his mind peeled for any sign of attack. The house creaked and groaned, sounds one would expect to hear in a hundred-and-fifty-year-old house. He heard faint footsteps across the floorboards overhead, but did not dare a peek that would draw his alert gaze from this new threat.

The man may be dressed in the black robes of a priest with a starched dog collar at his neck, but that did not mean he had ever been a man of the true God. Everything else about his appearance screamed suffering and death. He glanced around for escape routes, his heart sinking at the lack thereof. Just the door behind them and another across the room.

When Ellie took a step around him and toward the priest, Michael tried to stop her.

Fat chance.

"Father?"

The priest turned his attention to her for the first time. A flash of surprise exploded in his soulless eyes and was gone just as quickly. "Ellie. You got my note." He turned his evil gaze to Lucan. "I am disappointed you chose to partner with this abomination."

Wrenching her arm from Michael's grasp, she crossed the sitting room and stood before him. "Why are you...here...in this place? What happened?"

Michael wondered at the pain in her voice, at her bravery in the face of every child's Halloween nightmare.

If not for the macabre appearance of his features, Michael would have sworn the priest's face softened. "This is what happens when you rebel, my child. You must suffer in hell. That is the penalty." With another glare at Lucan that promised anguish and torment, he continued. "All who rebel against Him must suffer it."

He turned his freakishly sentimental gaze back to her. "But your mother was spared, and now you are here." His boney fingers twitched, but he did not reach out for her.

Then Michael understood. His talk of the one God, of rebellion. Of Ellie's mother.

She had called him *father*.

"You're no priest at all," Michael said.

"I was one of the heavenly host," he said. "Sent by the true God," he glared at Lucan, "to retrieve the weapon of power."

"Disguised as a priest?" Michael asked.

"Sadly, my perversions led to my downfall," he said. He lifted his arms and indicated the room in which they stood. "I am paying for my sins."

"Did she know?" Ellie asked. "That you were...in disguise?"

Michael marveled that she could absorb all of this. That she could remain cool and calm in the face of revelations that were beyond human imagining. Her strength was contagious. He felt like he could do anything. His admiration for her knew no bounds. He appreciated her open mind and clung to the hope that when this was over, there might still be a chance for them.

"She did not," the priest said. He grimaced, a gesture that could have been a smile. "She declared me her guardian angel, you how humans do. But she did not really know. She was eaten with guilt at falling in love with a priest. She felt she had lured me from the church. She would have really blown the whole angel thing out of proportion."

A soulless angel, eternally damned, with a sense of humor?

"At first, I needed your mother's help with the spear, as I could not handle it myself. I knew the spear's guardian, the Gray Man, lived here, in Savannah. Your mother was the perfect choice to get it for me. Easily seduced, I could get her to do anything." He paused. "I didn't expect to love her."

Ellie glared at him. "What kind of angel are you?"

"I was a soldier is His army." His hollow voiced filled the room. "Not some pansy-ass sworn to serve and protect."

He was quiet for a few long seconds. Remarkably, so was the rest of the house. A phenomenon that couldn't bode well.

"It was she who figured out where the guardian lived. Determined to ignore the ghost stories and search the house, she would have come alone. I *had* to come with her, to protect her.

"There was a struggle." He looked down at what was that left of his earthly body. "I lost." When he looked back up, the bottomless sockets of his eyes didn't seem quite as inky black as before. "That's what a warrior gets for trying to do a guardian's job," he said. "But your mother won. She lived."

"But she didn't succeed."

"Not entirely, no."

Now Michael stepped forward. The sooner they could get their hands on that missing piece, the sooner this whole thing would be over. "So it's here, the missing piece?"

"The Gray Man left years ago, hiding his treasures away until his return."

By now, Lucan was on his feet. "Where?"

"You have no need for the answer to that question."

"Please," Ellie begged.

After some thought, and plenty of glaring back and forth between the god and the angel, the angel spoke. "You will find the missing piece *oltre l'arcobaleno.*"

"What? What does that mean?" Ellie demanded.

"That's all I can tell you."

Michael held onto Ellie with one arm and supported Lucan with the other. "Let's get out of here."

Before he could blink, the priest manifested himself between them and the door.

"I'm sorry, Ellie," he said. "The pagans stay."

CHAPTER SEVENTEEN

Lucan pulled out his cell phone, pressed a single number, then held it up to his ear. After a brief pause, he said, "Sirona, I need ye. Bring Rhain." He slipped the phone back into his pocket just as all hell broke loose.

A blinding light filled the room. Ellie couldn't see anything at first, but she heard the slow beating of wings and the fading screech of evil. As the glare faded, she could make out the image of a beautiful woman in a flowing white gown with a mass of thick red hair that fell to her waist. Pearly white wings closed in around her back as she settled before them. Somewhere in the distance she heard…trumpets? An equally beautiful man, also dressed in white, with a mop of jet black hair settled next her.

Ellie had shoved the spearhead back in her pocket where it throbbed against her hip. The relic had never seemed so alive as it did now in the presence of these two.

Without a glance at anyone else, the woman addressed the priest. "Ye dare threaten my family?" The woman's Scottish brogue was thicker even than Lucan's.

The man with her closed in on the priest, a menacing threat despite his lovely appearance. To his credit, the priest did not back down, but stood his ground. "The master only wants what's owed him."

The fiery-haired woman curled her lip. "Ye call him master now?"

He huffed out what could almost be called a laugh. "Soon there will be nothing left of me. It makes no difference who my master is. I have given the girl what she came for—"

"You gave me a riddle," Ellie argued.

"It's more than your mother had," he snapped. "Now take your riddle," he turned to woman, "and your family, and get out!"

He faded into the wall only to unleash a horde of demons so foul they choked the very air. The two newcomers wrapped their snowy-white wings about the three of them. For a moment, time seemed to stand still. When they stepped back again, they were in the sitting room of the Dresser-Palmer house.

Lucan leaned on Michael's shoulder. "Neat trick, cousin." Then he promptly hit the floor.

The dark haired man lifted him and laid him gently on the worn sofa. Ellie finally let herself think about who these people were. This must be Lucan's cousin, Sirona. The goddess Arduinna had taken Lucan to her when he been exposed to the spearhead. Now she was here, some kind of guardian angel with healing powers. She assumed the man with her was an angel as well, since they were dressed alike. It shouldn't be so difficult to believe given all she'd seen in the last few days.

With a worried frown, the woman moved to sit beside Lucan. Her angelic attire morphed into a pair of white jeans and a silky cream-colored blouse. The wings disappeared. Her practiced hands moved over him pausing from time to time as she worked her healing magic through his body. At least Ellie hoped she was healing him. He was the only family Michael knew, and she didn't want him to lose that.

Her concern for Michael's family ties caught her off guard. She had never considered it before, but now that she thought back, she remembered that in high school, she'd imagined his life was so easy, free. He'd never contradicted that opinion. He didn't complain about being alone, or shuffled from one home to another. He never insisted on more of her time than she was willing to give.

It hit her suddenly that these had been defenses he had erected so she wouldn't realize how lonesome he was, so she wouldn't think he was too demanding and push him away.

What a fool she was. She realized now how important family was, how important it was to have your family around you, whether blood relatives or those you chose.

After several long tortuous minutes, Sirona sat back.

"He'll live, the wee jackass. Just needs a bit o' sleep."

Her companion moved behind her and began massaging her shoulders. She let her head fall back, the bulk of her red hair falling behind her back nearly to the floor. She reached up and squeezed one of his strong hands. "That's nice, baby." With that she stood up and fixed her gaze on Michael. With a warm smile, she crossed to him. "Hello, Michael," she said, taking him in her arms in a gentle hug.

Ellie almost choked at the blush that rose to his cheeks.

"I'm Sirona," she said pulling away and indicating the man with her. "This is my husband, Rhain." She laughed a soft, tinkling laugh. "We're kin from way back."

Michael cleared his throat, seemingly looking for his voice. "So I've heard," he finally choked out.

Sirona turned to her then. "And this lovely lassie must be our Ellie."

Am I supposed curtsey?

There was no need for her to have wondered as Sirona took her in the same familial hug she'd bestowed on Michael. The woman's embrace was so welcoming and nurturing, Ellie was disappointed when she pulled away.

"Ye're quite the anomaly, *a thasgaidh*. Usually angels aren't allowed to procreate."

"Angels?" Somewhere in her mind, Ellie had puzzled that out but couldn't make herself believe it.

"Aye. He fell hard, yer da." She patted Ellie's cheek. "But that'll make ye even more special, eh?"

She placed her hands on Ellie's shoulders. Warmth spread down her arms, across her chest, fanning across her lower back and falling down the length of her legs like a warm, soothing waterfall. All her aches and pains faded away, leaving her feeling restored and energized.

"Don't you have children?" Ellie asked.

"Aye," Lucan grumbled from the sofa. "A passle of hellions that would give Lucifer himself a run for his money."

Sirona sat down next to him. Her husband stood nearby like a silent sentinel. "Two can hardly be called a 'passle', now can it?" She rested a hand on his knee, an extra boost of her special medicine? "Besides, don' ye dare be talking bad about my children. Ye aren't the laird anymore."

She smiled up as Ellie. "I had my children in the years after Rhain and I married. A girl and a boy. They gave us six grandchildren, and one great-grandchild before we passed at the ripe old age of…well a ripe old age."

"And then you became an angel?"

"It was how we were raised," Sirona said. "I was a pious woman throughout my life. Thank the Lord I ascended first. I had to do some fast talking to save my heathen of a husband."

"So now you're both angels and not ... gods." Ellie glanced back and forth between them, searching for wings, a halo, something.

"'Tis awfully presumptuous to call oneself a god. There is only one." She stood and went to her husband's side. She slid her arms around his back and rested her head on his shoulder. "Rhain's not an angel yet. He has to prove hisself, ye ken."

With a smirk, Rhain spoke for the first time. "Now I'm in eternal purgatory."

"Tsk. Purgatory isn't eternal."

"It seems like it," Rhain said. "But as long as I get to spend it with you, *m 'aingeal*."

He pressed a quick kiss to her full lips before she pulled away with a giggle that made her sound like a girl. "Thanks to my healing skills, I was appointed as a guardian. So as long as Rhain has tests he must pass, I'll continue to do what I do best."

"Tests?"

"Rhain's family is forever trying to lure him back into the fold. Temptation is forever at our door, isn't baby?"

***

Michael was still struggling with the idea that he had family. Lucan had told him all about his Highland cousins. More than six hundred years ago, they had been children struggling to hide the powers they could neither understand nor control. Eventually, the four of them had embraced their god powers, even though they each followed a different path.

Michael hadn't met any but Lucan, so he hadn't let himself think of the possibilities. He'd lived so long with the knowledge that he was alone in the world, he'd given up on the notion of *having* a family. If he wanted a family of his own, he would have to create one.

"Why do they have to lure you?" Michael asked Rhain. "Don't you get along?" He couldn't imagine deliberately cutting himself off from his own family.

"My clan descends from the purest sort of evil, Lucifer himself."

"Sort of like demon royalty," Sirona laughed.

"I was not always as rebellious as I am now," Rhain continued. "I indulged in my share of debauchery."

Lucan joined in with more enlightenment. "The one ye encountered in Atlanta, Cael, is Rhain's nephew."

Ellie looked up then and all eyes fell on Rhain. "So you're a demon...in purgatory?" She shook her head disbelievingly. "That's what this is? Are we all in purgatory?"

Rhain shook his head. "Purgatory is different for everyone. While ye're there, Lucifer has free reign to try and lure ye to the dark side. If ye resist temptation, ye are then allowed to ascend into heaven."

"How long does it last?" she asked.

"For eternity," he said with a frustrated breath.

Sirona rose and went to stand next to him. "Tsk. It won't last that long," she assured him. Changing the subject, she asked, "What is that yer workin' on, Ellie?"

Ellie held up the notepad. "It's what my father said to me. The last thing he said to me," she trailed off, muffling the note of sadness in her voice.

Michael went to retrieve the notepad. When he reached to take it from her, she leaned against his thigh, sending a shockwave of pleasure straight to his groin. Was it an accident or was she drawing on his strength and proximity? He cleared his throat, trying to mask the emotion he felt.

"*Oltre l'arcobaleno*," he read.

Sirona looked at Lucan. "Italian?"

Lucan nodded, rising and going over to the bar to pour himself a shot of whiskey. "Over the rainbow," he translated. He indicated the decanter. "Rhain?"

"Ye know it," Rhain said, joining him. Michael, Ellie, and Sirona declined.

"What does it mean?" Ellie asked.

They stood around, each in his or her own thoughts, for several long moments, but no one had an answer. Finally, it was time for Sirona and Rhain to leave. When Ellie returned Sirona's hug, she didn't seem at all inclined to let go. Her reaction surprised him, although it shouldn't have. An embrace from an angel with the healing powers of a goddess was enough to make anyone feel like a new person.

"Where will you go?"

"While Rhain serves out his purgatory, I have accepted a position at a mission hospital in Bolivia. Everyone believes me to be a medical doctor, but *guardian angel* is my official title." She laughed. She bid her goodbyes to the rest of them, then she and Rhain were gone.

Ellie plopped down on the sofa. "This hasn't turned out to be a very lucrative venture," she said.

Michael sat beside her, unwilling to be any further away from her than necessary. He was determined to keep her safe, and get enough physical contact to sustain him for the future it case things didn't work out like he hoped.

He went rigid when she laid her head on his shoulder, berating himself as he sat like a marble statue for the fool he was. He was a demi-god. He'd fought demons. He was going to be brought down by a woman? A woman with no special powers except the power to crush his soul?

"No, not a good venture at all," Lucan said, nursing his second whiskey.

Ellie sat up and cocked her head to one side. "A good venture? Bonaventure?" She looked at Lucan hopefully. "Isn't that Italian?"

Lucan nodded.

"Bonaventure Cemetery. What does that have to do with 'over the rainbow'?"

Michael could hardly think with her so close, but he watched quietly as Ellie pulled out her cell phone and brought up the search engine.

"Is Judy Garland buried there?" She typed it in, clicked on the first of thousands of results, and started reading. "No," she said, her voice laced with disappointment. "New York."

"Isn't there a famous song writer buried out there?" Michael suddenly recalled. "Maybe he wrote *Over the Rainbow*."

She punched it in. "He wrote *Moon River*." She scrolled through and read a few more posts. "Little Gracie is the most famous person buried at Bonaventure Cemetery. But that was fifty years before *The Wizard of Oz*."

A sudden blinding pain struck Michael's temple. He grabbed the side table next to the sofa, jostling the lamp and sending it crashing to the floor. The tinkling sound of crystal floated up to him as he doubled over in pain. He pressed both fists to his closed eyes but couldn't block out the pain.

Nor the vision in his head.

"Michael!" Ellie's voice came to him as if on a breeze, from far away. Her hands clutched at him, but he dared not open his eyes or else the pain would make him pass out. Or worse, hurl all over her.

"Michael, what's wrong? Speak to me."

In some far off, perverted corner of his mind, he was pleased at the concern in her voice. He held up one hand, holding her off, but kept his eyes squeezed tight. When the pain finally started to dissipate, he was left with a vision that he had been dreading since Lucan first told him the story. Swallowing against the acrid taste in his mouth, he peeled his eyes open and fixed his gaze on his uncle.

"Neala's in trouble."

***

Lindsey Smith pulled two *pontarlier* glasses from the freezer and set them on the bar. "Sure you don't want to just share one to start?"

The couple sitting across from her looked like any other couple visiting Savannah on holiday. Rosy cheeks from their afternoon exploring Tybee Island. Crisp, new, 'vacation' clothes. A ready supply of cash and an eagerness to try new things.

Apparently one of those things was going to a swanky, secret club and imbibing in a drink that had been banned until recently. All nervous energy, the woman was practically sitting in the man's lap and chattering in a loud voice. She glanced around, like she was worried the police were going to raid any moment and cart her off to jail in the back of a paddy wagon.

Tourists.

The woman giggled, then pressed Lindsey with a droll stare. "I can handle it," she said. Her words expressed confidence. Her demeanor was anything but.

Lindsey cocked her head to one side. "Okay," she drawled. "You might want to write down the name of your hotel in case we need to give the info to your cab driver." She balanced a slotted spoon over each glass and topped it with a sugar cube.

"Oh, we have a car," the man said.

Lindsey eyeballed a shot of absinthe into each glass. The aroma of licorice wafted up to her as the cube of sugar soaked up the liquid like a sponge.

Mm-hmm. I've heard that before.

She held a flame to each cube, then stepped back as it flared to life, caramelizing the sugar, which dripped down into the glass. While she waited for the flame to die down, she poured a spare shot of the alcohol, reserved for the finale at the end of the show.

She watched the sugar melt, transforming to a thick, brown syrup, and tried not to think about all the homework she had tonight. Dr. Perkins, one of her professors at the institute, had the class working on a project that seemed impossible. All her research led nowhere. Every lead was a dead end. She was beginning to think it was a sick joke and he was leading them all on a wild goose chase.

Just as the flame would have gone out, she doused each with a final splash, igniting a small inferno and drawing hearty oohs and ahhs from the crowd. It was her own special trick at the end, not that she was the only bartender in Savannah who did it, but not many did. She had picked it up in…

…in Paris.

No, wait. She'd never been to Paris. Where *had* she picked it up?

A small pop from one of the spoons drew her attention back to her task. She doused the flame with water, transforming the clear absinthe into an opaque concoction with a sea-green tint, and set each glass on a saucer she had laid out earlier.

"See you on the other side," she said in a low voice as she slid the saucers across to the couple.

A bizarre sense of déjà vu washed over her. But instead of being the bartender, she was the bubbly woman, giddy with excitement over, not this dweeb, but a hulking beast of a man who sat beside her. Instead of a Savannah speakeasy, they were at a gilded Parisian nightclub. Women smoked cigarettes from slim, black filters. Smoke hung overhead in a thick cloud.

The vision was new.

The hulking beast of a man beside her was not.

He was always there, whether it was dream, a vision, or a moment of déjà vu—like now. Sometimes she thought she caught a glimpse of him, passing on the street, a news bite about some social function or charity event. But he was always gone so quickly, she couldn't be sure. Like always, flashes of memory came and went so quickly, Lindsey could never quite recall them later. They were soon forgotten, until the next time.

Except for him.

A premonition of her future?

No, that couldn't be. Her visions always seemed to take place in the past. Were they suppressed memories from another life? She wanted to think so. How romantic to imagine a bond so powerful even the elements of time could not break it.

She smirked when the man across the bar swayed on his stool after only a few sips of his drink. The woman giggled at absolutely nothing. *Yeah, good thing you got that car, buddy.* With a knowing smile, she set the leather pouch with their check on the bar between them. "I'll take that when you're ready," she said before stepping away.

Lindsey rounded the bar and crashed headlong into a man so familiar she didn't feel the urge to avoid him until it was too late.

"Ho-ho, Lindsey," he said, catching her in his arms and holding her there. "Careful where ye tread."

Unable to disengage from his embrace without causing a scene, she stared up at him trying to keep as much space between their bodies as possible. The certainty that she knew him made her reluctant to ask his identity.

He seemed to take her lack of recognition in stride. "I'm friends with Dr. Perkins. We met at your school the other day. My name is Cael. Cael Comyn."

That tidbit of knowledge did nothing to alleviate the discomfort she felt in his arms. "Oh, yes," she said, carefully working her way free. "I haven't seen you in here before," she said. *And I hope I never do again.* There was something off-putting about him. She couldn't say exactly what it was. He was certainly handsome enough. And that Scottish accent was enough to melt a woman on the spot. But her skin had crawled where he'd touched her. She sensed an evilness in him that was not readily apparent at first sight.

"'Tis my first time. It's all very mysterious. A secret club, special access only. I was lucky enough to acquire a key, but sadly have been forced to enjoy it on my own." He took a sip from his glass, his haunting gaze never leaving her face. "Perhaps ye'd take pity on me? Maybe go for a coffee when you finish work."

Not if you were the last man on earth. "Sure," she heard herself say. *No!* Her mind screamed. What was wrong with her? She shifted from one foot to another, jittery beneath his intense stare. "There's a coffee shop next door." *Have you lost your mind? Don't tell him that.* "I mean…if you don't mind waiting." *Shut up. Shut up. Shut up.*

He lowered his glass. The amber liquid left his red lips glossy. Her stomach flipped over a little when he snaked his tongue out to lick them dry. Had she really just agreed to have coffee with this snake?

She pulled her phone from her apron pocket and checked the time. Almost midnight. "We close at two." That was it. She should commit herself to a lunatic asylum now.

While she stood there trying to figure out how to slip out the back of the club at closing time without him seeing, he reached out and brushed her bangs from where they'd fallen into her eyes. The pad of his finger brushed her forehead sending a discomfiting wave of nausea to her stomach. She swallowed the bile that rose in her throat.

"I'll meet you out back," she choked out.

CHAPTER EIGHTEEN

"Where is she?" Lucan was already storming through the house.

"She's working. But you can't go there," Michael said, following close on his heels. "If you break your covenant, you'll never see her again."

Lucan stopped at the door. He had keys in his hand, prepared to go to his beloved's rescue. Her knight in shining armor. She glanced at Michael, *her* knight in shining armor. Her heart swelled with emotion she'd denied herself for years. Even now, she couldn't admit her feelings, not even to herself. To give in would only leave her weak and dependent, something she'd avoided all her life.

"She willna notice my presence," Lucan said. "She doesna ken me."

"She doesn't have to know who you are. If she sees you, talks to you, you will have broken your covenant with a God who sees everything. You'll live for all eternity, and she will be lost to you." Lucan seemed about ready to cave at the prospect. Michael kept trying to convince him he'd be making a mistake. "Let me go. I'll take care of it. I swear I'll protect her, just like you've taught me."

Lucan still seemed undecided.

"Even if things go bad for her," Michael continued, "it's only one life. You'll find her in the next one. That's the promise He made. But if you reveal yourself to her—"

With a growl, Lucan yanked open the back door. "'Tis no' happenin', lad. I'm goin' wit' ye."

With little choice, they followed him to the sleek, black Jaguar parked in the alley behind the house. He started the ignition as they climbed in. As she settled into the plush back seat, Ellie couldn't help but marvel at the luxury of the interior. She'd expected leather seats. It *was* a Jaguar. But this had to be the softest leather made. It was as silky smooth as warm butter. She got her seatbelt buckled just as gravel crunched beneath the custom wheels.

Before the car had come to a stop, he slammed the Jag into drive and took off like a shot, spraying dirt and gravel behind them. Ellie grabbed the seat in front of her and held on as he whipped the sedan through the narrow alley. He barely slowed down as they reached the end and turned right. Tires squealed when they caught the pavement. There were no squares on Drayton Street, so he ignored all indications of a speed limit and practically flew towards the river.

The reached River Street in record time. Lucan brought them to a screeching halt before an unassuming building, unmarked and dimly lit. Leaving the Jag illegally parked, he went to the door and rang the bell.

Ellie and Michael caught up to him and waited. The door was made of thick panels, held together by large, wood rivets. There was a tiny window at eye-level, covered by an iron grate. After a few tense moments, the window slid back and a pair of eyeballs stared out at them.

The eyes blinked several times, then the window closed. They could hear the sound of locks sliding open.

"Mr. Munro," said the man who opened the door. He stepped back to allow them entrance. "Sir, we close in fifteen minutes."

Lucan pushed past the man. "That's all I need," he said.

When they entered the bar, Ellie felt like she'd stepped back onto the 1920s. A lounge singer belted out the blues from a small stage. She wore a banana yellow dress that hugged every curve from beneath her bared shoulders to just below her knee. Yellow feathers adorned her hair. Her face was barely hidden behind a delicate web of black lace. Her smoky voice created the perfect ambiance.

Just beyond the performer, was the bar, where Ellie noticed the bartender was serving absinthe. This was one of the only places in Savannah it could be found, even though the ban had been lifted years ago. It wasn't as potent as it had been before the ban, but its hallucinogenic properties made it quite taboo even today.

They sat down at a table that miraculously became empty just as they walked up to it. A server spotted them immediately and rushed over, eyeballing the two men with a hungry expression.

"Hello, I'm Brooke. What can I get for you?"

Lucan started to speak, but Michael interrupted him. "Hey, Brooke. Is Lindsey around?"

Brooke shook her head as she laid out cocktail napkins. "She left early. She said she didn't feel good."

Ellie noticed Lucan clenching and unclenching his fists, but he remained silent.

"When did she leave?"

"Not long ago," she said glancing around. "I think you just missed her. She was supposed to close tonight, but it's been kinda slow, so no biggie. You guys want something to drink?"

Lucan was already on the move, but a voice behind them had him sinking slowly back into his chair.

"That didn't take as long as I thought."

Ellie felt the blood drain from her face. The demon they had encountered in Atlanta pulled up a forth chair, whipped it around and straddled the back as he joined them. Brooke faded away and disappeared to the other side of the bar.

"Where is she?" Lucan ground out. He gripped the side of the table so hard, Ellie wondered why part of it didn't break off in his hand.

"Where she belongs. With her family."

"Ye're not her family. Now tell me where she is, and I'll destroy ye quickly, instead of dragging it out overlong."

The demon held up one hand in a placating gesture. The move did absolutely nothing to placate the Celtic god who was poised to rip his head off.

"Neala is safe. For now."

Cael Comyn smiled, an evil smile that raised the hairs on her arms. Ellie scooted closer to Michael, drawing Cael's attention.

"Ye have something I want, lass, but I also need the missing piece."

"We don't know where it is," Ellie said. She was surprised at the strength in her voice. Inside, she was a mess, terrified of the danger this man posed and worried about what he'd done with Neala.

"Ye ken well enough," he said. When she made no response, he looked back and forth between Lucan and Michael, finally settling his gaze on his old nemesis. "Time's ticking," he said.

"'Tis at the cemetery," Lucan informed him.

His creepy smile split his face again, making Ellie want to run and hide. "Weel...I'll meet ye there in an hour."

"We doona ken where."

"Find it," the creepy smile was gone, replaced by a glare of hatred so foul, she half expected one of them to burst into flame. "Find it and bring it to me."

"What makes you think we'll do that?" Michael asked.

The demon pushed back from his chair and stood. Lucan and Michael stood as well, fully prepared to send him to hell if he made a move. He kept his gaze on the Highlander. "If ye want to see yer precious Neala again in *this* lifetime," he said to Lucan, "ye'll do exactly as I say."

***

The ride out to Bonaventure Cemetery seemed much longer than it should. After their ordeal at the Gray Man's house, none of them was eager to go to an old cemetery in the middle of the night. But it was the closest thing they had to a clue.

Michael glanced into the back seat. Ellie was engrossed in her research, looking for some tie to the *Wizard of Oz*. Her face was beautiful in the glow from her cell phone. Slim brows pressed together in concentration. Eyes sparkled as they darted from one side of the screen to the other. Her hair had fallen forward, framing her striking features.

He turned back, staring out the passenger window. It amazed him that she was still on her feet. It was almost three in the morning, and they hadn't had much sleep in the last few days. She'd always been cool and composed, confident in her ability to handle any situation. She'd certainly adapted to recent revelations with calm skepticism.

Michael would not have expected her to acquiesce so quickly. But what choice did she have? Some of the things they'd seen were hard to explain. He felt a sense of pride in her strength and determination.

Lucan cut the headlights when they pulled off and meandered down the unpaved road that led to the cemetery. Enormous gothic columns greeted them at the entrance.

"Now what?" Michael asked.

"Ye dinna ken anything?"

He took deep breaths. Sorted through the movie reel in his head. Tossed away visions of the abundant wildlife that would cross their path. "Nothing," he finally admitted.

Lucan pulled the Jag into the parking lot of the administrative building and cut the engine. He looked up into the rearview mirror. "Ellie?"

Michael turned again to look back at her.

She held up one finger. "Wait." She continued reading for several long minutes. Finally, she looked up. "It's a long shot, but Judy Garland had an affair with that songwriter who is buried here. John Mercer."

"Does it say where he's buried?"

She flipped through several screens until she pulled up a map. "Section H."

When she looked up, their gazes met over the glow from her cell. Michael's heart lurched at the wild combination of fear, eagerness, and trust in her eyes. He didn't want to let her down. No matter what happened after, he would see this to the end. He would be the man she needed him to be.

They got out of the car. What little there was of the moon shone brightly in the clear sky overhead. Michael had a sudden vision of he and Ellie descending into a dark place. Just the two of them.

"You should stay here," he said to Lucan.

"Why? What did you see?"

Michael shook his head. "I'm not sure, but I think Ellie and I are meant to go alone." He looked around. "You could hide somewhere in case our demon friend shows up."

Lucan was usually pretty trusting of his visions, if not his advice. He nodded once and ducked off into the shadows.

"Is there a map?" Michael lifted his chin in the direction of Ellie's phone, which she held up for him to see the screen.

"Right here," she whispered.

He laced his fingers with her. "Let's roll."

Even in the dark, the cemetery was beautiful. He'd heard it described as part natural cathedral and part sculpture garden. Said sculptures glowed as if they were lit from the inside.

Ellie's hand was warm in his. He could sense that she was more relaxed than she had been earlier tonight when they'd stood on the threshold of the Gray Man's house. Hauntingly beautiful, Bonaventure Cemetery was not nearly as frightening, but that did not mean it was any less dangerous.

Following her virtual map, Ellie led them down dusty paths, beneath the moss-draped limbs of live oak trees that were hundreds of years old. The dead were buried along either side, silently keeping Savannah's secrets. Stories of success, failure, love, betrayal, good, and evil were kept here.

At one point they came to the edge of the bluff overlooking the Wilmington River. The river moved past in a slowly meandering flow. Two cargo barges moored in the middle and an unassuming cabin cruiser was anchored below the bluff where they stood.

For the first time, Ellie let go of his hand. "I must have missed a turn." She held her phone out in front of her, turned in once direction then the other trying to find her mistake.

Michael felt cold and empty when she disentangled her fingers from his. How could such a small thing make him feel like a piece of himself had been ripped away?

She seemed to get her bearings and headed off in a new direction. After only a few steps, she stopped and waited for him to catch up. When he did, she slipped her hand back into his, making him feel whole again.

He was a goner.

After a few more missed turns, they found the section where famed song writer Johnny Mercer was buried. A low wall surrounded the half dozen gravesites of the Mercer family. There was a half-moon-shaped marble bench in one corner. Song titles were engraved around the edge.

"What now?" she asked as they stood there staring down at the graves. Uncertainty radiated from her, and no wonder. They could have read the clues completely wrong and not be any closer to finding the missing piece than they were when they started.

"I guess we look around," he said.

They spent the next fifteen minutes scouring the area. One of the headstones was so old, it lifted right up off the ground when Michael slid his fingers beneath the edge.

"There's nothing here," Ellie said. Frustration laced her voice. She stepped outside the enclosure and stood on the path, arms crossed, glaring at the dead as if she could intimidate them into giving up their secrets.

Suddenly she became fully alert. "What was that?"

Michael followed her gaze to an archway between the Mercer plot and the one on the opposite side. The arch was flanked by two ionic columns that rose to a height of at least twenty feet. The top was anchored by a decorative slap of marble which had been discolored over the years to a soft, earthy color. Except for its extraordinary beauty, nothing else about it was attention grabbing. "I don't see anything."

Ellie was already scurrying down the path and around to the other side. Michael followed her only to find another plot similar to the one belonging to the Mercers. The archway was in between the two plots. The only way to reach it was to step over the graves.

Ellie did just that.

She circled the archway, using the flashlight app on her phone to light the ground around the base.

"See anything?"

She looked up at him from the other side. "Nothing." She took three steps toward him, this time through the archway, and disappeared.

"Ellie!" Michael ran to the archway ignoring the disturbance he made to the gravesites. His heart roared in his ears. "Ellie," he called again. When she still didn't answer, he slipped through the arch.

And came out on the other side. Back and forth he ran, but there was no sign of her.

Ellie was gone.

***

Cael was so startled by the lass' sudden disappearance, he almost dropped the protective shield that hid his presence from the Munro's protégé. The bastard had already cost him time and effort. If not for him, the spear would be his by now.

But soon.

He could feel the spear's power. Soon it would be his. So would the lass. His entire body hardened at the wicked thoughts of what he had planned for her. She would be so much more fun that 'Auntie Neala'. Once Ellie had the spear intact, it would be a simple enough trade, one the Munro would be unable to resist.

He watched Michael raced back and forth in a frantic search for the lass. Cael enjoyed his panic, fed on it. He considered taking him out. He'd held off so far in case Michael had some role to play, but Cael was like a cat tired of playing with the mouse he'd caught.

Time to eat.

He slipped from behind the grave marker where he'd been hiding and worked his way closer to the archway. He wouldn't reveal himself until it was too late for the lad to react.

When Michael pulled out his cell phone, Cael hesitated, listening to the call.

"I need you to get over here. Quick."

Cael faded back into the shadows to wait. There was only one person he would have called.

All the elements were coming together.

CHAPTER NINETEEN

Ellie stood frozen in her tracks. She sensed the change the moment she stepped through the archway. Michael was gone, but she didn't feel the sense of urgency to get back to him like she should.

Where was she?

All around her, the cemetery was bathed in a soft glow. Not day. Not night. But somewhere in between. Soft tufts floated around her, some catching light from somewhere and twinkling like stars, stars she could touch. She reached out her hand and watched the tufts land on her skin like glistening snowflakes, before bouncing off and floating away.

Everything—the statues, headstones, trees, azalea bushes—had taken on a soft edge, blurring and blending and creating a peaceful scene she would not have expected to find in a grave yard, not even one as beautiful and tranquil as this one.

The only thing she found remotely disturbing was the silence. No chirping cicadas. No croaking frogs or hooting owls. Not even the dull hum of the distant city.

"Hello?" she said softly. She whipped around when she thought she heard someone coming, curious but not afraid. She choked back a little cry when a woman stepped out of the shadows.

"Mama?" Ellie's breath was barely a whisper. Tears clogged her throat. She wanted to run to her, to throw herself into her arms. She wanted her mother to take her in her protective embrace and tell her everything was going to be okay.

But now, Ellie *was* afraid. She didn't want to disturb whatever fantasy had taken hold of her. She didn't want to do anything to jeopardize this encounter. So she stood rooted to the spot, tears streaming down her face. When her mother held out both arms, it was all the encouragement she needed. Ellie ran into them, sobbing and holding onto the apparition as if she would never let go.

Her mother held her, stroking her hair and whispering soothing words in her ear, while she cried. She waited for Ellie to get her emotions sufficiently under control then led them to the bench in the Mercer Family plot.

"I'm sorry I wasn't there—" Ellie began.

"Don't, Ellie. It wasn't your fault. They would have gotten to me whether you were there or not. When they came, I was glad you were gone."

"But maybe I could have helped."

She shook her head. "No, you weren't ready. I'm the one who should apologize. I was so lost, so bitter about the task your father had left me to deal with...alone. I knew I couldn't protect you, so I did the only thing I knew to do. I left you with your grandmother and tried to draw attention away from you for as long as I could."

"But you sent for me. You had me come home."

Her mother made a phishing sound. "That wasn't home. Home is the place where you belong, where you are loved and safe and happy. I knew you would find those things here." She gave Ellie a sad look. "The evil inside that house on Calhoun square changed me, Ellie. I was weak and powerless to resist the commands of the demons who controlled me after I escaped. Since you were born, I've tried to block them out. Drinking helped some. Shameless self-degradation relieved some of the guilt. I hoped I would find peace if you joined me, but peace eluded me." She indicated their surroundings. "Until now. I should have come back instead of having you join me in Atlanta, but as it happened, everything worked out."

"Worked out?" Was she kidding? "You're...gone." She couldn't bring herself to say 'dead'. "Gran was nearly killed. I'm being chased by demons. I've been through stuff so scary...it's like a horror movie."

Her mother patted her on the arm. "I know it's been difficult, sweetie, but you're doing a great job."

"No, Mama, you're wrong. I could never have done any of this without help. I needed you."

"You have all the help you need, that you'll ever need. Your young man has been a boon I wasn't expecting."

"He's not my man. Just a friend from high school."

"I suspect it's more than that."

Ellie stared down at where their hands were joined and rested in her mother's lap. "I don't want to be left behind. Never again."

"Sweetie, you can't go your whole life without takings risks. There is no joy in that. Trust your own strength. Don't miss out on love because of fear. Your father and I had so little time together. It was a blink in time, really. Don't waste a single moment."

Ellie knew she was right. She could accept that her mom had left her behind to protect her. She admitted that she treasured the time she'd spent growing up in Gran's house. She *had* felt safe, happy, loved. She reaffirmed her vow to make up for the heartache she'd caused her grandmother over the years.

Then there was Michael. Ellie still was uncertain about her feelings. Of course, she cared about him. He had been there for so long. He had helped her through some of her roughest moments, even before her return to Savannah. She dreaded that something would happen during this ordeal and he might be hurt or worse. Was that love? True love that could sustain them forever? Did that kind of love even exist?

Did people even stay together for forever anymore? Morgan and Erica at the diner both came from broken homes. Ellie had known very few people whose parents were still together. Maybe such love wasn't something people found, but just happen to luck up on.

Could she be so lucky?

She pushed away those thoughts. There was no need thinking about the future when the present was so uncertain. First, get rid of this artifact that had caused her so much heartache. Then, maybe she'd have the luxury of contemplating her future.

Ellie reached into her pocket and pulled out the spearhead. "Where can I find the missing piece?"

Her mother reached over and curled Ellie's hand around the ancient stone. It was cool and warming at the same time. It sent a little tingle up her arm. She barely recalled using it at the Gray Man's house. Everything had happened so fast, and there'd been little time to think about it since.

But she remembered how it felt—like an extension of her arm. When she gripped the spearhead, she was strong, invigorated. Fiercely protective.

"You are the missing piece, Ellie."

Ellie screwed up her face. "What do you mean?"

"See how it fits," she answered.

Ellie hefted the ancient stone. She flexed her fingers, noting that they did indeed align perfectly with the grooves and notches on the 'broken' side. She held it over head, as she had done when she destroyed the creature at the Gray Man's house. Rising to her feet, she brought the weapon down again and again, waving her arm about and coming at her imaginary opponent from different angles. She turned it in her hand, now holding it next to her thigh and bringing it up in a thrust she suspected would take down almost any enemy she faced.

Ellie had never felt so powerful.

With a heavy sigh, she returned to the bench.

They had assumed the spearhead was broken, that they would find a jagged shard to make it whole again, and turn it over to someone else to worry about. "What am I supposed to do with it?" She wasn't sure she wanted to hear the answer.

"It's an ongoing battle we humans are fighting here on earth. We need someone to even the odds."

Ellie shook her head. "You want me to hunt demons?"

Her mother gave her a sad smile. "You won't have to hunt them, sweetie."

Her heart fell. Demons were going to be after from now on? She didn't want this responsibility. Protect humanity? Was she serious?

"You must return to the cathedral and dedicate your service to Father Neilson. He will guide you." She stood. "I have to go now," her mother whispered.

Now Ellie's heart jump right back up to her throat. She returned the spearhead to her pocket and threw her arms around her mother. "Not yet." She felt tears spring to her eyes. Pulling away, she asked, "Are you in...heaven?"

With a slight shake of her head, she stood. "Lucifer's followers consume human souls when they can. It's where they get their strength."

"So...is this hell?" She looked around. Even though they seemed to be in a dream world of sorts, it wasn't a place of suffering. That much Ellie could tell. Even in this alternate Bonaventure Cemetery, she sensed nothing that would cause fear or pain. Only peace and tranquility. The cemetery's beauty was not lost in here.

She gave a little chuckle. "This isn't real. The archway acts as a portal, a way for God's agents to interact with those in need." She pointed through the archway.

Ellie could see Michael on the other side, pacing. Her heart tripped. He was frantic with worry. When she looked back at her mother, her image faded. She was losing substance fast.

She had sudden idea. "Wait. What if the demon who stole your soul was destroyed? Can I get it back?"

A look of horror came over her face. "No, Ellie. You cannot go there. Promise me."

Ellie reached out to grab her hands, but there was no substance. She grasped at air. "Please, don't go.

"Your momma loves you, baby girl. Don't ever forget that."

Ellie stood there, watching the mist that had been her mother fade away towards the river. She waited for several long moments before accepting that she was gone. Swallowing the lump in her throat, she glanced around, found herself alone, and hurried back through the archway.

***

The look on Michael's face when she suddenly reappeared was priceless. She doubted anyone would ever look at her with such emotion. What was she holding out for?

He scooped her up against him and held her in a tight hug, only letting go when Lucan arrived with the car.

"What happened?" he asked emerging from the Jag.

Michael stepped back, but did not let go of her. "Ellie disappeared." He pointed at the archway. "Through there." Turning his attention back to her, he said, "I tried to follow you, but I couldn't."

"Where did you go? Did you find the missing piece?" Lucan asked.

Before she could answer, Michael practically jerked her behind him. He stared off into the trees, peering into the darkness.

Despite the powerful weapon throbbing against her hip, Ellie clung to him. "What is it?"

"He's here," Michael whispered.

Lucan stepped next to him, efficiently blocking her from any forthcoming danger. "Come on out, ye coward," he said in a firm voice.

Since both men were at least a head taller than she, Ellie watched from between them as Cael Comyn emerged from the shadows, dragging a petite woman along with him. Her hands were tied behind her back, and even though a hood had been placed over her head, Ellie could tell from her muffled cries that she was also gagged.

Michael had his knife in his hand. Like a light saber, it transformed into the medieval-looking sword Lucan had created for him. Lucan went stiff as a board. A sword more ancient looking than Michael's appeared suddenly in his hand.

Cael chuckled. "Ye willna be needin' that, Laird Munro." He held the woman with one arm around her small shoulders. Now he stroked the top of her arm, sending her into a struggling panic and provoking Lucan to raise the sword.

"When I bring him down," Lucan said in a low voice, "remove his head."

"Got it."

Not wanting to be left out, Ellie pulled the spearhead from her pocket. Closing her fingers around the edge, she let the energy surge through her.

Cael laughed again, an evil sound that made Ellie even more concerned for the woman's safety. By all reckoning, she had deduced that this was Neala, Lucan's beloved. The woman he had promised the one God he would not make contact with until her twenty-fifth birthday.

"Look at the three of ye, ready to do battle over one wisp of a woman. She must be verra special indeed. I canna wait to taste her." He leaned over and inhaled deeply, drawing a whimper from his captive.

With threat of the broken covenant and the possibility that his agreement would be void, Lucan stepped forward.

Cael slid his hand up to curl around Neala's throat, pulling her in front of him to use as a shield. The move served its purpose. Lucan froze.

"Ye ken I can snap her neck in an instant," Cael warned. He cupped one of her breasts with his other hand, squeezing viciously until she cried out. "It would be disappointing to kill her now, before I've had a chance to enjoy her."

Ellie's stomach turned. She could only imagine the turmoil Lucan was feeling right now.

"See how she struggles? I like a fighter. Of course, I can bend her to my will with just a touch, but this way is so much more fun."

Ellie could not hide behind the two men and do nothing. She knew the only reason they had not attacked Cael yet was because of concern for Neala's safety, as well as her won. She recalled her mother's words and the responsibility she had been given. She could no longer go through life worrying about herself and no one else. She would have to step up and use her gift to protect others from evil.

She stepped out from behind them before Michael could stop her. "Is this what you want?" She held out the spearhead, careful to keep her grip firm. If he got a hold of it, they were screwed. Ellie was no fighter, but all she need to do was nick him with it. She'd seen what happened when Lucan touched it. She didn't need to fight, but she had to be cunning.

Cael's eyes turned a sickening shade of yellow at the sight of the weapon he coveted. His excitement was evident in the way he licked his lips and ogled the weapon in her hand. When he met her eyes, Ellie felt what seemed like all the despair of the world land on her shoulders. Her skin crawled, and depression washed over her so completely she nearly burst into tears.

She dragged her gaze away just enough that she could see him in her peripheral vision and instantly felt better. She would have to remember to avoid eye contact with the demon if she was to have any chance at all.

"Ellie. Step. Back." Michael's voice behind her was commanding and left no room for argument.

For once, she wanted to do exactly as she was told. But she had to be brave. She had to save the innocent life before her.

"An even trade," Cael said. "One whore for another?"

Ellie swallowed, then nodded. "Let her go first."

"I doona think so, lass."

Out of the corner of her eye, she saw Michael take a step behind her, causing Cael to strengthen his hold on Neala. Lucan stopped Michael with a hand on his arm.

"If ye harm her," he said, "I will hunt ye for all eternity. And yer death will be much more than a simple fireworks display. Hell cannot compare to the suffering I will rain down on ye."

"Those are big words from one about to die," Cael teased. "Do ye have the missing piece?" he asked Ellie.

She nodded, careful to keep her eyes averted.

"Then come closer," he said.

As long as he had Neala, there was little any of them could do in the way of defense. All she had to do was get close enough to touch him. She looked over her shoulder then and regretted it almost immediately.

The anguish on Michael's face almost sent her scurrying back behind his protective wall. Had anyone ever cared so much about her?

He moved his head from side to side, silently imploring her to stay put. But how could she? Ellie was under no illusions that Cael would show Neala any mercy. With the greatest strength she had ever known, Ellie turned her back on him. This was as much for him as it was for the innocent in Cael's clutches. Michael had strength and power unlike any man she had ever known. But would he be able to defend himself from a demon with the full power of Lucifer? It wasn't a chance she was willing to take.

Cael Comyn had to go down.

***

Cael watched her take a step toward him, then another. She kept her eyes averted glancing around, at the ground before her feet, at the woman he held captive. The helplessness of her companions was the sweetest sort of revenge. It dragged on, wrenching torment from Lucan Munro at a sloth's pace. He savored every long moment of the laird's discomfort.

Tonight he would have it all. Destruction of his clan's greatest enemy. The weapon of power. And two delicious playthings to warm his bed. He would bend Neala to his will and use her to ensure Ellie's cooperation. His entire body hardened in anticipation. Oh, the fun he would have. When he finally took their souls, the infusion would compound his own strength, making him one powerful demon. His place at Lucifer's side was assured. Then it would be a simple matter to overthrow the big man himself.

When she was within arm's length, he commanded her to stop. She did. He noted the lad's relief.

"Let me see it," Cael said. She lifted her arm, unwrapping her fingers to show him the shard. "There is still something missing."

"I know where it is, but I couldn't get it by myself." She nodded back over her shoulder. "That's why I came back. I need help."

She was lying. He was sure of it. He studied her, forced to admit she was cool under pressure. She had the missing piece. Why had she not fit it to the shard before coming back through the archway? "Where is it?" he demanded. He tightened his grip on Neala's throat, lifting her off her feet. Her struggle energized him. "I will snap her neck," he looked at Lucan, "and devour her soul right before your eyes. She will spend eternity in a place so dark, she will never again see the light." He sneered with perverse pleasure. "Nor another lifetime."

While his attention was drawn away, the stupid lass charged him. He yanked Neala in front of him to act as a shield. She drew up just in time to prevent mortal injury. From his peripheral vision, he saw Lucan attack. The two men came at him, weapons raised. Swearing, he sent a blast into Ellie sending her flying through the air and slamming against a tree. She hit the ground and lay limp and still among the exposed, gnarled roots.

Still using Neala as a shield, he cursed them. He couldn't defend himself and keep a hold on her at the same time. Withdrawing his own weapon, he shoved her away, and faced his opponents, flaming sword clenched in both hands. By the time she hit the ground, he was already swinging this way and that deftly parrying everything Lucan and Michael threw at him.

Cael needed to take one of them out so he didn't have to defend against both at the same time. The lad was the least experienced of the two, and the least powerful. Cael had practically been born with a sword in his hand. He swung at Michael, screaming wildly in an ancient Highland war cry, but the cocksure lad met the blow on his blade and kept thrusting, driving him back. He was stronger than Cael had anticipated.

The added disadvantage of Lucan Munro on his other side was not something he could ignore. Cael was forced to the defensive again and again. Rage, pure and unbridled, infused him from his core, creating an inferno of hatred that surged through him and fed the fire he rained down on his enemies.

For a time, he held the advantage, but their combined strength and stamina began to wear on him. He felt himself fading. He should have fed on Neala's soul while he had the chance. Once again greed would be his downfall.

He made the mistake of changing the direction of his trust at the last moment. He flailed his sword into empty air, felt his balance slipping. He was going down.

By Lucifer, he was taking one of the bastards with him.

CHAPTER TWENTY

Ellie peeled her eyes open. She hurt everywhere. She lay there for a moment, trying to get her bearings and mentally giving her body a once over to see if anything was broken. Satisfied she was still in one piece, she moved gingerly onto her side and cocked her head back to see what all the ruckus was about.

A slew of memories flooded her at the sight she found. Cael had found them. He had Neala. Ellie had tried to get close enough to touch him with the spearhead, but he had attacked her with a blast of power unlike anything she would have thought existed in the real world. Having only recently found herself in this magical one, she struggled to reconcile the two.

But more urgent right now was the terrifying image of Michael and Lucan embroiled in a sword battle with the demon. Neala squirmed on the ground, moving away from the fray as best she could with her arms tied behind her and a hood over her head.

Ellie was in no position to help her, but she pushed to her hands and knees, where she knelt for several long moments and took in deep, deep breaths. She felt around and retrieved the spearhead, promptly tucking it back into the pocket of her jeans. With some small measure of strength restored, she used the rough trunk of the oak tree she'd crashed into to push to her feet—a painful, arduous task.

The world around her was spinning by the time she gained her footing. Stars burst behind her eyes, and she closed them, squeezing the bridge of her nose until she saw only black. She opened them again just in time to see Michael drive Cael to his knees. He brought his sword down with a cry of fury.

Instead of cleaving the demon's skull in two, the blade seemed be swallowed in a vortex of some kind, a gaping maw that seemed to assimilate the steel. Cael answered with a howl so filled with hatred and evil, Ellie's ears burned.

Fear and panic bubbled up inside her. She had already begun to run toward them when Cael faded into the vortex, taking Michael with him. By the time they disappeared, she let loose a blood-curdling scream that ripped through the silence of the cemetery.

Standing in the spot where he'd just been seconds before, she spun in a circle, first one way then the other. *Where is he?* her mind screamed as a new wave of panic flooded her.

She suddenly remembered Lucan when he appeared at her side and asked him. "Where is he?" She gripped his arm. "Where did they go?" Fear threatened to choke her. She'd never felt so helpless.

"I doona ken," he said.

Irritation flared within her. "What? What does that mean? Speak English for fuck's sake," she railed. Her gaze darted from one headstone or tree to another.

"Calm down, lass." His voice was low, quiet.

She dragged her hand through her hair. She didn't want to calm down. "We have to find him."

"Aye. And we will." He glanced at the woman still lying on the ground. "I will see what I can find out, but I need ye to get Neala to safety." He pressed the keys to the Jag into her hand. "I'll speak with Arduinna. Take her home, then wait for me at my house."

He pressed a kiss to her forehead and disappeared into the darkness.

Ellie stared off at nothing, tears clogging her throat. She didn't want to leave. What if Michael came back? What if he needed her?

A whimper nearby drew her attention. Resigned, she walked over and knelt beside Neala. She began to struggle when Ellie touched her.

"Shhh, you're safe now." She helped her sit up, then removed the hood and untied the gag. Moving into her line of sight, Ellie took her by the shoulders and tried to smile. She could only imagine the frightening grimace that resulted from her effort. She blinked away tears. "It's okay now," she said.

"W-what happened?"

Ellie stood, pulling Neala up with her. She turned her around and fumbled with the knot that bound Neala's wrists. "The man who kidnapped you is gone. My...friends...took care of him."

Freed at last, Neala faced her, rubbing her wrists and staring back with look of such concern, Ellie nearly broke down. "We have to get out of here," Ellie said. "I'll take you home."

She indicated Lucan's car, then followed Neala in that direction. Just as she reached for the sleek handle, she had a sudden thought. Whirling back around, she stared at the arch she'd gone through earlier. Maybe he was in there. "I'll be right back," she said as she hurried across the gravestones.

She crossed the threshold. All around her, the silence was deafening. This alternate cemetery was exactly the same as before. "Michael?" she called. His name on her lips brought a fresh wave of despair. "Michael!" she called again, this time she did nothing to squelch the desperation in her voice. With a choked sob she hugged her arms around her body. Was he truly gone? She stood there for a moment, listening to nothing and allowing the tears to stream down her face. She swallowed against the nausea that churned in her stomach.

And the despair that threatened to crush her.

Michael was gone. He'd vanquished a demon to protect her and with it, her heart

***

A week later, Ellie sat on the Johnny Mercer bench cradling the unremarkable urn that held her mother's ashes. She'd been staring at the archway for nearly an hour, trying to decide what to do. She'd stepped through, back and forth several times, but nothing happened. Bonaventure Cemetery was the same on both sides.

They'd held a memorial service at the beginning of the week, but it had been a sad turn out. The only people who had come were Morgan, Erica, and a few of Gran's friends. Lucan had come, as well, hiding in the shadows until he could speak to Ellie alone.

When she spotted him, hope had flared that he had answers to Michael's whereabouts and what they had to do to bring him back. With a sad look in his eyes, he'd told her that Michael was no longer a part of this realm, that there was nothing he could do bring him back.

Hope had vanished along with her reason to get up in the morning, something she'd had to force herself to do every day since Michael's disappearance. He was gone, completely and utterly as if he'd never existed.

With no more tears to cry, she stared down at the urn in her lap. She intended to spread her mother's ashes here, legally or not made no difference. Who would ever know? Ellie would have a memorial she could visit, a place she could lay flowers. There would be no marker for Mama or Michael, except the one she carried around inside her.

Resigned, she pulled back her drooping shoulders and stood, rubbing the heel of her hand against the ever-present ache in her chest. A week had done nothing to heal the pain. Not surprising. Ellie knew that the pain of Michael's loss would haunt her for the rest of her life.

She wondered briefly what would happen to her at the end of that life, something she'd never considered before. Now she knew there was so much more to the world than anyone knew. Heaven wasn't a guarantee. Hell was all around them.

Unscrewing the top of the urn, she proceeded to sprinkle her mother's ashes across the open patch off to one side of the archway. She would return here in the years to come and make an effort to connect with that other world. Despite Lucan's crushing news and lack of useful information, she wouldn't give up hope. She'd seen enough to know, that gone didn't always mean forever.

Afterwards, she made the long trek to the marina on her bicycle. Lucan had given her all of Michael's worldly belongings, which were his boat and his motorcycle. She'd need lessons to learn how to operate them both, but the boat was home now. For a little while, anyway. It was the first time Ellie had lived by herself. She'd been reluctant to leave Gran even though she'd made a miraculous recovery and was completely independent. Time for the bird to leave the nest.

Lucan had pulled some strings and gotten Ellie into the army. His cousin, Camulus, was a soldier in an elite military unit. Ellie's age and lack of education was 'overlooked'. A month from now, she would leave for Fort Benning and suffer through basic training before shipping off to flight school.

She slid open the door and stepped down into the living area. Every time she did so, she half expected to find Michael inside. Disappointment washed over her when she found the boat empty. She trudged through to the berth and fell onto the bed, finally letting anguish take over. Burying her face in the pillow, she let the tears come, sobbing out loud in her misery and despair.

She'd wasted so much time. She'd give anything to go back and do it all over again. She wouldn't have resisted him, would never have deserted him. She would relish each moment.

"I don't want to do this without you," she said out loud. Her voice was clogged with emotion, but she needed to hear the words, even coming from her own mouth. "I couldn't admit it. I didn't want to." Even a future that included flying planes, seeing the world, and killing demons would be a bleak existence without Michael Munro in it.

"I love you," she whispered.

Her tears came in a hot rush. She had to stop kidding herself. Michael was gone, and he wasn't coming back. She curled into a tight knot on his bed and wept.

***

Ellie woke with a start when the boat rocked. She sat up like a shot, banging her head on the low ceiling.

Rubbing the sore spot, she scrambled to her feet and checked that the spearhead was still in her pocket. Recalling that it wouldn't have much effect on a human, she grabbed the bat Michael kept behind the door.

Poised to bash the intruder in the head, she stepped out of the bedroom just as the exterior door slid open.

"Ellie, put the bat down," Michael said softly.

Hearing his voice, she nearly fainted. The bat clattered to the floor. She couldn't breathe. Her knees wobbled and she grabbed the table to keep from falling.

She stared at him, afraid he would vanish again. He was here. He was really here. He was real. If she reached out, she could touch him.

He must have sensed her hesitation. He jumped down into the cabin and took her in his arms just as Ellie flung herself at him. He ducked his head and kissed her. Once, twice, a dozen times.

"Oh, Michael. I thought I'd lost you forever," she mumbled.

More frantic kisses, deep and hungry. She clamped her arms around his neck, holding tight, determined to never let him go. She savored the hard press of his body against hers. *He's real*, she thought again. She couldn't believe it.

"You're the one who brought me back, Ellie. You did. When you said—" He broke off, sliding his hand up her arms and cupping her face in his strong hands. His golden eyes darted back and forth between hers. "Say it again," he whispered.

Ellie pressed her hands against his. "I love you. I love you, Michael."

He took her open mouth in a kiss so hot, so erotic she felt it right down to her toes. She leaned into him, tears falling freely down her cheeks.

It took a dozen more kisses before she was finally convinced. He was indeed real. She buried her face against his chest, sniffling. She was afraid to believe it, afraid that if she let herself, she would wake up, find herself alone in his empty bed.

Michael tilted her head back with one finger beneath her chin. "Open your eyes, Ellie. Look at me."

Worried he would disappear the instant she did, Ellie shook her head. A single tear escaped and trickled down the side of her face. He brushed the pad of his thumb over her cheek and kissed the corner of her eye. Then her closed lids, each in turn, the ticklish spot behind her ear, the tip of her nose, then back to her eyes.

"Ellie," he whispered. "I love you. Look at me."

She let her eyes flutter open. Drinking him in, she stared up into those golden eyes.

He kissed her, slanting his mouth over hers, his velvety tongue probing, gliding against hers. She gave in, letting herself believe she wasn't dreaming. He was here, and he loved her. If she couldn't believe in that, what else was there?

Her body flared to life, sizzling, hungry. She felt wild. Kissing him back with a frenzy, she pulled him to the bed and dragged him down on top of her. She kissed him and kissed him, with days of grief and yearning pouring from her.

Moments later, they were both naked and writhing around on his bed as he pushed into her. She forgot the heartache, the loneliness. He was here and she was never letting go.

~THE END~

About the Author

Bambi Lynn graduated from the University of Maryland European Division with bachelor's degrees in English and History. She writes Historical Paranormal Romances set in Scotland.

Connect with Bambi online:
http://www.bambilynn.net
http://www.facebook.com/BambiLynn.HotHistoricals
http://www.twitter.com/hot_historicals